The Destined Bond: Mystics of V'nairia ©2015 by J.C. Ritchie

The Fated Swords © 2014 by J.C. Ritchie

All rights reserved. This book or any portion thereof may not be reproduced or used in any manner whatsoever without the express written permission of the publisher except for the use of brief quotations in a book review.

This is a work of fiction. Names, characters, businesses, places, events and incidents are either the products of the author's imagination or used in a fictitious manner. Any resemblance to actual persons, living or dead, or actual events is purely coincidental.

Third Edition Printing, 2016

ISBN: 978-1539548232

Edited by: J.C. Ritchie

Cover design: Copyright © 2014 by J.C. Ritchie

Texts and illustrations: Copyright © 2014, 2015, and 2017 by J.C. Ritchie

THE FATED SWORDS

MYSTICS OF V'NAIRIA BOOK ONE

J.C. Ritchie

About The Author

J.C. Ritchie was born in the city of Norton, VA. He lives in Sevierville, Tennessee and spends most of his days reading, writing, and playing massive amounts of video games. His influences are Brent Weeks, Mark Lawrence, George R.R. Martin, J. K. Rowling, and J.R.R. Tolkien.

J.C. Ritchie Novels

The Mystics of V'nairia Series

I: The Fated Swords

II: The Crusader King

III: The Last Mystic

Novellas

The Destined Bond: Mystics of V'nairia

To my readers, thank you for all your continued support. May there be newer and bolder adventures to come.

THE DESTINED BOND
A MYSTICS OF V'NAIRIA NOVELLA

Part One

Zephyr sat in between the bushes, breathing steadily. He ran his hands through his short brown hair that had been dampened by the humidity in the air. He had been waiting several minutes for the others to make their move, but hadn't seen or heard a thing. He knew that even the slightest movement would cause a rustling in the bushes and his position would be given away. He couldn't afford for that to happen, there was a lot at stake. He could feel the sweat from his forehead making its way down to the tip of his nose. He fought the urge to wipe it from his face.

He was going to have to leave his spot soon, he had started becoming anxious. He dashed out of the bushes quickly drawing his sword. He heard the steel ring from the knives coming from a nearby tree and deflected them with his blade. A man jumped down from the tree above him and meant to strike Zephyr from above but was interrupted by Zephyr's firm gripping hand. He tossed the man over his head into a tree trunk directly behind him.

The man rose to his feet and rubbed the sore spot on his head, "Your perception is as keen as ever Zephyr." he said.

The man was tall with long black hair and had a small patch of black hair on his chin. They were both around the same height and build. They were both around eighteen years old and more mature than most young men their age. The man raised his sword and pointed it at Zephyr smiling.

"I guess we will see who wins then, the loser pays the price." Zephyr said.

The man nodded and quickly dashed towards him with his blade to his side. He lunged at his stomach but was blocked by Zephyr's blade. Zephyr's speed was incredible and there was hardly a man in the kingdom that could match it except for a select few. Zephyr appeared behind the man and delivered a kick to the center of his back, sending him forward off his balance.

"Flame Art: Flame Burst!" Zephyr shouted as he fired three fireballs from his mouth.

The hit was inevitable; there was no conceivable way the spell could have been dodged. "Stone Art: Mud Wall" a voice said. A wall of dirt and grass rose from the ground blocking the intense flames.

When the smoke finally cleared Zephyr could see another man standing a few feet from the other. This man was clean shaven and had red hair down to his shoulders. "You blocked my spell; I thought this was every man for himself?" Zephyr asked.

The red haired man drew his sword, "I had just joined the struggle, and I was looking forward to fighting you both" he said.

"I don't need your help Hyo, I could have deflected it myself." the black haired man said.

"Whatever you say, Vallerus." Hyo replied snidely.

Vallerus rose to his feet and flipped backwards, throwing knives at Hyo who blocked them with his blade.

"Flame Art: Great Fire Stream!" Vallerus shouted as he leaped into the air.

The flames flew through the air towards Zephyr and Hyo. They had looked at each other and had the same idea. They had both casted their own fire stream spells to counteract Vallerus' spell. The three fire spells had collided causing a bright yellowish-orange tint in the sky above them. They could feel the intense heat of the flames as the spells raged on.

After a few moments they had called off their attacks and walked towards each other. "Looks like another draw." Hyo said.

Zephyr sighed heavily and shrugged his shoulders, "It can't be helped were all on equal levels of strength." he said.

Vallerus stared at them for a moment and began to laugh. "We are not on the same level, I can assure you." he said.

"Let's just get back to the city and hope the girls have dinner ready." Zephyr said as they began their trek back to the city.

The three of them had finally made it back to Zephyr's house for dinner after their long walk through the forest. They opened the door to find Lillian and Aeria, Zephyr and Hyo's wives standing in the kitchen preparing a meal for them. Zephyr walked over to Lillian and kissed her on the cheek while the other two men sat down around the table.

"So who won the sparring match today boys?" Lillian asked.

"It was a draw again." Zephyr spoke up.
Vallerus rolled his eyes, "You two were lucky I didn't mop the floor with you. I'm just having an off day that's all." he said.

Vallerus had always seen himself as the strongest warrior in all of V'nairia. He was ranked top of his class at the academy and was already commander of their squad of three.

"Well maybe one of you will eventually win at sparring so we can all go out to a fancy dinner that we women don't have to cook." Aeria said lifting her right brow.

"Maybe that's why they make it a draw all of the time. None of them want to pay for dinner for everyone." Lillian suggested.

"Well maybe we would rather our wives cook it for us." Zephyr said bravely.

Lillian hauled off and punched him in the back of the head, "What the hell is that supposed to mean!?" she shouted.

Vallerus and Hyo began to laugh hysterically until they heard a knock at the door. "Come in." Lillian said politely.

The door opened slowly and in walked Tera, who was Vallerus' Fiancé and behind her was their friend Kiarra. "Sorry we are arriving so late, we couldn't figure out what to wear." Tera said just as any typical woman would.

"That's alright; we were waiting on you dear." Vallerus said kissing Tera's hand as she sat down next to him.

Lillian had carried over the large roasted chicken from the oven over to the table. Zephyr had gotten a knife from a drawer in the kitchen and began to carve the bird. He handed out plates to everyone and they had grabbed what food they wanted and sat down to eat with each other.

They passed around the jug of wine and filled their glasses preparing to eat the wonderful meal that was laid out before them. Lillian and Aeria had passed on the wine due to the fact that they were both with child and poured themselves a glass of water instead.

"Lillian, how has Vallus been today?" Tera asked.

Lillian smiled widely, "I had laid him down to sleep just before the boys got here, he has been wonderful all day." she replied.

"I'm sure the two of you will have wonderful babies just like him." Tera said smiling back at her as she sipped her glass of wine.

Kiarra sat at the far end of the table not saying a word. She often tried to keep to herself since her husband had left on a mission for the militia over a year ago and hadn't returned. She had become quite jealous of her two closest friends. She hadn't even received a letter from him letting her know how or where he was.

"Kiarra, has there been any word yet?" Aeria asked. She shook her head and remained silent.

"Well it's good to have you here dear." Lillian said smiling.

"Thank you." Kiarra said smiling back at her faintly.

Hyo sighed heavily, "Well he is one of the strongest men we know. The four of us are a force to be reckoned with, I'm sure he's doing just fine." he said smiling at her. His kindness caused her to smile weakly, but it was barely noticeable.

"Well old man, in just a few weeks you will lose all of your freedom." Zephyr said punching Vallerus in the shoulder.

Vallerus laughed looking over at Tera, "You're mistaken, I am free because I have her Zephyr. She is quite the treasure" he said admiring the warmth in her smile. Vallerus always had a way with words and could sweep her off her feet every time. They were perfect for each other; he loved to stare into her bright blue eyes and run his hands through her long blonde hair. She was the most beautiful thing he had ever seen and he was madly in love with her.

"Giving birth to our beautiful son only a month ago and now in only a few weeks I will be marrying the love of my life. What a wonderful time this is." Tera said feeling blessed as he kissed her cheek.

"I think we should toast to our good fortune, too friends and family." Zephyr said.

They all raised their glasses, "Too friends and family!" they shouted.

Suddenly there was another knock at the door, Zephyr rose to his feet and answered it. It was Lieutenant Jerriston; he was the commander of the entire V'nairian Militia. "Lieutenant, what a pleasant surprise." Zephyr said saluting him.

The other two rose to their feet and did the same. "Please take your seats, no need for formalities at this hour." the Lieutenant said.

The Lieutenant had been a tall older man with graying hair, but with the way he carried himself you could not tell his age at all. "What brings you out this late at night Lieutenant?" Vallerus asked.

The old man removed a letter from his side pocket and handed it to Vallerus. He opened the letter and began to glance over it. "It is a letter from Supreme Judge Baralai." Vallerus said.

"Yes, his lordship has requested that the three of you have a meeting with him at the Capital building tomorrow." the Lieutenant explained.

This was surprising news to all of them; they had never met the Supreme Judge in person before. "Do you know what the meeting is about sir?" Hyo asked.

"No unfortunately I do not, but I must be on my way. It is getting rather chilly, and my old bones cannot stand the cold." the Lieutenant said. They said goodnight to the Lieutenant as he walked out the door and shut it behind him.

"A meeting with the Supreme Judge that sounds interesting." Lillian said.

"Yes interesting and rather suspicious." Zephyr said curiously.

"Well at any rate our squad is finally getting recognized for its accomplishments." Vallerus said boasting.

"I guess we will just see tomorrow." Hyo said.

After dinner they had all helped the girls clean up the dining room and the kitchen. Once everything had been cleaned up Tera and Vallerus had gotten their son and made their way home. After a while Kiarra and the others left as well leaving only Lillian and Zephyr in their own house.

***

The next morning the men had gotten up early and put on their uniforms, and made their way to the gardens to meet up with each other. "Good morning men." Vallerus said as Hyo and Zephyr approached him in the gardens. "Morning boss." they said.

"Are you ready to head to the Capital building?" Vallerus asked them.

"Lead the way." Zephyr said. They followed Vallerus to the Capital building to meet with the Supreme Judge. They had never heard of the Supreme Judge setting up a meeting so early in the morning. They had already been on their way to meet with him and most of the city was still asleep in their beds. The streets of the Capital wouldn't fill with people for at least another hour or two.

When they finally reached the Capital building they walked inside and walked up to the front desk. "Commander Vallerus, how can I help you today?" the receptionist asked.

"My squad has a meeting with Judge Baralai." Vallerus said.

She had entered some information into the computer in front of her and waited for a reply. "Alright it does look like he is expecting you. Please ride the elevator to the highest floor, the passcode is five five four two." she said.

"Thank you very much." he said smiling at her as they walked over to the elevator.

"Is anyone else as nervous as I am?" Hyo asked.

"Shut up!" Vallerus said glaring at him.

"I mean come on Vallerus; it's a meeting with the Supreme Judge." Hyo said. "Aren't you the least bit curious?"

Vallerus looked back at him and faced forward without saying a word.

They boarded the elevator and input the passcode. The elevator began to rise; they patiently waited for it to stop at the top floor. There was finally a beeping noise and the doors opened up.

They walked down the long narrow hallway past the High Court's chambers where they hold legal hearings and Capital business. They had finally made it to the Supreme Judge's office. There was a gold plate on the door that read: "Supreme Judge Baralai." Vallerus knocked on the door slowly; he could hear a man's voice telling them that they could enter.

They walked inside the large office and saw the Judge sitting at his desk filling out some paperwork. Judge Baralai was a man in his early thirties with hair as white as the snow of the Kazarke Mountains and he had piercing blue eyes. His skin was darker than most of the citizens of V'nairia and he wore armor that matched his hair color. Beside his desk stood another man that the squad did not recognize. He was older with short graying hair. He wore a long black robe and carried a large staff with a white stone on the end.

The three of them lined up in front of the Judge's desk and saluted him. "Your Grace, it is an honor." Vallerus said.

Judge Baralai rose from his seat and walked over to the three of them. He walked around them examining them for a moment and then stopped in front of them. "So this is the squad that I have heard so much about? Lieutenant Jerriston speaks highly of you three." the Judge said.

"Thank you sir." Zephyr said.

Judge Baralai looked over at Vallerus and stared hard for a moment. "Well Commander Vallerus, you have quite the team. I believe Jerriston made the right choice in naming you his successor." Baralai said.

Vallerus and the others were shocked, "Wha-, what do you mean successor?" He asked curiously.

Judge Baralai smiled, "He named you the new Lieutenant of V'nairia's Militia. He is going to be the new Headmaster of the Academy." he said softly. "In his old age, he had thought it better to assume a less stressful position and I obliged."

Zephyr and Hyo patted him on the back, "Congratulations Lieutenant." they said.

"What will happen to my squad now?" Vallerus asked him.

"Well I assume they will be assigned to another commander." Judge Baralai said.

Zephyr and Hyo looked down at the floor; their squad had gone through so much together only to get separated. "There is one last mission I have for your squad before you take on your new duties as Lieutenant." Baralai said.

Hyo and Zephyr had immediately sprung back to life. It must be a very important mission for the Supreme Judge to assign it to their group specifically. "Of course sir, what is the mission?" Vallerus asked.

"Before I begin the debriefing let me introduce you three to someone." he said pointing to the gentleman in the robe behind him. "This is Hylkroft-" Judge Baralai started.

"The Godsage!" Zephyr shouted.

The judge smiled, "Yes this is Hylkroft the Godsage." he continued. "So you have heard of him Zephyr?"

"Yes of course, he is the strongest and wisest of all mystics." Zephyr said.

The man stepped forward, "It is an honor to meet V'nairia's finest." he bellowed in his deep voice.

Zephyr walked up and shook the man's hand. "No sir the honor is all ours. Meeting a legend such as yourself is a chance in a lifetime." He said.

Vallerus rolled his eyes and pushed Zephyr aside. Vallerus didn't particularly like mystics; they had always made him feel uneasy. The fact that he knew they were going to have to work with the legendary mystic made his skin crawl. "It is an honor Godsage." Vallerus said bowing respectfully.

"The honor is all mine Lieutenant, clearly." Hylkroft said giving him a look of skepticism

"So you're Grace, what are the details of the mission?" Hyo asked.

Baralai turned to look at him, "Oh yes the mission. Well there have been reports from some of our soldiers on the outskirts of Oaba Desert and the northern city of Rygoth that there is an army making its way to V'nairia." the Supreme Judge said.

"An army from the Foreignlands?" Vallerus asked.

"Yes it would appear so, an army dressed in all black." the Godsage explained.

"No one else has any other information to report about these strange soldiers?" Zephyr asked.

Judge Baralai shook his head, "No further information unfortunately." he said. "I understand that it isn't much to go on at all, but I don't believe our men would make up such a situation."

"Well I do have some information on who leads them; they call him The Shadow Mystic." Hylkroft said.

None of them had ever heard of such a warrior, they could only think that the origin of this mystic was from the Foreignlands.

"It is said that he can use demonic magicks and summon hellbound creatures." the Godsage explained further.

"So he is an abomination then, demonic magicks are forbidden for both human and mystic alike." Vallerus said.

The Judge sat back down at his desk, "Yes it is forbidden by law, and the accused parties will be executed for the use of such dark magick." the Judge said explaining one of V'nairia's oldest laws.

"Then you want us to find this man and bring him back here to try him?" Zephyr asked.

"No! We should just find the bastard and kill him, which would be the easiest way." Vallerus shouted.

"That plan certainly seems a bit rash Vallerus." Hyo said.

"I am the Commander you are the soldier you will do as I command!" Vallerus shouted.

"Enough! Gentleman, your task right now is neither to kill him nor subdue him." Baralai said.

"Then what will you have us do your grace?" Hyo asked.

"You are to report to the Baron of Talias to discuss the Order of the Cursed Blades and do nothing further unless you are instructed to do so." The Judge instructed. "I will send a letter if something changes.

"Why does the Baron want to speak to us about this order? What exactly is it?" Zephyr asked.

"You will have to reach Talias and ask him for yourselves, I have no further information for you." Baralai said.

"When do we depart?" Vallerus asked.

"You will leave at dawn; make sure you are well prepared. You may leave." the Supreme Judge said.

The three of them walked outside the office and down the hallway to the elevator. "Are you sure they will be enough?" Hylkroft asked.

"It appears they are all we have at the moment, so I sure as hell hope so." Baralai said unsure of his decision.

"That commander and his temper could be a real problem. I feel like he doesn't take orders well." Hylkroft said.

"I have read their files. They have been friends for a long time; I'm sure Zephyr and Hyo will keep him in check." Baralai said full of hope.

"I hope that you are right." The Godsage said taking his leave of the Judge and closing the door behind him.

***

That night the men went back home to prepare for their mission and to spend time with their family before they departed. At their home Zephyr was preparing to pack while Lillian prepared a small dinner for the two of them.

"So where do they have you traveling to?" she asked him.

"We travel to Talias to speak to the Baron about some of order of blades or something." Zephyr said.

"The Order of the Cursed Blades?" Lillian asked.

"Yes, how do you know about it?" he asked her curiously.

She took a drink of tea and placed the cup back on the table, "My father used to tell me stories about it all the time; it is an organization that protects the cursed blades Ebony, and Ivory." Lillian explained.

"I've never heard of them." Zephyr said.

"Ivory, the holy blade is said to purify all evil in ones heart and Ebony the devil blade is said to hold dark power and can manipulate the hearts of mankind." Lillian explained further.

"I don't understand why these swords are so important, why make an entire organization just to protect them?" he asked.

"The swords were used centuries ago to seal away Diaboro, the Demon King in the shrine in the northern mountains. The organization protects V'nairia from all evil that may harm its people." his wife said.

His bags were finally packed and he strapped his sword on his back. "Maybe we will become members of the order?" Zephyr said jokingly.

Lillian began to laugh, "I don't think you could protect the world from evil." she said smiling at him.

"I bet your wrong." he said before he kissed her. He placed his hand on her stomach, "Boy or Girl?" he asked anxiously.

"Girl." she said as she whispered in his ear.

He smiled and kissed her again and walked towards the door. "Her name will be Ashlyn." he said as he walked out the door and shut it behind him.

She smiled widely, "Come back to me Zephyr." she mumbled to herself.

***

The next morning Zephyr left before dawn and met his squad members at the city gates. "It's about time you got here." Vallerus said.

"You know me Vallerus, always fashionably late." Zephyr said as he and Hyo began to laugh.

"Yeah okay time to focus, our mission is to reach Talias and meet with the Baron. Is everyone prepared?" Vallerus asked.

"Yes sir!" they shouted.

They strapped their weapons on their sides and backs and gathered their bags and started down the trail into the forest.

"Remember to stay in position I will lead, Zephyr you follow in the middle, and Hyo you watch from the rear guard." Vallerus ordered. The other two agreed as they made their way through the forest unsure of what awaits them ahead on their mission.

Part Two

Vallerus led his squad through the Durean forests that lie on the outside of the Capital's great steel walls. The Durean forest was very thick and humid especially during the summer months; they could feel the heat from the sun as it shone through the trees. It had only been the start of their journey to Talias and they were already exhausted from the heat. Their squad had been on many missions through the forests before even during the summer months but this particular summer had been especially cruel.

"We still have miles to go, we should have taken horses." Zephyr said as had begun to sigh long and hard.

"The walk is good for us; you should quit complaining so much." Vallerus said. He want one to talk, the other could see the sweat dripping from his forehead onto the warm forest floor. They knew that being the biggest of the three of them he had been more exhausted than even they had been.

"You think with all this damn shade, it would be much cooler in the woods." Hyo said.

"Nature is often cruel and works in mysterious ways." Zephyr said smiling walking faster ahead and leaving them both behind.

"What the hell are you?" Vallerus asked "Some kind of poet."

"Maybe, but that would only be from Lillian's influence." Zephyr replied to Vallerus' snide comment.

They each had worn comfortable clothes all except for Vallerus who had donned his favorite black coat that stretched passed his knees. The others could just imagine how badly it must have been bothering him but they were just glad that it hadn't been them wearing the heavy black getup.

"I hope the girls will be alright, they could give birth any day now." Hyo said.

"Yeah I just hope it's not while we are gone, I want to be there when Ashe is born." Zephyr said proudly. Hyo could see the fatherly gleam of love in his eye, he was ready to be a father; hell they both were.

"If you two would shut up and focus on the mission, we could get there faster." Vallerus grunted.

"Yes sir, of course." Hyo said sarcastically looking at Zephyr and grinning. It had been evident that the two of them had a closer bond than they had with Vallerus.

He was never for the sensitive loving types. He was rough, and focused and only about battle unless it came to Tera. Even then he didn't want anyone else but her to see that side of him. Unlike Vallerus however, Hyo and Zephyr were the complete opposite. They were all about family and they would do anything to protect it.

Their current conversation came to a close and they went back to focusing on their mission. Along the dirt path of the forest there had been no sign of invading soldiers in black. They thought that perhaps the enemy was in hiding waiting for the right moment to act. They remained on guard at all times, prepared for anything. They also thought about what diabolical plan they had to destroy or enslave the kingdom of V'nairia. The kingdom itself hadn't seen any kind of war or invasion in almost two-hundred years. There had been peace up until the shocking rumors of the mysterious army and the squad had been eager to investigate.

Suddenly they had heard a rustling in the bushes. Hyo moved towards the bushes slowly while removing his sword from its scabbard. A large shadow shot out from the bushes and attacked him. The large black creature lay upon him breathing its fowl breath into his face. It had smelt of decaying flesh and sulfur, which had almost made Hyo sick.

Zephyr and Vallerus ran up to the beast to strike it, but before they could connect it swung its long claws at them, slicing Zephyr's arm, thus blocking their advance. The blood poured down his arm from the deep wound the creature had given him. He ripped off part of his shirt and quickly tied it around his arm to stop the bleeding.

"Flame Art: Fire Stream!" Vallerus shouted spewing fire at the beast.

The spell was ineffective and Vallerus was knocked out of the way by its claws. "You idiot! You can't use a fire spell on a hellbeast!" Zephyr shouted.

"Stop shouting at me and kill the fucking thing!" Vallerus shouted back. The beast had jumped off of Hyo who had for the moment been frozen in fear. He had gotten back to his feet and was able to move again.

The beast had faced them and firmly planted its feet on the ground in front of them. The beast then tilted its head back and proceeded to blow blue flames from its open jaws.

"Walls!" Vallerus shouted as the three of them casted their defensive spells to block the flames.

"If those flames hit any part of your body you're done for, be careful." Zephyr warned them. He had read many books on demons and otherworldly beasts, the hellbeasts being his favorite of all. The blue flames that it exerts from its body can melt through still after only just a few minutes. It was truly a formidable foe to even the most experience of Militia soldiers.

Even with the power of their magick, they could feel the heat from the flames. Their walls were deteriorating, and they wouldn't hold for long. "I have an idea but it's risky." Zephyr said.

"Well spit it out, we don't have much time!" Vallerus shouted over the roar of the flames.

"Were going to have to hit it with combined fire spells, It won't damage it but it will block the flames long enough for us to move behind the beast. "Zephyr said.

They didn't hesitate; all together they combined their powers. "Combination Art: Hellfire Pillar!" they shouted together.

The collision of their spells created a large pillar of fire blocking the blue flames. While the hellbeast was distracted they made their way behind the beast to move in for the attack. They took out their swords and began to strike its thick hind legs. The steel from their blades hadn't even dented the beast's hide; it was as strong as diamonds.

"There has to be a weak point." Hyo said.

"Okay so where is it?" Vallerus asked.

Zephyr stood and thought for a moment, he had observed every inch of the beast and their surroundings from afar. Suddenly he had remembered reading about its weakest point; he knew how to kill it.

"This is going to sound crazy but you need to run in front of the beast so it chases you, both of you." Zephyr said.

"Are you insane, those flames will kill us?" Hyo shouted.

"No, did you notice? The beast has to stay in one place to breathe its fire." Zephyr explained.

Vallerus grabbed Hyo and pulled him aside, "Let's go." He said. Without hesitation Vallerus and Hyo ran out to move in front of the hellbeast.

They had made their way in front of the beast and kept running waiting for it to follow. The flame pillar had finally subsided as well as the beast's flames. The beast noticed the two of them getting away and chased after them. Even for its enormous size, it was faster than any creature they had ever seen before. Vallerus looked back and could see Zephyr jumping from tree branches above them. "Clever Bastard." he mumbled to himself.

The beast planted itself once again to prepare for its flame breath attack. Hyo and Vallerus stopped and panicked they didn't have enough magick to cast sufficient defensive spells to block the flames. Their fate had been in Zephyr's hands now.

The beast tilted its head back and expelled the flames once more from its foul smelling mouth. Zephyr leaped from one tree branch to another keeping up with the beast from above while clutching his blade, waiting for the right moment to strike. He came down and stabbed the beast through the top of the head with his sword. The beast stumbled and shrieked for a moment before collapsing. Zephyr then cast a fire spell that had enveloped the blade on his sword, setting the hellbeast on fire. The beast's eyes had went from a rage filled red to pitch black empty voids.

Hyo and Vallerus had been saved from the deadly flames of the beast. Zephyr removed his blade and jumped off of its large black head. They watched as its body had turned to ash and had been swept away by the wind and carried throughout the forest.

"There is no question that the beast was summoned by a demonic spell." Zephyr said.

"It had to be the Shadow Mage the judge had warned us about." Hyo said.

Vallerus began to laugh, "It's like he is toying with us, he should have known we could kill the beast." he said boasting again.

"He probably has information on the Militia including us. He must know our abilities." Hyo said.

"So a diversion then?" Vallerus asked. "Well at least it's dead now."

Zephyr scratched his head, "Did you forget the part where we were almost incinerated?" he asked Vallerus who had a smug look on his face.

"You done a good job Zephyr, we killed the beast that's all that matters." Vallerus said.

He seemed to be acting like the victory had been all his, they were used to this with being on the same squad as Vallerus for years. He loved to take credit for any accomplishments he deemed worthy to steal to build up his own reputation. It seemed to be working considering he had just been promoted to Lieutenant of the Militia.

***

After a few more hours walking the path through the forest they had finally reached the top of the mountain. It was nearly nightfall and they were relieved that their destination had been just below them at the bottom of the mountain. The great city of Talias awaited them and they didn't spar a second more to reach it. All that ran through their minds were warm baths and hot food, nothing else seemed better at the moment.

Zephyr was the only one of the group who had ever been to the city before. He could remember the large buildings from when he was a boy; they weren't as tall as the buildings in the Capital however. The Capital's buildings seemed to reach the clouds sometimes looking at them from the right angle. Talias had many restaurants and shops where you could by armor and weapons or clothing and jewelry. It was one of the most popular tourist's spots in V'nairia. He could just see the Baron's Mansion in his mind and wondered if it was as magnificent as he remembered.

They had finally reached the bottom of the mountain and walked up to the gates of Talias. They noticed that the gates had been closed, which was unusual for such a popular tourist attraction. The three of them walked up to the two guards that stood in front of the gates. They removed their weapons from their scabbards and pointed them at Vallerus and his squad.

"State your business." The guard demanded angrily waiving his blade in Vallerus' face.

"Listen little man, I think you should put the weapon down before I hurt you." Vallerus said.

Zephyr cleared his throat, "Are you trying to get us killed, they are not the enemy we are on a mission." he whispered to Vallerus.

"I am the Lieutenant of the V'nairian Militia. We were sent by Supreme Judge Baralai to speak with Baron Tyran." he said.

The guards sheathed their weapons and opened the gates. "You may enter, I apologize for the inconvenience sir." the guard said as his tone quickly changed.

"Damn, and here I thought I was going to get some good practice in." Vallerus said looking back at them smiling. Zephyr and Hyo rolled their eyes and ignored him.

They walked on through the gates and down the streets of Talias. They could see the various shops and restaurants that were lit up with neon signs. "Over there is the inn, we should go acquire a room." Hyo said pointing to the large building on the right side of the street.

It was tall and wide with many windows, just below the roof was a neon sign that read "Inn." "*How original.*" Zephyr thought as he looked up at the sign.

Talias had changed a bit since the last time he had been there as a child, but they certainly weren't bad changes. "We should go see the Baron first." Vallerus said.

"It's after dusk, are you crazy?" Hyo asked.

"No this is a very important mission we should see him as soon as possible." Vallerus said. There had obviously been no reasoning with him. Zephyr and Hyo sighed and gave in.

"Alright follow me; I know how to get there." Zephyr said.

Zephyr led them down a side street between a couple of buildings that led to the main path to the large mansion. They could see it off in the distance. It was a large white building with burgundy colored shutters. The path to the mansion was lined with apple trees and lanterns that lit up their path. To one side of the mansion had been a large garden. The garden was filled with many different colored flowers as well as an assortment of different types of fruits and vegetables.

"So I take it you have been here before Zephyr?" Hyo asked.

"Yes, once when I was a boy." he said.

"Have you ever met the Baron?" Hyo asked him.

Zephyr shook his head, "No I never had the opportunity." Zephyr explained as they walked up the steps past the columns and to the front door.

Vallerus knocked hard and they waited for a moment. The door opened slowly and a short sharply dressed man walked outside. "Can I help you?" the man asked.

"We are here to see Baron Tyran; we have orders from the Capital." Vallerus said.

"It is rather late but we have been expecting you, please right this way." the short man said motioning them inside the door.

Inside the foyer, they stood and waited for the Baron. They looked around the room and could see the many paintings that lined the walls. His home was well decorated; they could tell he was a man that appreciated the arts. They looked up to see a large spiraling staircase that led to the very top of the mansion.

As they turned away from the staircase they could see a tall thin man accompanied by a young woman walking toward them from the hallway past the dining room. He wore a gray suit and had short graying hair and a gray mustache; they could only presume that this had been Baron Tyran.

The three of them saluted him and fell silent. "I was expecting the three of you half a day ago and to arrive this late no less." the Baron said smiling, shaking each of their hands.

"We ran into some unexpected trouble. I apologize for our tardiness." Vallerus said.

Zephyr looked at the Baron's left eye. It was clear and shining, the others hadn't noticed it but he had. The Baron's left eye was made of glass or some other clear gemstone.

"Yes I'd say that those hellbeasts are quite difficult to fight off." Baron Tyran said smiling.

The three of them were shocked, how could he have known that it was a hellbeast that they had fought? "What is he playing at?" Vallerus asked himself.

"I don't understand. How could you have known that?" Zephyr asked curiously. The Baron Had ignored his question.

"We shall have our meeting upstairs and I will explain everything. Please follow me." the Baron said as he led them up the winding stair case.

At the very top of the stairs they had saw a wooden door, the Baron unlocked the door with an old rusty key and motioned them inside. They walked inside to see what had looked like a library; books had filled the entire room. In the middle of the room was a square table with four chairs placed around it. On the table there was a map of V'nairia and to the left of V'nairia was the Foreignlands.

"Please have a seat." the Baron said.

The four men sat down around the table, while the young woman served them hot tea. "Oh how rude of me; this is my daughter Thesia." Tyran said pointing to the young woman.

She looked to be around eighteen years old and was tall and thin like her father with long brown hair that was braided; she wore a bright blue dress with a black bow in the back. "It is nice to meet you gentlemen." she said bowing courteously.

"So to answer your previous question, my left eye is how I saw your battle with the beast." the Baron explained.

"I still don't follow; do you have some kind of foresight?" Hyo asked.

The Baron sipped his tea and placed his cup back on the wooden table. "You could say that, while I am only partially a mystic my left eye gives me the ability to find anyone in the order." the Baron said.

"Wait, you said the order?" Zephyr said confused.

"Yes, the Order of the Cursed Blades. You three are now members." Tyran said smiling.

"I'm confused. How did we become members of the order, we have only just arrived?" Hyo asked.

This had certainly been news for the three of them; Baralai had mentioned the Baron discussing the order with them but nothing about becoming members themselves. "The Supreme Judge spelled your bodies and made you members without you even knowing and your wives and soon to be wives are as well." The Baron said looking over at Vallerus.

"How are they apart of all of this?" Vallerus asked. "I'm presuming that each of you touched your wives at some point before you left the city correct?" the gray haired Baron said.

"So the spell is through physical contact?" Zephyr asked.

Tyran nodded, "Yes and soon after they hold your children for their first time when they are born they will be members as well." he said.

"What do the women and children have to do with the order?" Hyo asked him.

"It is simple you three and your wives and children are a part of the Destined Bond. The prophecy says so." Baron Tyran said.

"The Destined Bond? What is this prophecy?" Vallerus asked.

"We are not here to discuss the prophecy Lieutenant. The order's concern is the goal of this shadow mystic and his army." the Baron said.

Zephyr rose from his seat after finishing his tea and looked around at the many books on a nearby bookshelf. There were books on wars and dark creatures from the Foreignlands; some were spell books for different elements. There was anything that one in the order would ever need to know.

"Do we have any information on his whereabouts or why he means to invade us?" Vallerus asked.

"We know that he is trying to find the cursed blades Ebony, and Ivory. So we assume he means to reawaken the Demon King Diaboro." the Baron said.

"The swords are sealed in a shrine in the northern mountains past Rygoth aren't they?" Hyo asked.

"So you know the story then? Yes you are correct and I have the only key to open the shrine." Tyran said pulling out a small silver key with an onyx stone in the top of it.

"So our job is to protect the blades and kill the bastard before he can get to them?" Vallerus asked impatiently.

"That is the mission yes, dispose of him anyway you wish. The rest of the Militia can handle his army." the Baron explained.

"Do we know if he and the army are currently in V'nairia?" Zephyr asked.

"We do not know, however that beast that attacked you was the product of a spell at his disposal." the Baron said.

"So demonic magick is his trait? Are there any spells that we need to learn to counter him?" Zephyr asked.

The Baron shook his head, "As far as I know there is no spell that I or anyone else could teach you that counter demonic magick. It is an ancient forbidden type of magick." Tyran said.

"I read about it once, it is as rare as healing magicks." Zephyr said.

"That's right, while healing magicks aren't forbidden by the kingdom; its users are few and far between." Tyran explained. "Most of its teachers have been dead for many years."

Vallerus and Hyo rose from their seats, "We will begin locating the Shadow Mystic right away." Vallerus said.

"No, you three have other matters to attend to right now. I can handle tracking his whereabouts for now." The Baron smiled.

"What is more important than finding this evil mystic and stopping his army from invading us?" Hyo asked.

Zephyr could see that the Baron was using his eye to see something. "It looks like you have just enough time to make it back before your children are born." Tyran said.

Zephyr and Hyo smiled widely, "Thank you sir." they said.

The Baron pulled out a letter and handed it to Vallerus, "Take this to the Supreme Judge please, it is confidential." Baron Tyran said.

"Certainly sir, you can count on us." Vallerus said as they saluted him and said their goodbyes.

It had now been time for them to make their way back home. Zephyr and Hyo couldn't have been more excited to finally hold their newborn children in their arms.

Part Three

After traveling another long and humid trek from Talias, Lieutenant Vallerus and his men could finally see the tall steel gates of the Capital ahead of them; they had never been so thrilled to be home. Their journey back had been a miserable one; the heat had taken a larger toll on their squad than it had previously on the way there.

The entire trip Zephyr had tried to wrap his head around the Baron's glass eye. Was it true? Could he really see the near future? This and other questions he had asked himself multiple times. They had never met a mystic with a power like that; mystic's abilities had normally relied on the elements of nature to fuel their magick. The three of them had thought it possible that Baron Tyran's foresight had been a sacred skill like that of healing magick.

Zephyr was curious, and often his curiosity got the better of him. Lillian had scolded him many times for sticking his nose in the business of others. He had told himself that it was none of his business and for now he tried to push it out of his mind.

As they walked up toward the gate, they were greeted by an anxious guard. "Lieutenant Vallerus!" the guard shouted waving his arm like a mad man.

"Yes?" Vallerus asked.

The man could barely speak he was so out of breath, "I was ordered to meet you three at the gate. Lady Lillian and Lady Aeria are in labor, they were taken to the hospital a few hours ago." the guard said.

Zephyr and Hyo's eyes had widened, "Did anyone accompany them to the hospital?" Zephyr asked.

"I believe Lady Tera had accompanied them but I'm not sure." the guard said.

Zephyr and Hyo hadn't waited a moment longer, they ran passed the gate and down the street towards the hospital. "Go alert Judge Baralai and let him know that I am on my way with the report." Vallerus told the soldier.

"My apologies sir, but Judge Baralai is currently away and said to tell you to go to the hospital as well to be there for your friends." the guard explained.

"What!? What kind of order is that?" Vallerus asked confusedly.

The guard pulled out a note from his pocket and handed it to the Lieutenant. "It is an official order from Judge Baralai himself, you will see he also signed the bottom." the guard said pointing to a spot on the paper.

"On with you then and take this letter to Judge Baralai's office." Vallerus said angrily handing the guard the confidential letter. The guard looked frightened and ran off down the street. Vallerus let out a long sigh and preceded passed the gate and down the street to catch up to Zephyr and Hyo.

***

Zephyr and Hyo had finally made it to the hospital; they ran inside eagerly wanting to see their wives. They had almost mowed down a group of people standing outside the entrance.

They rushed up to the front desk so quickly it startled the nurse sitting before them. "Excuse me, were here to see our wives. They are in labor." Zephyr said panting heavily.

"Names please?" the nurse asked.

"Lillian and Aeria." Hyo said.

The nurse began to type on the computer in front of her and finally found the locations of the women. She called over another nearby nurse and began to whisper something to her. "Please, follow me." the other nurse said leading Hyo down the hallway to his wife's room.

"You can follow me, Lillian's room is this way." the nurse behind the desk spoke up breaking Zephyr from his daydreaming.

"Thank you er- Darla." he said looking down at her name tag and smiling awkwardly.

She led him down a darkly lit hallway; he had the strangest feeling come over him. He had felt a strong magickal force. On a nearby bench in front of the door he could see Tera sitting and waiting on the doctor. She saw him out of the corner of his eye and immediately ran over to him and wrapped her arms around him.

"Thank goodness you're here." she said.

"What's going on? Why aren't you in there with her?" He asked.

She had a terrified look on her face, Zephyr had feared the worst. "Lillian is alright but the baby; there is something wrong, a complication." Tera said.

"What do you mean?" he asked confused.

"The doctor had asked all family and friends to leave the room, there is some risk with the birth. The baby's magick is powerful beyond measure. More powerful than any other newborn he has ever seen the doctor said." Tera explained.

Zephyr didn't know whether to be happy or concerned. He had no idea that he and Lillian could have created such a powerful mystic child. Maybe this is what the Baron had meant when he mentioned the prophecy? Zephyr thought to himself.

He walked towards the door and tried to open it but the doorknob was so hot it burned his hand. "Damn!" Zephyr shouted pulling his hand back quickly.

Through the closed shades in the windows he could see flashes of red light filling the room. He could hear Lillian's screams from behind the door. He couldn't imagine the pain she was feeling. The massive amounts of magick the child had would take a toll on her body. The birth could end up killing her.

He needed to be in the room with her. He didn't care what orders the doctor had given, he was going in. He grabbed the door knob once more and fought through the searing pain.

"What are you doing!?" Tera asked. "Stop!" she added urgently.

Zephyr burst through the door and immediately saw Lillian lying in the hospital bed, sweating profusely. She had looked weak; there had been no color in her face. He looked down and could see a pool of blood in the floor below the bed. The room was hot from the intense heat of the infant's magick. He could smell the iron in the blood and it made him sick. He fought the urge to vomit then looked over and could see the doctor poke his head from between Lillian's legs.

"What the hell are you doing!? It isn't safe in here!" The doctor shouted.

Zephyr's face turned red with rage, "I'm her husband goddammit!" he shouted at the doctor.

No more was said and the doctor and nurses went back to work. He walked over to Lillian and grabbed her hand. "Your here, I'm so glad." she said smiling at him barely able to breathe.

"Of course I'm here I wouldn't miss this for the world." Zephyr said kissing the top of her hand.

"Doctor, how is everything looking?" he asked anxiously.

The doctor let out a long sigh, "The baby's magick is too powerful and if she continues it is likely your wife will die." the doctor said softly.

He couldn't even look Zephyr in the eye. Zephyr looked over at Lillian and tears began to fill his eyes. He didn't want to lose the love of his life. He knew something had to be done, there had to be another way. "It's okay Zephyr, you will have Ashlyn. She is more important." Lillian said selflessly as she stroked her husband's cheek.

"No! There has to be another way!" He shouted slamming his fist on the table beside him.

"There is one way but it is risky." The doctor said.

"What is it?" Zephyr asked.

"We can use a sealing spell on a part of your daughter's magickal essence." the doctor said.

Lillian and Zephyr were unaware that such a thing could be done; there were still questions to be answered. "So our daughter will be half as powerful as she would have been?" Lillian asked.

The doctor nodded, "Yes half as powerful and less dangerous. Her magick at this point is frightening." he explained.

"So what are the risks?" Zephyr asked.

"In order for the seal to work we have to bind part of your daughter's magick essence with half of her mother's soul." he said.

It definitely sounded dangerous and the doctor wasn't even sure if it would work but they had to try, he didn't want to lose Lillian.

"What happens then?" Lillian asked before shrieking once more in pain.

"With only half of your soul, your life expectancy will be altered dramatically and the chance of you having another child is almost impossible." the doctor warned them.

Zephyr didn't hesitate, "Do the spell." he said.

"Zeph-" Lillian started.

"No! I'm not losing you!" he shouted interrupting her.

She gave in, it was what he wanted and for him she would do anything. They both accepted the risk and responsibility of the choice they had made.

The doctor and nurses formed a circle around Lillian's hospital bed. They began chanting and Zephyr couldn't understand what they were saying. He could see a green aura surrounding each of them. It was their healing magick; the spell was so powerful their magick had manifested itself into a green light. The light passed through Lillian's body and she began to scream due to the intense pain. The magick of their daughter was fighting the spell.

After a few moments the light had faded and Lillian had fainted into a deep sleep. "It is done, the spell appears to have been successful." the doctor said.

They began to work on her and hurried to get the baby out before any complications had risen. "Is she sleeping?" Zephyr asked.

"Yes it is a side effect of the spell; it helps with the healing process. She will be fine." the doctor said.

He was relieved; Lillian was going to be okay. Now all that was left was for their beautiful little girl to enter the world. After a few moments he heard crying. He looked over saw the doctor holding his daughter in his arms.

The nurse handed him a pair of scissors, "It's time to cut the cord daddy." she said smiling at him.

He took the scissors from her and proceeded with the cutting then the nurse wrapped her up in a blanket and handed her to him. She wiggled around inside the blanket and opened her eyes and looked up at him. Her eyes had a red tint to them; they had glowed brightly in the light of the room. On the side of her little arm he could see the red streak on her skin which meant that she was a fire magick user.

"Hello Ashlyn, I'm your daddy." he said softly kissing her on the forehead.

The nurse walked back over and grabbed Ashe from him and walked out of the room. "We are going to do some routine testing and then we will bring her back." the doctor said smiling.

"Thanks doc, you are amazing." Zephyr said smiling back at him.

"Comes with the job lad." the doctor said as he cleaned his glasses with a cloth from his coat pocket and walked out of the room.

He looked over at his wife who was still sleeping and tears began to stream down his face. "We did good honey, real good." he said kissing her on her forehead. He rose from his chair and slowly walked out of the room so he wouldn't wake her.

Outside the door, Tera and Hyo were sitting and waiting for him. "Well how did it go?" Hyo asked.

Zephyr hesitated for a moment; he thought it best not to mention everything that happened to their friends. "Everything went well, she is sleeping now." he said.

"What about Ashlyn?" Tera asked. "The most beautiful thing I had ever seen, besides her mother of course." Zephyr said smiling.

They each took turns hugging and congratulating him. "Oh I almost forgot how is Aeria?" Zephyr asked.

"She is doing great, I can't wait for you guys to meet little Heiro." Hyo said smiling.

"Heiro, that's a great name." Tera said.

"Thanks, Aeria picked it out." Hyo said.

"So what marks does he possess?" Zephyr asked curiously. Hyo smiled widely, "He had the marks of fire and stone." he said proudly.

"We have a little fire user as well." Zephyr said.

"Come to think of it Vallus was also a fire user, he has the wind mark as well." Tera said.

"Just like his dear old dad." a voice said from behind them.

It was Vallerus walking towards them with the same smug look on his face. "Where have you been?" Tera asked.

"I stopped by headquarters to find out why Judge Baralai had left the Capital but those idiots at the office never know anything." Vallerus said.

"Oh I'm sorry dear." Tera said. "So I heard that both of the children are fire magick users. They would be considering we are the strongest men in the militia after all." Vallerus said laughing.

Hyo and Zephyr looked disgusted, "Vallerus is that all you do is boast?" Hyo asked.

Vallerus ignored his question and turned to Tera, "I will be late tonight dear I have a report to finish and then I'll be home." he said.

"Alright I will have dinner ready then." Tera said. He kissed her on the cheek and turned around and walked down the hallway out of sight.

"Tera have you heard from Kiarra?" Hyo asked.

"That's right; I forgot she's probably in the waiting room. We should go tell her the good news." Tera replied.

"Alright then let's go." Zephyr said as they began to walk down the hallway and passed the nurse's station.

After a few moments they had reached the waiting room and could see their friend Kiarra sitting reading a magazine. She noticed them and immediately stood up to greet them. The three of them had noticed something different about her, she was smiling.

"Hello everyone." she said greeting them warmly.

"Kiarra you're glowing, what happened?" Tera asked.

"I received a letter today. An actual letter from him." she said with excitement.

They hadn't seen this much happiness from Kiarra in a very long time due to her husband being on an important mission for the Militia. This had been the first time she has heard from him since he left the Capital.

"We'll sit down and tell us what it said." Zephyr said.

The four of them sat down in the waiting room, surrounded by sickly people waiting to be taken back to be seen by their doctor. Hyo had hated hospitals and especially hated sick people. He became very paranoid and tried to ignore the coughing and hacking that was going on around them.

"He said that he would be back within the next six months, He will finally be home for good." Kiarra said smiling.

"That is great news; I can't wait to hear the stories of what he has seen in the Foreignlands." Zephyr said.

"Well enough about me how are the girls and the babies?" she asked eagerly.

"They are doing wonderfully; we can't wait for you to meet Ashlyn and Heiro." Hyo said proudly.

"It's probably best if we all go home and get some rest, we can all come back and see them tomorrow." Tera said.

"Yeah you're probably right; Hyo and I definitely need some sleep after that mission and coming straight to the hospital." Zephyr said.

The Fated Swords

"I need to go make some last minute wedding plans, we only have a week from today." Tera said.

Kiarra jumped out of her chair, "That's right we have so much to do! Let's go!" she shouting as she grabbed Tera and dragged her down the hallway of the hospital.

The men waved goodbye to them and had started home themselves. For a moment all was right in the world, no one had even thought about the Shadow Mage or his army but soon that was all about to change.

***

One Week Later,

"Where is that damn tie?" Zephyr asked as he began to frantically look around his house.

"Where did you have it last?" Hyo asked.

"I'm not sure; if Lillian were here she would know." Zephyr said.

Vallerus walked into the room dressed to the nines in his suit and tie ready to go. "Hey Black and White looks good on you old man." Zephyr said looking at his outfit.

"I don't understand why we couldn't have just worn our Militia uniforms." Hyo asked.

"It's what Tera wanted, and believe me what that woman wants she gets." Vallerus said laughing.

"Happens to the best of us I guess." Zephyr said.

"You'd think that with combat skills as good as yours, you would be more organized Zephyr." Vallerus said pointing to his white tie lying in the floor next to the coffee table.

"You would think so." he agreed as he picked up the tie and put it on.

"Now are you ready we were supposed to meet the girls at the Capital Building twenty minutes ago." Hyo said looking at the clock on the wall.

"Yes I'm ready let's going." Zephyr said as he opened the door. The three of them walked out of Zephyr's house and started off down the street toward the wedding venue.

***

Back at the Capital building the girls were helping Tera get ready for her big day. "Have the boys arrived yet? It's almost time. I'm kind of nervous to say the least." Tera asked putting on her makeup.

"No I haven't heard anything yet; they will be here don't worry." Lillian said rocking Ashlyn in her arms.

"Hold still Tera, I can't fix your hair with you moving so much." Kiarra said.

"Sorry." Tera apologized.

The girls all wore black dresses with white ruffles on the bottom all except for Tera whose wedding dress was as white as freshly fallen snow with diamonds that covered the entire dress.

"You couldn't have picked a better venue than the High Court's Chambers." Aeria said holding Heiro trying to soothe him.

"The Supreme Judge suggested it; he said it would be a great honor to even perform the vows at the ceremony." Tera said.

For a moment she had sounded just like her soon to be husband, and the other girls had noticed it all too well just as the guys had when they were around Vallerus.

"Well we are definitely happy for you and glad to be a part of your special day." Lillian said. Out of the four of them

Lillian had had the biggest heart and when it came to truth and love she had been the purest.

Suddenly there was a knock at the door, "Yes?" Tera asked.

"My lady the men have just arrived we are almost ready to begin." The wedding coordinator said from behind the door.

"Alright we will be right down." Tera replied. Tera stood and walked towards the door, "Well girls, it's time to get married." she said as they walked out the door.

All was quiet in the chamber, the large double doors opened as Zephyr and Lillian walked in arm and arm followed by Hyo and Aeria and then Kiarra and Headmaster Jerriston from the academy. As they proceeded down the aisle they could see all of their family and friends from near and far that came to see the wedding.

Vallerus stood up at the altar with Supreme Judge Baralai. At the Alter each man and woman parted ways and stood on their respected sides. The piano began to play and Vallerus could see Tera step into the door way. Her beautiful blonde hair shone brightly in the light coming from the windows. Her dress sparkled all over from the many diamonds that covered it. To him and the rest of the room she was certainly a sight to behold.

She walked down the aisle slowly and gracefully until she met him at the altar. He took her hands into his and turned to face her captivating beauty.

The Supreme Judge cleared his throat, "Thank you everyone for being here on this wonderful occasion. We are here today to join together Vallerus and Tera and take part in the beginning of their lives together." he said.

Vallerus and Tera smiled at each other blissfully. "Would you please make the sacred sign?" the Judge asked the two of them.

They held the palms of their hands together and raised them up high until their arms formed an arch. "Marriage, whether it is between human and mystic or in their own respected races is a magickal bond that should never be broken. That is how it is treated as such in our beautiful kingdom of V'nairia. With this sacred binding spell, I bind these two souls as one." Baralai said raising his hand to theirs as a blue aura began to envelope it.

A bright light flashed in the room and in that moment the two were now one. "You are now husband and wife. You may kiss your bride Lieutenant." Judge Baralai said smiling.

Vallerus had taken his wife into his arms and kissed her passionately. Everyone in the room began to clap and cheer to congratulate them on their marriage.

Suddenly there was a loud crash and all of the windows in the room burst open with glass flying everywhere. Black smoke began to fill the room. People began to run out of the chamber screaming.

"What's going on!?" Zephyr yelled over to Vallerus.

"I bet I know." Vallerus said angrily.

"Judge Baralai, you need to get out of here. We can handle this." Hyo said.

The black smoke circled the room and quickly closed the doors behind them. The Judge ran for the doors and tried to open them, but they were shut tightly. A powerful force shot out from the doors and sent the Judge flying backwards.

He pulled himself up off of the ground, "We can't get out the doors have been spelled." he said panicking.

The smoke had begun to clear, and what had appeared they weren't at all surprised. Out of the smoke came a man of average size. He wore a long black robe and had short black hair. His eyes were as black and lifeless as the colors he wore. "Good evening." the man spoke.

"Who the hell are you?" Vallerus asked.

"I guess since I know who all of you are I might as well introduce myself, I am the dark mystic Yaigamat." the man hissed like an evil serpent.

"I was expecting you to show your face at some point Yaigamat." The Judge said.

The robed man walked around the room surveying his captives. "Yes better late than never I'm afraid. It's wonderful to have you all in one place." he said.

"You're never going to release the Demon King, we will stop you." Zephyr said.

Yaigamat began to chuckle, "Oh will you, well let's see then. Come on show me what you've got." he hissed.

"Flame Art: Fire Stream!" Zephyr and Hyo shouted spewing their fire spells at Yaigamat.

With one hand the dark mystic harnessed their spells into a ball of flame and hurled it back at them with great force. The two of them dodged the fireball just before it hit a row of chairs behind them, catching part of the room on fire. The Judge cast a water spell to put out the fire before it had spread.

"With only his bare hand? How is that possible?" Hyo asked.

"Anything is possible with dark magick my friend." Yaigamat said glaring at him.

"I can't have you two interfering with my plans." the dark mystic said looking over at the Judge and Jerriston. "Demonic Art: Shadow Binding."

Yaigamat's shadow extended and connected with Baralai and Jerriston's shadows. This formed a black casing around their bodies to where only their heads were visible. "Now you two will not be able to participate." Yaigamat said.

"Girls get to the back of the room now!" Zephyr said.

"The only person that is going to lose their life today is you Yaigamat." Vallerus said.

"Oh really now, well actually I had someone different in mind." He said glaring at Tera devilishly.

He stretched out his hand and black smoke began to surround her, transporting her within his grasp. Yaigamat grabbed her by the hair and yanked hard.

"Let me go!" Tera shouted in pain.

The more she struggled the harder he pulled. "Let her go you filthy piece of shit!" Vallerus shouted.

"You're not in any position to make threats Lieutenant. That kiss you gave her will be your last I promise you." Yaigamat said as he pulled out a steel dagger from his pocket and held it to her throat.

Sweat began to pour from Vallerus' forehead and tears had entered his eyes, but he remained calm. "Don't harm her mystic, we can discuss this." Vallerus said.

"Ha that's the thing with you V'nairians, you always want to negotiate. Sadly that time is not now." Yaigamat said licking the blade of his dagger.

Tera was whimpering and no longer struggled. She stared into Vallerus' eyes, she loved him so and on this day of all days her life was uncertain to her anymore. She could tell just by Yaigamat's voice where his intention had lied. She simply closed her eyes and remained silent

"Please, let her go Yaigamat. I will help you get the swords. I know where the key to the shrine is." Vallerus said.

"Vallerus, stop!" Zephyr shouted.

Yaigamat began to laugh hysterically. "You would commit treason against the entire kingdom for the love of a woman?" the mystic asked.

Vallerus couldn't even look him or anyone else in the eyes, "Yes." he whispered shamefully.

"Well it's too bad I already knew where the key was, that was actually my next stop once I was finished here." Yaigamat said.

The Fated Swords

"Let her go!" Vallerus shouted.

"So be it then." the evil mystic said as he ran his blade through Tera's neck down to the bone.

A crimson mist sprayed from her neck onto the floor and blood ran down her snow white dress. "Tera, no!" Vallerus shouted in anger and disbelief.

Yaigamat threw Tera's body aside and stood and watched in awe at the horror that befell on the rest of the room. Zephyr and the others watched as Vallerus walked over and knelt by her body sobbing. He picked her up in his arms and held her, weeping and wishing for the nightmare to end.

Yaigamat stood laughing at the weeping Lieutenant, "How touching, sadly she didn't have much fight in her I'm afraid." he said.

Vallerus looked up Yaigamat but this time his expression was different. He was enraged and the others had never seen such hatred in someone's eyes before. "You!" he shouted pointing to the dark mystic. "I'm going to run my blade through every inch of your body. I'm not going to kill you; I'm going to destroy everything you are!" Vallerus said angrily.

His rage began to build up his magickal essence until a red aura had manifested around his body. The floor and the walls around them began to crack. Vallerus ran at Yaigamat, he ran so fast he picked the mystic up and ran him through the wall of the chamber and out the other side.

Yaigamat was falling, nearing the ground when Vallerus cast a fire spell that resembled a large flaming dragon that flew through the air and chased the mystic as he was plummeting to the ground. Yaigamat hit the ground with a hard thud. The flame spell had connected with his body and exploded on impact.

The explosion shook part of the city and could be heard and felt by many. Vallerus landed on the ground just below the large crater that the explosion had made. He stood there waiting for the smoke to dissipate so he could see if his enemy was still breathing. The smoke finally cleared and he could see Yaigamat walking out of the rubble.

    Yaigamat turned his head slightly so that his neck would pop. One of his arms was popped out of its socket and he was unable to move it. He used his opposite arm to quickly pop it back into place. It was as if he barely felt any pain at all. It was in that moment that Vallerus was no longer fighting a mystic nor a human like creature, Yaigamat was a monster.

    "Well you can pack quite a punch I see." the robed man said.

    "I haven't even begun tearing you apart demon." Vallerus said removing his sword from its scabbard.

    "You can try Vallerus." Yaigamat said grinning at him.

    Vallerus ran towards him as fast as he could. He quickly utilized his magick to teleport himself behind Yaigamat so he could get a clear shot at his blind spot. "Demonic Art: Shadow Claw!" The evil mystic shouted as his shadow extended just as it had before only this time it had formed a hand and caught Vallerus by the neck mid strike.

    Using his demonic power he picked Vallerus up and threw him into a nearby building. "Demonic Art: Slicing Darkness." the mystic said as his shadow transformed itself into a long black whip of black aura.

    Yaigamat's magick was so dark and so powerful that the crafted a weapon out of his own magickal aura. Vallerus walked out of the hole in the side of the building, cuts and bruises covered his body. Yaigamat swung his whip at Vallerus, striking his arm. The whip sliced through his skin with ease just like a knife through butter. The pain from the wound was searing and had been more intense than any burn he had ever felt before.

"I shouldn't take to many hits from that whip, who knows what damage it could really do." Vallerus said to himself.

The two warriors stood facing each other, neither of them moving not even an inch. As skilled as both of them were, they knew that the slightest mistake could cost them their lives.

Yaigamat would never admit it but he did have some respect for his opponent. "What will you do after claiming V'nairia?" Vallerus asked the evil mystic curiously.

Yaigamat chuckled at the question he was asked and instantly envisioned V'nairia's fall at his hands. "I will offer up every last human soul to the Demon King Diaboro, I hear he likes them flesh and all." Yaigamat said grinning.

Vallerus looked down at his reflection in the blade of his sword. He didn't see the man he had been before, he saw someone else. He didn't even recognize himself anymore. If he was to be honored for anything in his miserable existence even if it cost him his life; it would be this battle. "It must be a pity that I will be the last face you look upon before you die." Vallerus said confidently.

Suddenly behind them, they could hear the sound of a thousand marching soldiers entering the city. The Supreme Judge had made a mistake by lowering the city's defenses during the wedding. It had been a decision he had now regretted. As Vallerus looked on ahead he could see the legion of black armored soldiers moving towards them. He could hear them chanting something, but it was too difficult to make out what they were saying. As they moved even closer he could finally hear them. They were chanting a single word, a name. "Yaigamat." They chanted it over and over as they moved in like a dark plague that would soon inhabit the entire Capital.

"You see I have an army of at least a thousand soldiers Lieutenant. You are but one man and we have already taken out the Capital's primary and secondary defenses. What will you do now?" The Shadow Mystic asked.

This had been no army of mere foot soldiers; they were far better trained than that. Vallerus knew that he alone could not take out Yaigamat and his entire army. Two thirds of the city's soldiers and defenses were gone and Zephyr and the others were tending to everyone else that had been evacuated. There was nothing more to do than fight until he could fight no longer. He had already used up half of his magic strengthening his spells. Time was running out and he was running out of options.

"Are we too late?" said a voice from behind him.

Vallerus had turned to see Zephyr walking towards him accompanied by Hyo, Judge Baralai, and Hylkroft the Godsage. Marching behind them was the rest of the Militia's soldier left in the city.

"You're just in time actually." Vallerus said.

"Jerriston and a few of the soldiers are guarding the women and children at a hidden location in the city; we saw the army and thought we would lend you a hand." Zephyr said.

Vallerus turned to face the dark mystic once again. "That is fine, but Yaigamat is mine. Understood?" he asked.

"Whatever you say Lieutenant, just don't die on us." Zephyr said just before running out to face the army of black armored soldiers.

Hyo and the others quickly followed behind him. Vallerus and Yaigamat stood and faced one another as the two armies clashed and began to battle. They could hear gunfire and the collision of cold steel all around them.

"There is nothing more arousing that the sound of your enemies getting hacked to pieces." Yaigamat said.

The very sight of him disgusted Vallerus to no end. He stood before his wife's murderer full of hatred and little to no remorse for what he was about to do. Vallerus was born for battle and he wasn't merciful or forgiving. He was a vengeful bastard and he wanted Yaigamat to know just what that had meant. Vengeance would have been running a dagger through the mystics neck flesh and reveling in the sight of the blood as it poured out of his lifeless body. Vallerus was about to make this daydream a reality, he wasn't about to be sorry for any of it.

Zephyr locked swords with one soldier; and quickly removed a dagger from his boot and stabbed the soldier in the leg. The man fell to the ground and closed his eyes just before Zephyr's blade had pierced his heart; killing him instantly. He reached out and grabbed another soldier; head butted him and then ran his blade through his chest.

Hyo grabbed a man by the head and shoved him down onto the tip of his sword and watched as the blade went through his eye socket and pierced his brain. "Flame Art: Fire Stream!" he shouted as he set a small group of soldiers on fire.

"Water Art: Tidal Surge." Judge Baralai said as he used his magick to conjure a giant tidal wave that came crashed down on top of the soldiers before him.

Hylkroft leapt into the air and threw his staff into the crowd and used it amplify to strength of his lightning magick; electrocuting the already soaked soldiers. They had already taken out quite a few hundred enemy soldiers while losing some of their own. Zephyr and the other had hoped Vallerus could quickly dispose of their leader and join them on the battlefield.

Vallerus charged at Yaigamat with his sword but was quickly blocked by the mystic's whip that he had fashioned into a sword of his own this time. Sparks flew from their blades as they hit one another. Yaigamat's sword had transformed back into its previous form and latched onto Vallerus' leg. The aura from the whip had burned deep into his leg, the pain almost unbearable.

Yaigamat lifted him up off of the ground and threw him high into the air. He lashed out with his whip once more and latched onto his body this time. With great force, the evil mystic ran him into the ground. As the dust had settled, Yaigamat had noticed that Vallerus was gone. He looked around but couldn't find him anywhere.

"Where are you bastard!?" he shouted.

"I'm right here." Vallerus said as he quickly appeared behind Yaigamat and forced his blade through his back and out his chest.

Yaigamat had begun to cough hysterically spraying blood along the ground below him. "So you used a replacement spell?" the dying man asked.

"You let your guard down thinking that you had me, you wanted to destroy me so badly it clouded your judgment." Vallerus explained "Big Mistake."

"So it seems." Yaigamat said coughing up more blood.

Vallerus gently pulled his sword out of Yaigamat's back and walked around to see his pathetic face. He grabbed him by the hair and lifted him up off the ground. "There will be others; they will come to destroy your kingdom just as I had." The mystic said spitting blood at Vallerus' feet.

"I will be here waiting on every last weak piece of shit like you that threatens this kingdom." Vallerus said smiling as he shoved his sword through the bottom of Yaigamat's chin and out the top of his skull.

Yaigamat's horrified face had given great pleasure to Vallerus, his vengeance was complete. Tera could finally rest in peace. He removed his sword from his enemy's corpse and placed it back in its scabbard. Without even looking back at the Capital he walked on towards the gates. He had no idea where he was going but he had to get away. The memories of his wife were too overwhelming for him to stay. He left his friends, his son, and his home behind not knowing when he would return.

***

With the death of Yaigamat, the remaining enemy soldiers had turned to dust and were swept away by the wind. Zephyr and the others stood in the center of the Capital looking around at the devastation that Yaigamat and his army had caused. They were thankful the battle was over.

"So it appears that even these soldiers weren't human." Hylkroft said.

"Yaigamat was more powerful than we anticipated, however Vallerus prevailed and that's all that matters." Baralai said.

Zephyr and Hyo walked over to Yaigamat's corpse but couldn't see their friend anywhere.

"What happens now? Where is Vallerus?" Hyo said.

"Well we will start rebuilding the city and have a proper burial for Tera." Zephyr said.

"What about Vallerus?" Hyo asked.

"For now we wait, that is all that we can do." Zephyr said looking off into the distance wondering what his friend was going to do now and if he would ever return home. "He is going through a lot right now and needs time to think."

"Your right, we should get back to our families." Hyo said. They walked over to regroup with Judge Baralai and the Godsage.

"You're Honor?" Hyo asked.

"No it is okay, you should find your families." The Judge said gazing around at the devastation surrounding them.

"Thank you sir." they said saluting him and turning back to find Lillian and Aeria.

"Now that the battle is won, I can't help but shake the feeling that this isn't over." Hylkroft said turning to the judge.

"Your right, I would like for you and I to meet with the other judges of the High Court. I found out some troubling news while in Talias." Judge Baralai said.

The Godsage was confused by Baralai's words, "What news do you speak of?" he asked.

"I had met with Baron Tyran." The Judge said gravely.

"I see, so it was another vision then?" Hylkroft asked.

Judge Baralai didn't answer for a moment he thought back to his conversation with the Baron and he could feel a cold chill enter his body. "Yes, the future has changed with the events that have happened today." Baralai said. "It was foretold that Vallerus was supposed to die at the hands of Yaigamat and the four of us were the victors against him."

"I see. The fact that the future has changed is unsettling, we must meet with the other judges at once." The Godsage said.

"Yes, I will call a meeting immediately." The Supreme Judge said as he turned to walk back to the Capital building leaving the Godsage with his thoughts.

Part Four

Two Years Later,

Zephyr woke up early and slowly got out of bed. He looked over at his wife who was still sleeping peacefully. He quietly walked through the room and down the stairs of their home so that he wouldn't wake Lillian or the children up. It had been very early in the morning and he had to hurry and get ready for work. He walked into the kitchen and started a pot of coffee then proceeded to the bathroom to turn on the shower. He stood motionless whilst the hot water beat down on his body.

He thought back to the day they had won the battle over Yaigamat and his army, the day that Vallerus had left the Capital without saying anything to anyone. It had been two years since they had seen their friend. He had often thought about that day and never quite understood why Vallerus had taken it upon himself to just leave and abandon his home. He was the Lieutenant of the Militia and even though that his wife had been killed right before his eyes he threw that all away and even left his only son behind.

He stepped out of the shower and put on his uniform. He had been promoted from a soldier to a commander in the

Militia now so his uniform colors were black and red. He slicked back his short brown hair so that he looked more presentable, and even trimmed what little facial hair he kept. He hated facial hair but Lillian made him keep it regardless.

He walked back up the stairs and into his bedroom, he bent down and kissed Lillian on the cheek. He had picked up his sword from beside his nightstand and strapped it on his side, walked back downstairs and walked out the door.

Outside he could see the sun peeking up over the large walls that surrounded the city. The city was very quiet and not very many people had been out this early in the morning, thatis how Zephyr liked it. He walked down the street in the direction of the Militia's headquarters when he was suddenly stopped by one of his squad members.

The young man with short blonde hair in his black soldier's uniform ran up to him urgently. "Commander Zephyr!" the soldier saluting his commanding officer.

"At ease Tai, what's going on?" Zephyr asked concernedly.

The boy was out of breath and could barely speak, "Sir some of the other soldiers had said they saw Vallerus down at the café." Tai said excitedly.

Zephyr hadn't believed him at first but he thought that it may have been a good idea to confirm the sighting for himself.

"Tai I need you to notify Commander Hyo of the sighting and let him know that I will be a bit late to headquarters." Zephyr ordered.

"Yes sir! Right away sir!" the boy said saluting him once again and turned to run down the street.

Zephyr walked down the street further towards the café hoping to see his friend inside drinking a cup of coffee and reading a newspaper. It had been two years since they had heard from their friend, he could only hope that he had finally returned. He was getting close he could smell the aroma of fresh coffee coming from down the street. He turned the corner to find the café in front of him. He walked up and opened the front door and could hear the bell chime as he walked in. He couldn't believe his eyes, sitting right in front of him had been Vallerus drinking a cup of coffee.

"Are you going to sit down or are you just going to stand there and look stupid?" Vallerus asked. Zander walked over and sat down in front of him.

"What happened? Why did you leave?" Zephyr began asking impatiently.

Vallerus gave him the death stare, so he knew to instantly shut his mouth. "My wife had just been killed, what did you two expect me to do?" Vallerus asked.

"We expected you to take up your duty as Lieutenant and do your job!" Zephyr shouted.

Vallerus gave the same look once again, "If you don't lower your voice, I'm going to cut your tongue out of your head." Vallerus said angrily.

"I just don't understand you even left your son behind. I have told him every day that you would be coming back not knowing if you were dead or alive. "Zephyr said softly.

Vallerus looked down at his cup of coffee that was no longer hot, "I know and I haven't forgiven myself for abandoning Vallus and everyone here in the Capital." he said.

The waitress walked over and asked Zephyr if he would like a cup of coffee and he agreed. He watched her as she walked behind the counter, poured the coffee and brought it back over to him.

"Thank you." he said smiling. He turned back to Vallerus, "So where did you go?" he asked.

"The Foreignlands." Vallerus said his eyes filling up with shame as he said the words.

Zephyr's eyes had widened, "Are you out of your mind? That is illegal! Unless we are sent on a mission we are not suppose to leave the kingdom!" Zephyr shouted trying to keep his voice down.

"Don't you think I know that? Anywhere but here is where I wanted to be." Vallerus said.

"Listen, this stays between you and me, no one else is to know where you were. You were staying at the inn at Rygoth under an assumed name so no one could find you." Zephyr said.

Vallerus rolled his eyes as he watched Zephyr sip his coffee. "Fine." Vallerus agreed.

"On a lighter note, looks like you made Commander." he added.

Zephyr smiled, "Yeah, Hyo made it to." he said proudly.

"Well both of you done just fine, how is everyone? How is Vallus?" Vallerus asked anxiously.

"Everyone has been doing alright aside front being worried about you and Vallus is in the troublesome two's." Zephyr explained.

"That's great I can't wait to see everyone." Vallerus said.

Zephyr rose from his seat and had laid some money on the table for his coffee. "I believe we may want to go see Judge Baralai first, he's going to want to know your back." Zephyr said.

Vallerus also got up from the table, "That sounds like a good idea. Err- you think you can spot me for the coffee?" Vallerus asked.

Zephyr began to laugh, "Don't I always." he said jokingly as they both walked out of the café.

The Fated Swords

Zephyr and Vallerus walked into the Capital building and approached the front desk. "How can I help you?" the receptionist at the desk asked.

"Commanders Zephyr and Vallerus to see Judge Baralai." Zephyr said.

Vallerus thought it odd that Zephyr had addressed his as a commander but he had ignored it thinking it had been a simple mistake. "Take the elevator to the top floor please, Judge Baralai is expecting you." the receptionist said.

They walked past the front desk and stepped into the elevator. Zephyr punched in the correct passcode to take them to the top floor. Zephyr had begun to get even more nervous with each floor they had passed on the way up. He knew that Judge Baralai wasn't happy with Vallerus' behavior and would want to know where he has been for the past two years.

They had reached the top floor and stepped out just as the elevator doors had opened. "Remember to stick to the story." Zephyr said to Vallerus.

"Alright." Vallerus agreed as they walked down the long hallway and past the High Court Chamber doors.

Zephyr knocked on Judge Baralai's office door at the end of the hall and listened for the judge to tell them to come in. When he had opened the door, they could see the Judge sitting at his large wooden desk signing paperwork.

He looked up at them and smiled, "Have a seat gentleman." Baralai said motioning them to the chairs in front of his desk.

They walked over and sat down in front of him. The judge stood up at his desk and stared long and hard at Vallerus, "So good of you to return Vallerus." he said.

Vallerus looked up at him and smiled faintly, "It's good to be back sir."

Baralai's smile had instantly faded, "Is it? Where have you been for the past two years?" the judge asked skeptically.

"I was in Rygoth, I stayed at the inn. I was in mourning and needed to clear my head." Vallerus said lying just as he and Zephyr had rehearsed at the cafe.

"Well that's all well and good, but next time don't take two years." Baralai said.

Vallerus was nervous to ask his next question but spit it out anyway, "So am I being released from the Militia sir?" he asked.

Judge Baralai sat back down in his black leather chair and sighed. "Of course not, your one of the best soldiers we have. Unfortunately we did have to remove your rank; you were gone so long we had to find another Lieutenant." Baralai said.

"So what rank am I being assigned?" he asked.

"You're going to remain a Commander until further notice; we will be watching you Vallerus. Remember that." Judge Baralai said with a raised eyebrow as he handed Vallerus his red and black commander uniform.

Suddenly there was a knock at the door, "Come in." the judge said politely.

The door swung open and in walked a short, bald man with a short brown beard and mustache. Vallerus had noticed he was wearing a black and white uniform and carried pistols on each side of his belt.

"Ah just in time. Men this is Omak the new Lieutenant of the V'nairian Militia." Judge Baralai said.

Vallerus instantly became enraged; Zephyr could see veins appear on the right side of his neck. Vallerus quickly contained his anger and saluted the new Lieutenant. Zephyr had done the same and they shook the man's hand.

"At ease men." Lieutenant Omak said in a thick accent. They could tell he had had been in his early thirties and from his voice that he had smoked quite a bit, cigars if they had to guess.

"From what I've heard your squad was the best damn group of soldiers the Militia had ever seen." Omak said.

"Thank you sir, we are honored by your kind words." Zephyr said.

"I also heard what happened with your wife Commander Vallerus and I know that out of grief you left the city. I'd just like to say that I'm sorry for your loss and I hope we can put all of this mess behind us." Lieutenant Omak added.

Vallerus bit his tongue; he had already pulled one ridiculous stunt. It had been best to keep his mouth shut and just make the best of his position for now.

"Of course sir, we look forward to working with you." he said lying yet again although he was very good at making it go unnoticed.

"I think that will be all gentlemen. For now you are free to go." Judge Baralai said.

Zephyr and Vallerus turned and walked out the door. The judge looked over at the Lieutenant in shock, "I suppose that went rather well." he said.

"Yeah, and here I thought he was gonna try and kick my ass." Lieutenant Omak said. He removed a cigar from his pocket and lit it with a match and inhaled just before blowing out a cloud of smoke.

"Keep an eye on him closely Omak. He isn't stable, he was lying most of the conversation." Baralai said.

Omak flicked the ashes from his cigar in an ashtray on the Judge's desk. "Don't worry about Vallerus your grace, I've got a handle on it." he said.

***

Zephyr and Vallerus rode the elevator down to the ground floor of the Capital building and proceeded to walk outside. "So where are we going now?" Vallerus asked.

"Well I guess we will go to my house, I'm sure that everyone will want to see you." Zephyr said.

"Everyone knows that I'm here?" Vallerus asked surprised.

"Yes before I went by the café to look for you I had one of my squad members relay the information to Hyo." Zephyr said.

"So I'm sure everyone else knows by now."

"Alright." Vallerus said smiling faintly.

He was excited to his son Vallus. After two years he could finally hold his son in his arms, he still hadn't forgiven himself for leaving him behind but he had hoped that as Vallus had gotten older he could have forgiven his father. Luckily for Vallerus, his friends had done an excellent job of talking with the boy about his father.

As they walked down the street towards Zephyr and Lillian's house, Vallerus took in the beauty of the Capital at sundown. It was just as he had remembered; he loved to take walks through the city at this time of day. He certainly had a different side to him at times, a side he didn't want just anyone to see. Tera had been the only one to ever see his passionate side, and to Vallerus that one person was enough for a lifetime.

After a few minutes the men had made it to Zephyr's home just outside the industrial part of the city next to the gardens. They could see Lillian outside messing around in her flowers on the side of their house. Vallerus could see the bright colors of her tiny garden as he approached their home, There were a variety of colors; red, blue, pink, and purple. Lillian had loved to garden and plant flowers, she was the only one in the group with a green thumb. Seeing the flowers seem to warm his heart a little, he had softened up even if only for a moment. Somehow their beauty had reminded him of his wife.

Lillian had quickly noticed them approaching, "Hyo! Aeria! They are here!" she shouted calling to them from outside the kitchen window.

Hyo and his wife Aeria quickly ran outside to greet them; they had taken one look at Vallerus and were very surprised. "Well I'll be damned, he's back." Hyo said.

"Long time no see stranger." Lillian said looking up at Vallerus' furry mug.

"Hello everyone." Vallerus said looking around at each of them. He looked around at everyone and noticed that Kiarra wasn't with them. "Wait, where is Kiarra?"

"A year after you left, Mik showed up and had taken her away to train, something about her wanting to be trained in combat because of her ancestry." Lillian said.

Hyo came up and patted Vallerus on the bad, "How ya been you big lug? We haven't seen you in two years." Hyo asked curiously.

Seeing their faces only reminded him of Tera, he could picture her beautiful smile and the way she laughed. Seeing them pained him, but he knew that he couldn't shut out his only friends and family. He couldn't stand the thought of being alone, not after losing the love of his life.

Suddenly they could here an infant crying from inside the house. "Oh he's awake ill go and get him for you Lillian." Aeria said.

"Thank you." Lillian said.

Vallerus looked over at Zephyr and smiled, "Do you?" he asked.

Zephyr nodded, "Yes we do." He replied.

Aeria walked outside the house carrying a baby in her arms. It was wrapped in a black blanket that had been made out of wool. "His name is Zander." Lillian said taking the child from Aeria and showing him to Vallerus.

He had short brown hair that had perfectly resembled his father's, and had eyes just like his mothers. "Congratulations to the both of you, what elements does the boy possess?" Vallerus asked.

"He's human, there aren't any markings." Zephyr said taking his index finger ad tickling the underside of Zander's chin.

"Well mystic or not he will be a fine soldier someday just like his father, and uncle Vallerus of course." Vallerus said laughing. There it was, Zephyr had been waiting on the old Vallerus to appear. They all began to laugh with him.

"Mommy! Heiro keeps poking me." A tiny voice said.

Running toward them from around the house came little Ashe followed by Heiro. Ashe was the spitting image of her mother down to the freckles on her face and her long red hair. Vallerus was sure that her temper would be just as terrible as her mother's had been. Vallerus could also see a little of Hyo and Aeria in Heiro as well. They were both growing up so well.

Another young boy walked up behind them, "Uncle Zephyr I told Heiro to leave her alone, but he wouldn't listen." Vallus said looking up at them.

The boy had black hair down to his shoulders; he had bright blue eyes and was just a hair taller than the other two children. "My son." Vallerus mumbled under his breath.

Vallerus was stunned; he didn't know how to react. He stood in amazement as he looked upon the life that he and Tera had created. "Vallus this man here is your father." Zephyr said pointing to the man beside of him.

"You're my papa?" Vallus asked.

Vallerus nodded in silence and smiled widely. He held back the tears so no one would see him cry. Without a second thought Vallus ran over and hugged him tightly. Vallerus bent down and picked up Vallus and held him close.

"My son, I have missed you." Vallerus whispered.

"I was waiting for you papa." Vallus said softly.

"I thought about you everydayVallus." Vallerus said overcome by emotions. He was finally happy again after two long years grieving his wife, Father and son had finally been reunited.

***

Later that night Vallerus sat in the windowsill of his bedroom. The room seemed empty at night without Tera. He had just tucked Vallus into bed and watched him fall asleep. He was still amazed at how big his son had gotten while he was away. It had been particularly quiet in the Capital that night. Normally up until the late hours of the morning you could hear people wandering the city. Vallerus had loved to stay up late and just watch the city from his bedroom window. The Capital and all of V'nairia had been his sole purpose for joining the Militia, he loved protecting the kingdom. It was his home and wouldn't dare allow anyone to threaten his home or his family.

He looked over at Vallus who was sleeping peacefully and began to weep. He held his face in his hands, "Tera I wish you were here, a boy needs his mother. I miss you." He said sobbing.

The pain had come rushing back, the thought of Vallus growing up with only one parent killed him and he knew that it was going to be hard for both of them from that moment on.

"Oh how touching, the big bad soldier has a heart." A voice called out from the other side of the room.

Vallerus jumped up and grabbed his sword, "Whose there?" he asked searching the room.

He looked around the room from one end to the other and couldn't see anyone. A shadowy figure appeared in the darker part of the room that had been away from the window. He appeared to be a cloaked man, Vallerus couldn't see his face.

"What if I told you, I could take your pain away Vallerus?" the shadow asked.

"What the hell are you talking about? Who are you?" Vallerus asked.

The man shifted closer to him, he moved just like a ghost only he seemed more real. "That is not important; the only thing you need to worry about is being released from your pain." The mysterious figure said.

"Get out of my house!" Vallerus shouted removing his sword from its scabbard.

"Kill me if you must, but I'm not leaving." The man said.

Vallerus thrust his blade through the man, but he was not a solid being. It was like Vallerus had struck the air. He jabbed at him repeatedly, but it was no use. Vallerus' blade could not make contact.

"What are you?" he asked curiously.

The figure had begun to laugh at his stupidity, "A friend." The shadow simply replied.

"The last time I checked, friends don't appear as cloaked beings in the darkness." Vallerus said skeptically.

The figure chuckled, "I guess that is true but things aren't always what they seem Vallerus. Just like Zephyr and the others." The shadow continued.

Vallerus didn't understand what the cloaked man had been talking about, his words were confusing him. "What do they have to do with you coming into my house in the late hours of the night?" Vallerus asked.

"Yaigamat killed your wife did he not? Was he not a mystic?" the figure asked.

"You son of a bitch!" Vallerus shouted.

"Calm down, just hear me out." The man demanded.

"You are only a half mystic, while Zephyr and the others are pure blooded mystics. It was a pure blood that killed your wife Vallerus."

"So you are saying it is my friend's fault that a demon killed my wife?" Vallerus asked.

"Not entirely no, but they are of the same breed. They long to dominate this kingdom as well as the rest of the world; you are just too dimwitted to see it." The cloaked man said.

"I never could stand mystics but I would never harm my friends because of my hatred, I see them differently." Vallerus said thinking about Zephyr and the others and the memories he had made with them.

"Vallerus, I can see that you are a man that desires power, craves it even. You would even kill for it. Would you not?" the shadow asked.

The very mention of the word excited Vallerus, he did crave power. He had wanted to become Supreme Judge and rule V'nairia, it had been his dream. "Yes given the right circumstances." Vallerus said allowing the man to get inside his head.

"What if I said that I could give you the power that you need? All you have to do is kill Supreme Judge Baralai." The man asked.

Evil thoughts began to surround Vallerus' heart and mind. The man pulled out a vial of purple liquid from under his cloak and placed it on Vallerus' nightstand.

"If you desire such power, then all you would have to do is drink this, but be warned. Do not drink unless you can perform the task that I have asked of you." The man said before his body evaporated into thin air.

Vallerus sat and thought for a moment. He looked across the room at Vallus who was sleeping soundly in his bed. Vallus did want a better kingdom for not just his son but for all of the people of V'nairia. He walked over to the nightstand and picked up the vial. He thought it absurd that one tiny vial of liquid could give him the power to take over the kingdom for himself. He removed the cork from the top of the vial and turned it up and drank its contents.

The taste was terrible, the only thing he could compare it to was horse piss that he had drank on a dare once back during his days at the academy. For a few moments he had felt nothing, and then he quickly began to feel a sharp pain in his chest. The only thought he had at the time was that the cloaked man had poisoned him. The room began to spin and he had fallen to the floor writhing in pain.

After a few moments the pain had subsided. He stood up and walked over to the bathroom and turned on the light. He looked in the mirror and couldn't notice any changes to his body externally. He could tell however, that his strength and magick aura had been strengthened. For a mere potion to give him this much power was astonishing. Looking in the mirror he had noticed a difference in his face, he was smiling. Smiling devilishly like he had been looking back at a completely different person. He thought it very strange but ignored it. He turned the light back off and walked back over to the windowsill and sat down. He sat there the rest of the night watching the city lights, thinking about what his next move would be.

All he knew at that moment was that he had to kill The Supreme Judge of V'nairia, and it wouldn't be an easy task.

***

Two weeks later,

Zephyr, Hyo, and Heiro had just returned from a fishing trip on the outside of Durea. They were gone only a few days to camp and relax from their previous mission that had sent them all the way to Rygoth.

"I bet Aeria won't know what to do with all of that fish you caught Hyo." Zephyr said.

"Yeah, I feel sorry for poor Lillian though. Her husband can't fish worth a damn." Hyo said laughing.

Heiro followed behind then carrying the couple of fish that he had caught. Even for a child that was two and half years old he could fish pretty well.

They had finally made it back to Hyo's house to unload the many fish they had caught when they had seen Militia soldiers standing outside. Lieutenant Omak was talking to Lillian who was crying hysterically. Both of them were shocked at what was going on. They ran over to the Lieutenant and Lillian, "What is going on?" Zephyr said.

Lillian began to cry even harder all she could do was point to Hyo's home. "Zephyr, watch Heiro please." Hyo said.

He proceeded to walk towards the house, "Hyo stop! You can't go in there!" Lieutenant Omak shouted.

He walked back over to them, "What the hell is going on? Where is my wife?" Hyo asked angrily.

Omak looked down at the ground and back up into Hyo's eyes. He placed his hand on his shoulders, "Aeria is dead, and we found her lying in her bed this morning, her neck sliced open. Lillian found her and notified us, Hyo I'm so sorry." Omak said.

Tears filled up Hyo's eyes as he sank to the ground. He had wondered if this was real, was his wife really dead?

He jumped up and ran past the soldiers guarding the door and burst in. He ran into his bedroom and saw Aeria's lifeless body lying on the bed covered in blood. He could see the open cut in her throat, the wound was wide and deep, he could tell that it was made by a sword and not a dagger. It was an unusual form of death to use such a weapon for that specific act.

Hyo fell on top of her and held her weeping, "Aeria, no!" he shouted. Zephyr and the others didn't walk back inside; they allowed Hyo to mourn in peace.

"What happened?" Zephyr asked.

"There didn't seem to be any sign of forced entry, but by looking at the evidence it was murder." Omak said looking back and Zephyr and Lillian.

"Was there a struggle?" Lillian asked.

"No there wasn't any sign of a struggle, they simply cut her throat and left it seems like." The Lieutenant replied.

"We will find them, someone maliciously killed Aeria and they will pay for it." Zephyr said looking over at Hyo's house and then down at Heiro.

"It will be alright Heiro, don't be afraid." Zephyr said softly.

Heiro smiled widely not knowing what had been going on. "The innocence of children." Zephyr thought, "It's a truly amazing thing."

Part Five

Over the next couple of days, Zephyr and the others held Aeria's funeral. All of their friends and family had attended, all except for Vallerus. They hadn't really seen much of him lately and they thought it had been strange. Out of all of their friends Vallerus was the only one who had lost a wife, so Zephyr and Lillian had hoped that Vallerus would have helped Hyo through this difficult part of his life. They had also thought that Aeria's passing had reminded him of losing his wife so they hadn't blamed him for not attending the funeral.

He had always worked late or even sometimes ignored the others. Zephyr and Lillian had brushed it off as him being emotional because Tera had died and then one of his best friend's wives as well, so they had just let him be. Hyo had been distant as well even around Heiro, so after the funeral they had prepared the boy to go live with Aeria's parents in Rygoth for awhile. Things had been pretty bleak and they had hoped that the darkness would subside and they could go about their everyday just as they had before.

"Where are you going?" Lillian asked watching Zephyr quickly put on his uniform.

"Hyo and I have a meeting at Militia Headquarters for the briefing for our squad's next mission." Zephyr said.

"Lieutenant Omak said that its going to require both of our squads."

"Sounds like it may be a difficult one." Lillian said while continuing to wash the dishes from their lunch together.

"I should be back in time for dinner, I love you." Zephyr said as he walked over and kissed his wife goodbye just before he walked out the door.

"I love you dear." Lillian called out to him.

Ashe walked in the room clutching one of her favorite dolls that had bright red hair just like her and her mothers. She sat in the floor playing without a care in the world. Lillian often looked at her in amazement; she was so young and had no idea just how cruel the world could be at times. Lillian reveled in the thought of her daughter having a bright and happy future, and she had hoped everyday that her dream was made a reality.

Zander had lain in his crib beside of the kitchen table, sleeping peacefully; he had looked just like his father with his short brown hair. Lillian had hoped that he would grow up breaking a few hearts just as Zephyr did before they met. She wanted the very best for her children just as any parent would. A mother's love knows no bounds and is some of the most powerful magic in the world.

Suddenly there was a knock at the door, she walked over and opened the door; it was Vallerus.

"Vallerus, what a surprise. Come in." Lillian said.

Vallerus walked inside without saying a word, Lillian could tell that there was something wrong with him by the way he was acting. He sat down at the dining room table and looked up at her still silent.

"Would you like me to make you something? Are you hungry?" she asked.

"No thank you, I'm alright. I just came to talk." Vallerus said.

"Zephyr just left to meet Hyo at headquarters; he will be back in a couple of hours." She explained.

"I came to talk to you actually." Vallerus said.

Lillian thought it strange that he had come to her instead of one of the other men. Something was off about him and it had made her nervous.

"What did you come to talk about?" she asked cautiously.

"I have to tell someone, I have to get it off of my chest. The very truth is ripping me apart." He said hysterically clawing at his head. He stood up and began to thrash about like an old drunk. He was knocking over chairs and pushed the table against the wall.

"Vallerus just calm down and tell me what's wrong." Lillian said frightened.

"I killed her, I killer Aeria." Vallerus said.

The very words had almost made Lillian sick, to think that he could have done such a horrific act. "Ashe go to the closet and hide." She said to her daughter who was playing on the floor behind her.

"Mommy." Ashe said.

"Go now!" Lillian shrieked.

Ashe jumped up from the floor crying and ran and hid in the closet. Lillian cast a spell on the closet door so it could not be opened from the outside.

"How could you do such a horrible thing to Hyo? To all of us?" Lillian asked angrily.

Vallerus slowly began to walk over towards Lillian who was walking backwards to the wall of the kitchen. Vallerus grabbed her before she could run and gripped her by the throat with his large hands. He began to squeeze tightly until she was gasping for air.

"It had to be done; I wanted Hyo and Zephyr to feel the same pain that I have felt for over two years now." Vallerus said. "It isn't fair."

"You don't have to do this." Lillian said whimpering trying to get the words out.

"I'm going to kill you, then Zephyr and Hyo, and then Judge Baralai. Mystics don't deserve to live in this kingdom anymore." Vallerus said talking out of his head.

Lillian couldn't even speak to try and calm him down, his grip kept tightening. Her vision was blurred; she could see Vallerus look over at Zander in his crib who was now crying after being woken up by the struggle. Tears ran down Lillian's face as she mouthed the word, "No."

He removed a dagger from his belt and jabbed her in the stomach and released her. She fell to the floor bleeding profusely. Vallerus walked over to the crib and picked up Zander and walked out the door. Vallerus then proceeded to cast a fire spell on the house to set it on fire. He walked off with Zander in hand and made his way to the center of the city where he would find Judge Baralai.

Zephyr was still on his way to headquarters when he saw the smoke rise from the east, where his house had been.

"Lillian." He said under his breath.

He ran back as fast as he could toward their home. All he could think about were his wife and children and hoped that they remained safe. He had taken a shortcut through the garden and had finally reached their burning home. He burst through the front door, "Lillian!" He shouted over the roar of the flames.

Smoke filled the room, he couldn't see anything. He had heard a whimper and looked over toward the kitchen. He saw Lillian lying on the ground; he ran over and sat down beside her. He picked her up and held her in his arms. He looked down at her stomach and saw that she was losing blood fast.

"Baby, hold on. It will be alright." Zephyr said as tears ran down his cheeks.

Lillian shook her head, and looked up at him with saddened eyes. She knew that she was dying.

"Who done this to you?" he asked frantically trying to keep her from fading. She looked at him and then down at her hand that was covered in blood. She had taken her index figure and began to write on the floor. She had written the name of her attacker, it read:

Vallerus

Zephyr was surprised, why would his friend have done this? What is going on? Zephyr was confused and needed answers. Lillian grabbed him and pulled him closer, she then mouthed the words "I love you always."

"No! Lillian don't leave me please!" he shouted.

It was already too late, her head slowly tilted to the side and he had watched the light leave his wife's eyes. His soul mate, his best friend was dead. He held her body close as he wept, parts of the ceiling came crashing down and he knew that he would need to get out soon. He picked up Lillian's body and walked outside the house. Outside Hyo had led a group of soldiers over to their home after seeing the smoke from the fire. Zephyr quietly carried his wife's body over to Hyo and the others and laid her on the ground.

"Is she?" Hyo asked unaware of what happened.

Zephyr nodded and looked up at him, "Yes she gone, I couldn't find Ashe or Zander so it's likely she had gotten them away in time. I'm not sure." He said brokenly.

"Who done this, did she say?" Hyo asked softly.

"It was Vallerus, so I'm guessing he was the one that killed Aeria as well." Zephyr said.

The news had struck Hyo hard, their best friend that they had trusted; their leader had killed their loved ones without remorse. They knew that he had to pay.

"Take my wife's body to the hospital; I have something I need to do." Zephyr said looking over at the soldiers.

They nodded and lifted up and her body and began to carry her. Zephyr motioned Hyo to follow him and they ran off toward the center of the city.

"Where are we going?" Hyo asked.

"Something is telling me he is going to the Capital building. We have to stop him before he can get to Judge Baralai." Zephyr said.

"Alright I'm with you Zephyr." Hyo said as they raced off together after Vallerus.

***

After a few moments they had finally reached the Capital building. There were already dead soldiers lining the steps of the building. They looked like bloody ornaments placed for decoration. They could see Vallerus at the top of the steps about to walk inside the building.

"Vallerus!" Zephyr shouted.

\Vallerus turned to face them; he was smiling with a crazed look in his eye. "Zephyr, I thought you were at Headquarters?" he asked.

"We know Vallerus, Lillian told me just before she died." Zephyr said angrily gripping the handle of his sword.

"That bitch did have some fight in her after all." Vallerus said.

Zephyr ignored his comment about his wife, "Why? Why are you doing all of this?" he asked.

"Mystics don't belong in this world, and once I become the new Supreme Judge of V'nairia they will all be destroyed." Vallerus said laughing.

"So he means to murder the High Court Judges," Hyo said.

"Not before we take him down." Zephyr said removing his blade from its scabbard.

Vallerus removed his sword as well, "Fine ill consider you both target practice." He said dashing towards them.

Vallerus was too quick for Hyo, he had appeared behind him and grabbed him by the arm and threw him across the lot. Zephyr ran up to him and clashed swords with his former friend. Sparks flew from their swords with each connecting strike.

Vallerus pushed Zephyr back with all of his weight, "Wind Art: Gale Storm!" Vallerus shouted as the current from his tornado spell has swept Zephyr up into it and threw him against a nearby building.

Out of the corner of his eye he could see Hyo running up to strike him with his sword and immediately jumped backwards just before Hyo could attack. "Flame Art: Fire Stream!" Vallerus said spewing the flames in Hyo's direction. The spell burned the left side of his body and he was barely able to move. He fell to the ground in pain. Vallerus walked over and struck him in the stomach with his sword.

"That should be enough to kill you." Vallerus said.

Zephyr came out of nowhere and delivered a powerful kick to the side of Vallerus' head knocking him to the side. Vallerus rose from the ground slowly wiping the blood from his mouth.

"Its gonna take a lot more out of me to kill you." He said.

"Your gonna pay for what you done to them." Zephyr said.

"Flame Art: Great Fire Stream!" both of them shouted.

Their fire spells collided causing a struggle between them. Both of them could feel the intense flames of each other's spells as they pushed against each other. Zephyr could tell a difference in Vallerus' strength now than what it had been before. Something had happened with him to make him so powerful and so full of hate. With a final rush of power he strengthened his fire spell to envelope Zephyr and knocking him backward.

Zephyr slowly rose to his feet even though most of his body had been badly burned, he held up his sword to defend himself and waited for Vallerus to attack.

"Fine if you intend to stand in my way, then I will show you a technique that I have been developing. It is meant for a must larger enemy but it will do just as well." Vallerus said holding up two fingers to his face. Zephyr watched as the blade of Vallerus' sword had vanished.

"Sacred Art: Dance of One Hundred Blades!" Vallerus shouted snapping his fingers

Vallerus watched as Zephyrs flesh was cut to ribbons before his very eyes. His spell was so powerful it left him unrecognizable. Zephyr was dead; no one could survive such a powerful spell from such an extraordinary warrior. Vallerus sheathed his sword and turned to walk inside the Capital building. He had finally killed the friends he had sworn to protect. He was now all alone.

***

The flames had subsided at what was left of Lillian's home. A carriage pulled by horses had pulled up in front of the wreckage. The horses were guarded by soldiers from Talias.

The door from the carriage had opened and Thesia had stepped out onto the ground. The guards led her through the wreckage that was once a home to a wonderful family. The only thing that had been left standing untouched had been the closet near the kitchen. Thesia waved her hand in front of the closet door, dispelling the enchantment Lillian had placed on it. She had opened the door to see a scared little red headed girl inside.

She motioned the little girl outside but she had been too terrified to move. "It is alright little one. I will not hurt you." The young Thesia said softly.

Ashe slowly stepped out of the closet and into Thesia's arms. She looked up at Thesia with tears in her eyes, "Where is my mommy?" she asked.

Thesia smiled widely, "Your mommy is gone little one but she told me that she loved you very much and that I could be your new mother." She said stroking her beautiful red hair.

Ashe held Thesia close and giggled, "I love you mommy."

"And I you little Ashe, let us go home." Thesia said.

Ashe nodded and held Thesia's hand as she led her back to the carriage. "Everything is going to be alright now my little dragon, just you wait and see." Thesia said smiling as she lifted Ashe into the carriage.

Thesia walked back over to the wreckage and pulled a letter out of her pocket; she kissed it and laid it on the ground.

"Watch over us Lillian, give us your strength." She said as she walked back and got inside the carriage.

***

The Elevator doors had opened and Judge Baralai stepped out into the narrow hallway that led to his chamber. What he saw when he stepped out hadn't shocked him. The other five Judges of the High Court were hanging from the walls of the hallway, dripping blood onto the carpet below. Each of them had been decapitated and strung up like decorations. The Judge walked down the hall until he reached The High Court's Chamber doors. He pushed open the double doors and had saw Vallerus standing at the other side of the large room.

"So Vallerus, it has come to this?" Baralai asked.

"Yes, Zephyr and the others are all dead." Vallerus said smiling.

"What about the human boy? You undoubtedly know how important he is to The Prophecy by now" the Judge asked.

Vallerus pointed to the table on the other side of the room where the boy laid on the table wrapped in a blanket asleep.

"Once I kill you and take the kingdom, I will raise him as my own alongside Vallus. He will never know of his parents or what happened. He is not a mystic" Vallerus said.

"I knew all along that you would be here waiting, Baron Tyran's powers are truly useful." Baralai said.

Vallerus reached into his pocket and pulled out a glass ball, "Oh you mean this? Well doesn't do me much good. He screamed like a bitch when I cut it out of him though." He said throwing the glass eye across the room.

"Let's just get this over with, I will not allow you to take my kingdom and destroy it." Judge Baralai said.

Vallerus grinned devilishly cracking his knuckles, "Oh I'm going to enjoy this."

They both removed their swords from their scabbards. So began the fight for V'nairia…

THE END

THE FATED SWORDS
MYSTICS OF V'NAIRIA BOOK ONE

PROLOGUE

V'nairia, a once peaceful kingdom filled with magick and wonder, a place where humans and mystics had lived together in harmony. Its cities were largely populated and more modern and advanced than some of its smaller towns and villages. There were many different hotels, restaurants, and businesses that lined the streets of the cities. There were no longer any mystics that possessed healing magicks so the hospitals of V'nairia had to resort to more practical methods in treating their patients.

V'nairia was technologically advanced in some areas such as computer systems to compile and store data for the hospitals and militia's records. These advanced technologies were not released to the public and mainly kept for the Militia's use. The V'nairians were unfortunately lacking in more important parts of everyday life such as travel and communication. The people of V'nairia still rode in horse drawn carriages and wrote letters that were sent by winged carriers.

The Kingdom itself was divided into two different races; Humans and Mystics. The mystic race was made up of those who possessed extraordinary abilities and could call upon the elements to do their bidding. It was not the entirety of the human race that despised the mystics because of their abilities; most had only envied them for the gifts that they had possessed. V'nairia itself was united under one governing body, which was and always had been The High Court. For over two centuries the government and its laws had prohibited any type of segregation between the races.

The High Court itself consisted of six judges; each a powerful warrior clad in armor that governed and protected V'nairia and its people. The sixth judge; who had been the most powerful of The High Court had led the rest as the Supreme Judge of the kingdom. Each judge was a chosen mystic who controlled a specific element of magick.

There was no religion or gods for the people of the kingdom to worship, humans as well as mystics followed the leadership of the High Court and had revered the judges as their saviors. Upon promotion to their new rank, each judge is to take a sacred vow to protect V'nairia from any evils that may disturb the V'nairian's way of life.

Anyone that came from the Foreignlands to live within V'nairia's borders had to take on a new name and a new way of life. They had to leave behind their families and their false gods and accept the ways of their new home.

One fateful day a man would step forward to challenge all that V'nairia had known, a man who would soon rule over the kingdom and its people. One of the most powerful mystics the kingdom had came to know.

His name was Vallerus Arvello; a previous Commander of the Militia, which was the military force that V'nairia's High Court had created to help the judges better maintain the order and protection within the kingdom. The Militia was made up of both mystic and human men and woman that wanted to serve their kingdom and protect its people from any foreign evils that may invade and threaten its residents. Vallerus had always hated the mystics even though he was born one himself. He ignored his lineage and left his home and family after tragedy had befallen him. He was the product of a mystic and human and was often ridiculed for being a "half-breed" as they had called them. Vallerus trained day and night for years to grow strong enough so that one day he could become the Supreme Judge and enslave all mystics. He wanted all of the mystics eliminated; he had seen them all as an abomination. It disgusted him to no end, seeing humans speaking to them or courting them. He thought it his duty to put an end to it all. No one had ever truly known where his hatred for the mystics had risen from, not that anyone had ever cared to know.

One day Vallerus challenged not one but all six judges to combat. He swiftly defeated each of them with ease and had erased them from the world to make sure none of them could ever challenge his reign. He had chosen five of the strongest mystics he could find and bestowed upon them the title of judge while he became the new Supreme Judge. The kingdom was finally at his command. With his new power he exiled all mystics to the Foreignlands and made them swear to never come back to the kingdom again or they would pay with their lives.

One mystic had sought a resolution to the races problem, he believed in going to war with the humans and taking back their home. They called this mystic Hylkroft the Godsage and he was the most powerful of his race. He was the only mystic that ever lived who possessed all five elements of magick. He had once befriended the human race until he had seen the evil and devastation that Vallerus had brought to the kingdom.

The Godsage had challenged Vallerus and his army to war and marched with his soldiers into V'nairia from the Foreignlands. Vallerus led his army to meet the enemy. The Five Year war as the people of V'nairia had called it; had been a bloody and tireless battle. Countless humans and mystics had lost their lives during the chaotic conflict.

Both sides were getting nowhere, until finally Vallerus and the Godsage had proposed a contest; whichever could defeat the other in one on one combat their side would be the victor of the war. The two warriors were powerful; the fight went on for days neither man tiring, running on only their will to win. Finally Vallerus had defeated the Godsage in battle. He decapitated the Godsage in front of a thousand of his own men. He raised the head high as the Militia's soldiers cheered him on. Then with his most powerful spell he wiped out the entire mystic army. That one technique struck fear into the hearts of man and mystic alike, after that no one ever dared to oppose him or they would face a gruesome death.

    He had killed many mystics and vowed to find the rest. He had organized what he had liked to call, "The Hunt" and sent out extermination squads to find and eliminate any and all mystics hiding within V'nairia's borders. All remaining mystics scattered to different parts of the kingdom, living in secret until the day when the judge would be defeated and the peace would be restored to V'nairia.

CHAPTER I

Zander sat under his favorite tree in the city's garden, it was the only place in the Capital that hadn't reminded him of war or death. He could smell the many types of flowers around him and he felt happy, happier than he usually felt. Zander hadn't had very many things to be happy about at all. The garden was a very calming place and he had come there at least once a day to take in its incredible beauty. He didn't quite understand why this specific spot in the entire Capital had been his favorite. It was a peculiar feeling that he often had but he didn't know why. He had grown up without a true family, without loving parents to encourage him everyday unlike the other children at the academy. He often sat and wondered what his parents were like, or about becoming a war hero like his father. He often had reoccurring dreams of receiving medals for winning fierce battles, or saving beautiful women.

He was a normal teenage boy born from a military family. Zander's parents had been a part of the kingdom's Militia and had died in battle while he was still very young, so it was unclear to him what his mother and father were actually like. He hadn't even known the names of his parents.

Zander was sixteen years old and of average build, he never participated in many things outdoors besides sitting in the garden. He often kept to himself; he liked it better that way.

He was a very avid reader, he loved to feed his vast wealth of knowledge of the world and how it worked. V'nairia's various wars and history had fascinated him, he had liked to think that his father was somewhat of a hero that could have gotten himself in the history books. He always was picked on in school for how smart he was, but he didn't mind it at all. He had always seen the world in a different light than most and the select few that actually knew him had known just how special he truly was.

He had short brown hair, and through his baby blue eyes you could clearly see his hopes and dreams as well as the overwhelming pain he kept inside. Today was a special day for Zander, because today he was to graduate from the Militia's Academy. He had always said it was his calling; to protect all of V'nairia just like his parents had done before him.

"Sitting there daydreaming again are we?" Vallus asked Zander as he approached him in the garden. "You think you would at least want to be on time for a day like today."

Zander looked up and saw his best friend standing over him. Vallus was more than a friend to Zander, they were more like brothers. Vallus' father had taken Zander in after his parents were killed and he had been with their family ever since. It had just been Zander, Vallus, and Vallus' father since the passing of Vallus' mother. Vallus' father had told the boys that she had died due to a terrible sickness that didn't have a cure. They were too young to remember anything about her or Zander's parents. Neither Vallus nor his father ever talked about her much.

Vallus was a tall and strong eighteen year old who had already graduated the academy two years earlier. He was now a commander in V'nairia's Militia and led the Mystic Extermination Squad. He had long black hair that he kept in a neat pony tail at all times; the only time you ever seen his hair down is when he was angry.

"That's why I have you as my own personal clock Vallus." Zander said smiling.

Vallus gave him a disappointed look, "Are you ever going to address me as your commanding officer?" Vallus asked.

"I don't believe its official just yet." Zander said knowing he would get "the look" from his friend.

They both stared at each other for a moment and then let out a hearty laugh. Vallus took Zander's hand and pulled him up off the ground, "Are you ready brother?" he asked the already nervous Zander.

"Yes Commander Arvello, let's go!" Zander shouted happily as they walked out of the garden and onward to the Militia's Academy.

The Academy was a very large building, pyramid like in shape. Not very many of its students even passed the entry exam, as it had been a very strict and prestigious school but Zander was determined to follow in his father's footsteps and become a war hero. In just two short years he had finally been able to graduate. He had advanced faster than the other students; he pushed himself every day to be the best that he could be. He had never been more excited or proud of himself.

Zander and Vallus had arrived at the Academy and walked inside the glass double doors. It had been a short trip from the gardens. They had walked over to the elevator and pushed the button and waited for the doors to open. They rode the elevator to the floor where the Headmaster's office had been. They walked down the darkened corridors of the academy; it was late in the afternoon so all of the classes had been dismissed for the day.

There was a knock on the headmaster's door, "Come in." Headmaster Jerriston said eagerly.

Vallus and Zander walked inside the office to find the elderly Headmaster waiting for them. Zander glanced around the room looking at the various medals and achievement awards that the Headmaster had received in his days of service; but as with all good things once they're old they are retired.

"Ah Commander Arvello; I see you've brought our most advanced graduate." The old man said standing to greet Zander with a firm hand shake. Firm wasn't the word for it, more like ironclad. It was quite impressive for an eighty-five year old man.

Zander gave a salute to the headmaster and grinned. "Sorry if I was late sir, nerves got to me I guess." He said.

"I wouldn't say it was nerves, more like daydreaming in the garden again." Vallus said grinning.

The headmaster laughed, "Not at all my boy, after all, your parent's house stood right beside the city's garden at least until the incident. It's expected that you would have taken a liking to the gardens."

Vallus glanced over at the Headmaster suspiciously. "Incident?" he asked.

"Oh don't mind me, just the ramblings of an old man." Jerriston said.

"Of course sir." Vallus said.

"So that is why I love being in the garden so much. It's because of my parents." Zander thought to himself ignoring them.

"So Mr. Kyre, how does it feel to graduate the academy with honors?" Headmaster Jerriston asked him.

"It feels great sir; I am honored to have learned so much from some of V'nairia's finest." Zander said politely.

"That's good to hear my boy." Jerriston said smiling at him.

Another knock came to the door, another man walked inside the office. He was much taller than Zander or Vallus, had a muscular build and had long black hair with a goatee and mustache. The man was Vallus' father, the Supreme Judge that ruled over all of V'nairia.

"There you boys are." Judge Vallerus said.

They both had saluted the Supreme Judge as he turned to close the door behind him. "Yes father, I had to search for him, his mind seems to wander quite a bit lately." Vallus said.

Zander lowered his head, "My apologies your honor." He said nervously.

Vallerus began to laugh, "Nonsense my boy, it's just your nerves. Today is a very important day for you, it is normal to be nervous." Vallerus said. Zander had always looked up to Vallus and his father; they were the perfect role-models in his eyes.

Vallus turned to Zander, "Being as I see you as my own blood, it is only right to give you this as a graduation gift." He said handing Zander his very own sword.

The Scabbard was the color of snow and the blade seemed to sing as it was released from its white scabbard. Zander felt a chill run up his arm upon releasing it, it felt like a quick burning sensation but he had ignored the feeling and went on to admire his gift.

"But isn't this-?" Zander asked as he gazed down at his gift.

Vallerus cleared his throat, "Yes that weapon is Ivory the twin blade to Vallus' Ebony. These swords are the two cursed blades of legend."

"Where did you find them?" Zander asked.

"I had actually bought them from a traveling merchant in Rygoth. The damned fool didn't know what he was selling." Vallerus said laughing.

Vallus pulled out his sword, the only difference between them being the scabbard was black. "I know you will use it well. The cursed blades work well together that is why I had Lieutenant Omak put you on my squad." Vallus said.

"Thank you so much Vallus, I will do my very best." Zander stated.

"But be warned for there is a curse on these blades, the wielders are said to be eternal rivals." Vallerus said.

Vallus and Zander stared at each other like they could communicate with thought, vowing to be stronger than the other. They stared at each other to see who would break first, this was their usual game. Neither one could keep a straight face, they both started to chuckle. Vallus rarely let anyone see his more playful side. With Zander it had just come natural, however most of the time he was always about business and only business.

Vallerus placed his hand on the boy's shoulders, "Your both men now do all of V'nairia proud." Vallerus said.

"Yes sir." They said saluting in unison.

"I must be off but I will see you both later." He said saluting them respectfully just before turning and walking out the door.

Vallus and Zander began to walk out the door when the headmaster stopped them, "Excuse me Zander but your forgetting these." He said handing Zander his new uniform and badge.

"Thank you headmaster, I won't let you down." Zander said as they saluted him and were on their way out of the office door.

Outside the academy, Zander and Vallus had saw their friend Kerra waiting for them by the side of the building. She ran up to Zander and embraced him.

"Congratulations Zander, you did it! Your father and mother would be so proud." Kerra said praising him.

Kerra Lyale was sixteen and the third in their group. When it came to Zander and Vallus nothing else in the world mattered. She loved them both equally and that often brought her great pain, she knew that she couldn't have them both but it was hard to choose between them. She was just a tad shorter than Zander and had short, brown wavy hair that came down to her shoulders. Kerra was quite mature for her age and often got the boys out of many a sticky situation. She wore a black tank top with white shorts and on her hands were black leather gloves that she never left home without. The credit for her maturity was often given to her mother who was also a judge on the High Court, who had taught her very well. Her family possesses lightning magick and the trait had been passed down from generation to generation.

"Have you been waiting long Kerra?" Vallus asked.

Kerra shook her head and smiled, "No not that long but you could have been quicker about it." She said.

"Sorry." Zander apologized with a half smile.

Zander pulled out his sword and showed it to her, "Is that Ivory?" she asked.

"Yes I had given it to Zander as a graduation gift." Vallus said.

The blade glistened in the sunlight and Zander could feel calming warmth when he touched the blade. "Well then here is my gift to you." Kerra said kissing him on the forehead.

"What was that for?" He asked jumping backwards blushing.

"It is for good luck." She said smiling.

"Well we best get home before dark." Zander said feeling embarrassed.

"Yes you need your rest for tomorrow; we have the debriefing for our first mission." Vallus said.

That had made Zander extremely excited and extremely nervous at the same time. "Well I'm gonna head home, Vallus will you walk me?" Kerra asked.

Vallus took her hand and nodded, "Of course."

Zander hated how she favored him, or so he thought. Vallus was just more skilled in combat and could protect her better in case someone had decided to jump her on her way home. Kerra hugged Zander once more and they said their goodbyes. Zander started in the opposite direction to head home to get some sleep.

***

That night Zander lay in bed gazing at his sword. He loved to listen to the blade sing as he pulled it from the scabbard. It was like hearing the wind blowing in the dead of the night, so peaceful and yet so powerful. It had quickly become his most prized possession. Vallus had still not gotten home, which was very unlike him to be late doing anything. Out of the corner of his eye Zander noticed a note folded perfectly lying on the nightstand beside him. *"How could I have not noticed it before?"* He thought to himself. It was from Vallus he could tell, the signature was worse than that of any doctor's. He opened the note, it read:

Meet me in the gardens at midnight,
And don't tell anyone – Vallus

Zander knew something was up; this wasn't like Vallus at all. Zander got up out of bed and quickly threw on a white t-shirt, a pair of black pants and his favorite brown leather jacket. He fastened Ivory to his side and went down the stairs and out the front door.

The night was so quiet; you could hear a pin drop. He walked on towards the gardens trying to think of why Vallus would ask him to meet him in the middle of night. This late at night everything in the city had died down and everyone had finally gone home. This would have been the best time to come to the gardens to think if he could have ever gotten away with it.

He made it to the gardens but there was no sign of Vallus anywhere. He looked all around him but he was alone. Zander stood next to his favorite tree and waited. Maybe he had gotten there before Vallus had? Suddenly he had heard some footsteps through the grass coming from across the garden. Zander looked off into the distance and saw Vallus walking towards him; he had Ebony fastened to his side.

"Vallus, why are we here so late?" Zander asked.

Vallus stopped about ten feet from Zander's position. "You aren't quite ready for your first mission Zander." Vallus said. Zander was confused, he didn't even know what the mission was yet so how is he supposed to know whether he was prepared or not?

"What will you do if you have to take a life? You know we hunt mystics and kill them. What if you have to kill one?" Vallus asked.

His friend was right in asking this question, Zander had joined the Militia and after all this time he had never thought about the fact that he may have to kill someone.

"Why must we kill the mystics? They don't mean us any harm?" Zander asked.

Vallus shook his head disappointed. "Do you know nothing brother? The mystics have the means to overthrow the government and enslave us all." Vallus explained.

Zander was one of the few people in the city that did not believe this, for Zander knew that the judges themselves could use magicks but are not persecuted for being different. The government was already quite corrupt the way it was. He had already known Vallus' opinion on the matter as well; he hadn't hated the mystics either. He was just following the Lieutenant and his father's orders.

"I'm here to see how you will fare on the battlefield, fight me!" Vallus shouted as he released his sword. Zander noticed a change in Vallus' eyes, they were dark and cold.

"No! I won't fight you!" Zander shouted back.

The wind began to pick up in the garden; Zander could hear the leaves rustling in the trees. Quickly, in an instant Vallus had appeared behind Zander.

"*He's so fast.*" Zander thought to himself as Vallus delivered a kick to his side. Zander fell to his knees,

"If you don't fight, you will end up dead and your dreams will mean nothing." Vallus stated as he lunged at Zander with his sword,

Zander had quickly blocked it with Ivory, which was still locked away in its scabbard. "You're crazy, what is wrong with you?" Zander asked him but there was no reply. Vallus knocked Zander off his balance, and grabbed him by his shirt lifting him up above him.

"You have to realize pain in all its forms, not just emotional but physical too." Vallus said as he launched his fist into Zander's gut so hard he couldn't even let out a whimper. He threw Zander to the ground on his back, Zander tried to get up but it was useless, he couldn't move a muscle.

Vallus hovered over him blade in hand, "The strong survive, whilst the weak die!" Vallus shouted as his sword came down towards Zander's face.

Zander closed his eyes because at that moment he realized Vallus could have meant to kill him, and if he did he couldn't do anything to stop it. He was weak, he never realized just how weak until this very moment. The blade made a sudden stopped on the top of his nose. Blood made a narrow stream down the side of his face which mixed with the salty stream of tears coming from his right eye. Before Zander fainted he looked up at Vallus and thought to himself, he wasn't dead he was very much alive. Vallus wasn't trying to kill him; he was trying to show him the intensity of a real battle. Suddenly everything had gone black.

CHAPTER II

Zander awoke the next day, lying in his bed asking himself if what he had experienced the night before had been a dream. He walked over to the mirror and examined the small scar on the top of his nose. He had barely touched it with his fingertip and it burned. He could tell that someone had tended to it while he was asleep. It must have been Vallus; it's obvious that was how he had arrived back home and placed in his bed. There was a tap at the door,

Vallus entered in his black and red uniform. "Ready to go soldier? You don't want to be late for debriefing do you?" He smiled looking at Zander.

Was this the same person? The same Vallus that Zander had met in the garden last night? It couldn't have been it was as if he had two completely different personalities. Zander had thrown on his black Militia uniform and packed his things while remembering to grab Ivory from the top of his dresser. They both walked downstairs and out the door. Together they headed off to headquarters for their mission debriefing.

"Zander I want to apologize about last night, I just didn't want you to go into battle unprepared." Vallus explained himself. "I feel like I was a lot tougher on you than I should have been."

"I thought you were going to kill me!" Zander shouted at him.

Vallus laughed, "Are you kidding? I was going easy on you." He said.

A chill came over Zander's body, *"Going easy?"* He thought. *"If that's easy I couldn't imagine him being serious, I feel sorry for any mystic willing to cross his path."*

They had made their way into Militia Headquarters and boarded the elevator. The Headquarters had been a large skyscraper with many floors that housed different departments within V'nairia's military. The knots in Zander's stomach had become even larger, he wondered what their first mission was going to be and how difficult it would be to complete. Zander knew that if Vallus had taken it on it was definitely not going to be easy.

"Vallus, what unit are we exactly?" Zander asked.

Vallus smiled and looked down at him, "Extermination Squad." He said.

Zander's eyes widened, "Extermination eh? That's um…cool." He said and swallowed really hard. The Extermination Squad's missions were fairly simple. Their objective usually meant that they had to locate a rogue mystic and eliminate them or bring them in for questioning. The more difficult missions require the squad to take out an entire group of mystics that have been hiding out in a remote location. Zander had hoped it wasn't the latter of the two. He definitely wasn't prepared for anything of that magnitude.

As the elevator doors opened they walked down the narrow hallway towards the Lieutenant's office. Zander kept getting sidetracked by all the computers and gadgets he had seen in the many rooms that lined the halls behind thick bullet proof glass. The Militia was always ready for anything. Most soldiers in the Militia carried guns, but Vallus preferred good old fashioned steel for his weapon as did his father and most of the remaining judges of the High Court. Judge Vallerus had always told them growing up that guns kill too quickly. He had been a good father but a cruel soldier, and killed the mystics without mercy.

They walked into the command station, and inside both of them saw Lieutenant Omak smoking a cigar and looking through some paperwork at a nearby desk. He was a middle-aged, bald muscular man with a thick accent which Vallus didn't particularly care for; it had often made him cringe. He had come to the Academy and spoke to the students at special presentations they sometimes held throughout the year. Zander couldn't stand the man; Vallus hated him too but had to respect him because he was the one that gave the orders. Vallus and Zander walked in, saluted the Lieutenant and sat down in the two chairs in front of the Lieutenant's desk.

"Well Commander Arvello is this our new graduate I've heard so much about?" Omak asked.

"Yes sir this is Zander." Vallus said. "He was top of his class; he will make a fine addition to the Militia."

"Well let's hope he survives longer than the last one." The Lieutenant sighed.

Zander felt a sudden awkwardness, "He's kidding Zander." Vallus said as he and the Lieutenant started to laugh.

Vallus' tone began to change, "Now that the introductions are out of the way, what is our mission sir?" Vallus asked. Straight and to the point, just as Vallus always has been.

The Lieutenant had pushed a folder towards him that read *Confidential,* "You're going to the desert village of Oaba, there's a thief that is suspected to be a mystic by the name of Heiro and we need you to scope it out. If the story checks out, kill him. It's as simple as that" Lieutenant Omak said.

"You know as well as I do that you never give my squad easy assignments Lieutenant." Vallus said.

"Ha, maybe you're right. Although wouldn't you rather have a mission that entertains you?" Omak asked him flicking his cigar and watching the ashes fall into the ashtray in front of him.

"Good point. Not that I'm complaining I love a good challenge." Vallus said.

"Just remember that this one's a special one, it came directly from your father." Omak added.

"From my father?" Vallus asked curiously "But why?"

"Dunno. Have you ever heard of The Mystic Rogue of Oaba?" The lieutenant asked.

"Maybe once or twice, I've heard he has an extraordinary ability." Vallus said.

"If that's the phrasing you wanna use go ahead, deadly as hell is what I'd call it." Omak said. "Unfortunately for us we don't have much info on him or what he can do."

"That will be the challenging part of the mission I guess." Vallus said smiling. "Going in blind."

Lieutenant nodded and began to laugh as he took another drag of his cigar.

Vallus and Zander stood up and were ready to leave, "Are those two even here yet?" Vallus asked.

"Yeah they should be waiting outside, you leave immediately. Dismissed." Omak said as they saluted him and walked out of the command center and down the hall towards the elevator.

Zander looked up at Vallus, "Who are we meeting again?" Vallus looked back at Zander and smiled.

"You will see." He said smirking.

They walked outside of Headquarters and could see two unusual characters waiting for them standing beside of the building. These men were the other two members of their squad, Blitz and Ace. These two soldiers unlike Zander and Vallus preferred guns as their primary weapon of choice but they had also carried swords just in case they came into close combat with the enemy. Not much was known about the brothers, but what they lacked in common sense they made up for with battle skills. To Zander that pretty much meant that you could be retarded in the Militia as long as you can fight. The more he thought about it the more he wanted to laugh, but he resisted the urge.

"Hey boss it's about time." Ace said waving at Vallus.

"Sorry I took so long guys had to let the Lieutenant meet the newest recruit, this is Zander. Zander this is Blitz and his brother Ace." Vallus introduced them.

"Hi guys." Zander said shyly

Blitz and Ace saluted Zander, "So Zander how good are ya in battle buddy?" Ace asked.

Zander felt a knot in his stomach form; he didn't want to tell them he was just a weakling who has never been in a fight in his life. Zander began to speak but nothing came out.

"He will be a valuable asset to this squad guys, Zander is quite the warrior. Seen him take out a small group of mystics all by himself" Vallus said smiling at them.

Zander looked up and gave Vallus a look that pretty much said *"You're fucking crazy."* Vallus looked back at him with the same dumb grin he always had.

"Well I guess it's on to Oaba then." Zander said as he looked over at the brothers then to Vallus.

The four of them walked on through the city until they had reached the gates that led to the forest outside of Durea. Zander didn't know what was going to happen when they got there but one thing was for sure he was afraid, Afraid to fight, afraid to fail, and afraid to die.

***

The next day the squad had made their way into the scorching desert, to Zander the heat had felt like it had been two-hundred degrees. Many fears were in the back of his mind like dying of starvation or dehydration and the buzzards picking their bones clean. But he didn't have time to think such thoughts; the only thing that mattered at that moment was the mission at hand.

Blitz and Ace were on what seemed like their thousandth game of paper, rock, and scissors. Zander was getting pretty annoyed and didn't care much for the two of them. Vallus didn't seem to mind them at all; perhaps he was used to their stupidity. For soldiers they didn't exactly seem all that bright. Then there was Vallus who didn't seem to be bothered by anything. No matter what the situation he had always kept his cool, Zander wished he could be more like him; the Stronger, more attractive friend of Vallus'. Being the son of the Supreme Judge of V'nairia he could have virtually anything he wanted.

They came to a broken bridge that had once stretched over the large crater in the sand, "Well it seems like a dead-end." Zander said.

Vallus laughed, "It only seems that way, the village is in the middle of that crater. We have to climb down the side." He said as Zander swallowed hard and nodded.

Vallus had taken out a rope from his bag and fashioned the end of it into a noose. He had staked the rope into the top of the cliff and pulled tight to make sure that it would hold the weight.

One by one they made their way down the side of the crater, slowly but surely they made their way down safely.

After a few minutes, the dust in the air had settled and they could finally see the sign that read *Oaba Village*.

"Everyone be careful, this village is a poor one but it is also quite rough when it comes to its people." Vallus told them.

They walked on through the entrance to the village, there were many merchants selling trinkets and cheap weapons on the side of the street. Everyone seemed to be wearing rags, Vallus was right this was poor town. Oaba Village had been the main source of all of V'nairia's drug supply. They were smuggled in from the Foreignlands apparently someone had been paying off the guards at the gates to let them into the kingdom. They still hadn't been caught in the act.

The squad walked by the local bar making their way down the street looking for clues and asking the locals if they had seen any mystics around the village. A suspicious looking man that had been glaring at them from afar and walked up and had gotten into Vallus' face. The man's breath smelt of cheap whisky and cigars, Zander could smell it from behind Vallus and it had almost made him sick. Vallus didn't seem to be bothered by it at all.

"What the hell are you doing here? Your kind isn't welcome here." The man said.

"I'm sorry friend, what exactly do you mean by our kind?" Vallus asked politely.

"Militia soldiers dumbass." The man said practically spitting in Vallus' face.

Vallus smiled at the man, "We came to investigate a mystic sighting, and we want no trouble. We will be on our way once our mission is complete, please stand aside." Vallus asked.

The man became angry and drew his sword, "Okay wise guy let's see what color you bleed, I said you don't belong here!" The man shouted as he swung his sword towards Vallus, who caught it with his bare hand.

Vallus' expression quickly changed, "I asked you nicely to let us through, I don't want any trouble but if you insist on causing it I will feel obligated to stop you." He said releasing the blade of the man's sword.

The man began to laugh heartily, "Bring it pony tail." He said and spat at his feet.

Suddenly Vallus vanished just like in his fight with Zander, utilizing his incredible speed. He appeared behind the man and placed his hand on his shoulder. "You seem to do much harm with this arm, what if you weren't able to use it? What a pity that would be." Vallus said calmly as he used two fingers and struck the man's right arm in multiple pressure points.

The man's arm fell to his side limp and lifeless. The man shrieked in surprise. Zander again fought the urge to laugh.

"Now I'd suggest that you make your way to your local hospital quickly, or you'll sustain permanent paralysis and lose function of that arm." Vallus said.

The man clearly couldn't move his arm as he ran off screaming, flailing his arm from side to side. Zander was amazed at his friend's incredible abilities and had grown even more jealous.

Suddenly a man ran past them and almost knocked Zander out of the way. "Stop that thief!" a merchant shouted from across the street.

"Looks like we found our guy boss." Blitz said as the four of them began to run after the man. They chased him to the edge of the crater where they had climbed down.

"Look Vallus he's up there!" Zander shouted pointing to the top of the cliff.

They began to climb back up the cliff and when they reached the top they saw the man standing before them. He wore green tattered rags, with short red spiked hair and was almost as tall as Vallus. He couldn't have been much older than him either.

"Why the hell are you four following me?" the man asked.

"We have come to eliminate the mystic in this village and it is our suspicions that you are the man were looking for." Vallus said.

The man began to laugh, "You heard correctly I am Heiro, The Mystic Rogue of Oaba." He said.

Zander grabbed his sword and held it tightly. "You are hereby sentenced to death for the use of magicks in the kingdom of V'nairia." Vallus explained.

Heiro drew his sword, "One lone mystic against four Militia lackeys? I have had worse odds before." Heiro said taunting them.

Zander wasn't sure what was going to happen to him or his squad but he was sure of one thing; this time the battle was for real and dying was definitely a possibility.

CHAPTER III

Vallus and the rest of the squad stood before their opponent trying to size him up. They weren't informed of any of the mystic's abilities so they had to play it by ear. The only thing that Zander had remembered the Lieutenant telling them was to not take this enemy lightly. Zander stood frozen in fear as Vallus and the brothers ran towards the rogue mystic with their weapons drawn. There was only one thought on his mind; the fact that he could die. It was a crippling feeling, hypnotizing even. He couldn't move or speak; he could only stand and watch as his squad met their opponent in battle, braver than he would ever be. They weren't afraid; they knew that they could die at any moment. The only difference between them and Zander was that they didn't care.

"Strike the enemy together!" Vallus shouted as he used his flash step ability to suddenly appear behind Heiro to strike him in his blind spot. The three of them had come at him from different directions.

"Stone Art: Stone Wall!" Heiro said as a wall of solid rock appeared before each of them blocking their sword strikes. Even with Vallus' incredible speed was not enough to get a clear shot at the mystic. Heiro was unlike any enemy Vallus had ever fought, mystic or human.

The Fated Swords

"He conjured three walls at the same time." Vallus thought to himself. *"Even a judge would use a considerable amount of magick casting a defensive spell like that."*

Suddenly, Heiro ran up one of the stone walls and leapt into the air above them, "Flame Art: Fire Stream!" He shouted as the flames cascaded down the rock wall like a raging dragon. The heat coming from the flames were intense and the three of them had begun sweating long before the fire had reached them.

Just before he had been engulfed by the flames, Vallus managed to flee unharmed using his flash step once again. Vallus looked back and noticed the others hadn't escaped, he had feared the worst.

"We are fine, worry about the enemy!" Ace shouted over the roar of the flames.

Vallus was relieved as he looked over and saw Blitz and Ace blocking the spell with their swords. For the moment he didn't have to worry about them and could focus easier on getting the enemy. He dashed toward Heiro at top speed and clashed swords with him. There was a mighty crash as their blades collided; with all his body weight Vallus pushed Heiro backwards. "Now I have you!" he said.

Heiro shrieked as he spat flames once more. Vallus pressed against the flames with his blade; he could feel a searing pain from his hands all the way up to his wrists. After a moment the flames had stopped, Blitz and Ace were fine. The smoldering rock wall had crumbled and smoke enveloped the battlefield.

Zander was amazed at the level of skill they displayed; he wished to be that powerful one day. Heiro stood with his devilish grin and glared, "Don't you all know how to give up and die!" he shouted in anger.

Vallus still hadn't got over the amount of magick energy that Heiro had dispensed so early in their fight. By this time he should have at least been tired out, but he had kept his composure. Vallus had thought that maybe he had taken some sort of drug to amplify his magick. They were hard to come by, but even so he could have gotten one from somewhere.

Vallus was aware of his friend's fear and he couldn't complain, after all it was Zander's first real battle; of course he would be unable to think or react. Vallus also knew that if Zander did help that he would have to protect him and that would be a distraction. That was something that they couldn't afford to happen especially in a fight this difficult. The three of them had a plan; Vallus looked over at the two brothers and nodded.

"T-formation now!" Vallus shouted at them giving them the signal.

They ran around Heiro forming a triangle and each had taken out a scroll and unrolled it on the ground in front of them. Heiro was unaware of this technique and was trying to read their movements to no avail. They each had taken their swords across the palm of their hands cutting themselves and allowed the blood to drip onto the scrolls.

"Sacred Art: Restriction Binding Seal!" Vallus said as chains sprang up out of the earth and wrapped themselves around Heiro constricting his body. "This is a two-hundred year old sealing technique you will not be able to break yourself out." Vallus explained. "It's over mystic."

Zander had learned about spells that required scrolls in history class at the academy. They were an ancient form of spell casting; mystics no longer required them to use their magick like in the old days. However this particular spell Zander remembered reading about. It was by far one of the strongest sealing spells ever created. Not even a judge could break themselves free. Vallus had been taking a large risk by using it; he was only a half mystic and the spell required three mystics which Blitz and Ace were not. Given the circumstances Vallus had to provide enough magickal energy for all three of them.

Zander looked over at Vallus who had a slight smirk on his face, however Zander could see through his friends' solid composure. He was sweating and breathing heavily. He was being drained of his magick at an alarming rate. Zander turned his attention to Heiro, his expression had completely changed. It was blank, the smart ass grin and attitude had faded.

Vallus raised Ebony's blade out in front of Heiro's body from across the cliff, "Sword Art: Extending Blade!" Vallus said as Ebony's blade grew longer until it had pierced Heiro's heart. Heiro struggled for a moment, before becoming motionless. Vallus had commanded Ebony to revert to its original form and the three of them had regrouped in the middle of the cliff while Zander remained off to the side. Vallus looked over and noticed that Zander was able to move again, he was no longer afraid. Vallus walked over to Zander to see if he was alright.

"I'm so sorry Vallus, I was terrified." He said feeling ashamed of himself. "I just couldn't move."

Vallus patted Zander's head and smiled. All tension and fear suddenly faded, Zander knew everything was going to be okay. "It's alright now, were gonna be just fine." Vallus said comforting his friend.

Suddenly, laughter was heard from behind them, Zander's fear had instantly flooded back in. They had looked over and saw Heiro dusting himself off, he was alive and had broken the seal. "That's impossible! That seal is indestructible." Vallus said in amazement.

Heiro laughed hysterically, "You lowered your guard when you thought I was dead so it weakened the seal, I have to say that was impressive." Heiro said. "It's too bad that I can harden any part of my body to withstand damage or even prevent it altogether." He said.

"This guy is invincible." Zander sighed.

Heiro dipped his index finger in the pool of his blood lying in front of him and drew a symbol on the ground. He then began to draw the same symbol on his wrist. Vallus didn't recognize the symbol but knew it meant trouble for them. This had to be the ability that no one had ever seen.

"Demonic Art: Blood Sword." Heiro said. "I'm going to end this here and now."

Blood came from the cracks in the ground, and ran up Heiro's body until it had reached the palm of his hand. The blood had crafted itself into a crimson blade before their very eyes. One the sphere was the symbol that he had written on his wrist in blood.

"What the hell is that!?" Ace shouted looking over at his brother and then to Vallus.

"This is a forbidden technique that I created; I can manipulate my blood into any shape and can also harden it." Heiro explained.

"*He's some kind of monster.*" Vallus said to himself, terrified with fear. "*No normal mystic can produce demonic spells.*"

"Vallus! What do we do!?" Zander shouted trying to get Vallus' attention. Vallus couldn't hear him; he was now frozen with fear just as Zander had been before. He didn't know what they should do; he had never fought a mystic with demonic abilities.

"Now fucking die!" Heiro shouted with rage raising his hand to command the sphere to attack.

Vallus didn't know what to do, his body had just reacted. It had told him to turn around and shield his friend. He had swung his body around and held onto Zander tightly. The sphere of blood exploded and hardened shards of blood made their way towards them. Zander had felt Vallus' body jerk violently a few times.

After a mere moment, everything had gone quiet. Zander felt something warm dripping down onto his face. He looked up and saw Vallus hovered over him; his mouth had blood running from the side. He mumbled Vallus' name under his breath almost as if he didn't mean to say it as if he was in a trance. Vallus fell to his knees and Zander caught him. In Vallus' back were shards from the sphere digging into his skin, carefully Zander pulled them out one by one. The blood from his wounds began to flow more quickly now. With each shard, Vallus shrieked louder from the pain.

"Vallus why did you protect me?" he asked.

Vallus had the usually dumb smile, "Because you are my best friend. It is my duty to protect you with my life." He said with tears in his eyes.

Zander's eyes began to tear up; he had never seen his friend in such a weakened state. It had sickened him, not because he was weak but because there was a person who could have done this to his friend. Vallus was the strongest and bravest person that he had ever known.

"*Where is Blitz and Ace?*" he thought to himself. About ten feet from where they were sitting was where Blitz and Ace had lain motionless. Zander walked over to them and checked to see if they had a pulse, they both were dead. They had suffered extensive damage to their internal organs; there was no way they could have survived.

All the fear Zander had felt before had vanished, it had been replaced by anger. He drew his sword and pointed it at Heiro, "You bastard I'm going to kill you!" Zander shouted.

"Well, it looks like the runt of the litter has some guts after all." Heiro said grinning devilishly. Zander could see the darkness and thirst for blood in his eyes.

"Shut up!" Zander shouted angrily, his sword shaking in his hand. By this time Vallus had passed out from the pain and it was up to Zander to finish the fight.

"If you think you can fight me alone, be my guest." Heiro said confidently.

Zander knew this guy was on a whole other level than he had been but he had to try. If he didn't do something soon neither he nor Vallus would make it out alive.

Zander ran towards Heiro with nothing but his sword. Ivory had collided with Heiro's sword; he could feel the immense pressure coming from the mystic's strength. Zander thought of his friend and how badly hurt he was and that made him even angrier.

With all his might he pushed against the blood sword and managed to find an opening and slashed right above Heiro's left eye. His blade had actually damaged him but he had lost his focus for the moment and Heiro delivered a kick across his face sending him to the ground.

The cut above Heiro's eye seared like is whole face was on fire. He winced at the pain and shook it off.

"You can't defeat me!" Heiro shouted, as he ran towards Zander.

Zander threw Ivory into the air, just before Heiro had gotten to him. Heiro came down with his blade but Zander rolled to the side barely dodging the blow. Zander grabbed Ivory as it fell from the sky and sliced Heiro diagonally down his side. With the blow came a flash of light.

The two of them stood face to face glaring at each other not saying a word. They were both breathing heavily at this post. Right before Zander had collapsed he had noticed a change in Heiro. The evil in his eyes had faded; he was no longer looking at darkness. In Heiro's eyes he could see a glimmer of light. Zander fell to the ground, out cold. He had hoped that Vallus had been okay, losing his best friend would mean losing an important part of himself. An important part of himself that he was sure he would never get over.

***

Zander woke up and rolled over onto his back. He rubbed his eyes and yawned leaning up in bed. He had noticed that he was back in the Capital and had been put in the hospital. *"How did I get here?"* Zander asked himself.

He then thought back to the fight with Heiro on the side of the crater in the middle of Oaba Desert. It was then that the thought had hit him. *"Vallus."* He said to himself. *"I wonder if he is here too."*

After a few minutes Zander could hear talking coming from outside the door and watched as the door knob began to turn. The door opened slowly and in walked Kerra with the doctor. "I see your better." She said smiling, she was happy to see that he was finally awake.

"Yeah I feel much better." He said. "What happened exactly?"

"You had fainted from heat exhaustion, although some of your symptoms were consistent with depleted magickal energy." The doctor explained.

"That's not possible, I'm not a mystic." Zander said.

"No Zander you don't have to worry, we know that you're not a mystic. It was more like a freak occurrence." The doctor said trying to ease his mind. "Your body had just mimicked the symptom that's all."

Zander looked over at Kerra; she was a sight for sore eyes after his difficult mission. "So what happened? How did I get here?" he asked her.

"You defeated the mystic and then the Militia had sent out a search party." Kerra explained. "They found you and brought you here."

"*Defeated? More like dumb luck.*" Zander said to himself. He had only struck Heiro twice during their fight and neither blow was fatal. He had also remembered the flash of light that appeared when he struck Heiro the second time.

"Where is Vallus?" Zander asked. Kerra had a grim look on her face and Zander feared the worst.

"He is down the hall, he still hasn't woken up." the doctor said. "He had extensive injuries, he's lucky to be alive."

Zander got up and out of the bed and began to look for his clothes. "What are you doing?" Kerra asked him.

"I need my clothes; I'm going to see Vallus." Zander said.

"Young man you are finally awake after three whole days. You should be resting." The doctor said.

Zander had finally found his uniform in the closet next to his bed. "I understand your concern doctor but my best friend is down the hall and I need to go see him." Zander said taking his hospital gown off.

Kerra quickly turned around blushing, in his rush to see his friend he had forgotten that she was in the room.

"Are you finished yet?" Kerra asked impatiently.

"Yes, I'm sorry about that Kerra." Zander said grabbing Ivory from beside the bed and strapping it to his back.

"I can't stop you from leaving but please be careful and don't overdo it." The doctor said.

"Thank you doctor, I'll be fine." Zander said. "Kerra lets go see Vallus."

Zander walked over to the door and opened it, they had walked outside the room and began to walk down the hallway of the hospital towards Vallus' room.

Zander stopped at the door to Vallus' room. "Kerra, what if he doesn't make it?" Zander asked.

"You know as well as I do how strong he is." She said. "He will pull through this."

"You weren't there; he had lost so much blood." Zander said.

She grabbed his hand and held it tightly, "It's okay to be afraid, and he's like a brother to you." She said smiling gently. "Let's just go in and see him."

"Your right." Zander said agreeing with her.

He opened the door slowly to find his friend lying across the room sleeping peacefully. There were a couple of fresh scars on his face however they weren't that noticeable. They had taken his long black hair out of its pony tail; it was strange seeing him with his hair down. The only thing that came to mind was Zander looking up at Vallus as he shielded him from the blood sword's attack.

"It's my fault, he would have been fine if I helped them; Blitz and Ace would be alive too." Zander said. "I just stood there like a damned fool."

Kerra placed her hand on his shoulder, "It was your first real battle no one is blaming you for anything." She said trying to comfort him.

He became angry and punched the wall beside him, "That isn't an excuse!" he shouted.

She could see the pain in his eyes she couldn't imagine what he must have been feeling seeing Vallus lying there in that hospital bed. "Come on we will get you something to eat, you must be hungry. We will come back later." She said smiling at him.

He turned to her and nodded; "I should probably take Ebony to Vallus' father." Zander said. "He will keep it safe for him until he wakes up."

"That's a great idea." Kerra said watching him walk over to the bedside table and pick up Vallus' sword. They both turned and walked out the door and left Vallus to rest.

***

A few hours later, a cloaked figure slipped into Vallus' room and stood over him examining his body. The figure pulled out a vial of purple colored liquid from under his cloak. He had opened Vallus' mouth wide enough to pour the contents of the vial inside his mouth and down his throat. After waiting only a moment or two Vallus had began to cough violently.

Vallus opened his eyes and looked around, "Where am I?" he asked startled.

"You are in the hospital." The figure said. "That was quite the battle that you were in."

Vallus looked up at the figure standing over the side of the hospital bed but he could not see his face, "Who are you?" he asked.

The man waved a finger in front of his face, "That is not important at the moment; I have come to offer you a proposition." The man said.

Vallus sat up and looked around he didn't see Zander, Kerra, or his sword in the room. "Where are my friends?" he asked.

The cloaked man laughed, "Friends, oh you mean the friends that haven't come to see you since you have been hospitalized?" The cloaked figure lied. "The friend who left you in the desert to die and took your sword for his own?"

Vallus shook his head, "No that isn't true, you're lying!" Vallus shouted. "Zander would never do that."

"Don't you know anything about the cursed blades? Only those that already possess one sword can wield the other." The man explained.

He was right Vallus remembered his father telling him the story of the two swords. "You have no friends now Vallus, but I can give you what you want." The figure said.

Vallus became curious, "What do you mean what I want?" He asked.

The figure sat down on the side of the bed and took out a black sphere. "I know you're longing to stop your father and this ridiculous government, I can give you the power to do it." The man said.

He was right Vallus did want to stop his father's thirst for genocide, hell he wanted the kingdom all for himself. Power was what Vallus craved and he would do anything to get it. He had always kept that side of him hidden from his family and friends.

"What do you want in return?" Vallus asked skeptically. "It's clear that this power that you possess wouldn't come free."

"Simply acquire Ivory from Zander and bring the two blades to the shrine inside the northern caves." The man said handing Vallus the sphere.

"The northern caves past Rygoth?" Vallus asked.

"Yes of course." The figure said.

Vallus sat and thought for a moment, to have the power to change all of V'nairia had always been his dream. By accepting this newfound power he was finally going to get his wish. He was too full of greed at the moment to think about any consequences. The thirst for power outweighed the love for his friends and his love for his kingdom.

"Alright I shall do as you say." Vallus said as he took the sphere, it began to glow and he could feel the power from it surge within him. He felt ten times as powerful as before.

"I feel incredible." Vallus said. "Where does this power come from?"

"That isn't anything for you to concern yourself with." The figure said. "What's important is that you have the power to change V'nairia's future."

"What comes with these new powers?" Vallus asked curiously.

"Your body will get used to your newfound power and your mind will gain the knowledge it needs to utilize it to its full potential." The cloaked man said excitedly. "Trust me it will come to you in time."

He got up out of bed and stretched, he had never felt more alive. "Where are my clothes?" he asked.

"You don't plan on wearing your uniform do you?" the man asked him. "We are against the current V'nairia."

"Your right." Vallus said.

"Here are some clothes I acquired for you, they should fit nicely." The figure said handing Vallus his new clothes. Vallus threw on the white t-shirt and black pants. He laced up his new black boots and slipped on his long black trench coat.

"The new look suits the new you." The man said. "Remember acquire the swords and bring them to the caves."

"Yes." Vallus nodded.

Suddenly the cloaked man disappeared without a trace. It was as if he wasn't human at all. Vallus walked across the room and opened the door. Standing outside the door was the doctor. "Vallus you're awake." The doctor said not expecting to see Vallus out of his bed.

"Yes I'm feeling much better, now if you'll excuse me." Vallus said trying to leave the room.

The doctor didn't move out of his way. "I don't believe you should be going anywhere in your condition." The doctor said insisting that he stay.

Vallus reached out and grabbed the doctor by his throat and lifted him up off of the ground. "I don't remember asking you for your opinion." Vallus glared looking up at him. "You should have moved out of my way."

Vallus tightened his grip until the doctor blacked out. He laid the doctor inside the hospital room and shut the door behind him. He walked down the hallway and out the entrance in search of Zander.

***

Zander and Kerra rode the elevator to the Supreme Judge's office in the Capital building; they walked down the long hallway and had finally reached his door. Zander knocked on the door of the Supreme Judge's office.

"Come in." a voice said from behind the door.

Zander turned the knob and pushed the door open. They entered the room to find Vallus' father standing near the window in the back of the room.

"Zander and Kerra what a lovely surprise." Vallerus said greeting them warmly. "Have you visited Vallus in the hospital yet?"

Zander saluted him, "Yes sir, he still hasn't woken up yet." He said.

"I had feared as much, but we have the finest doctors in the city it's only a matter of time before he wakes up." Vallerus said assuredly. "Zander are you feeling better?"

"Yes much better thank you." Zander said.

"I would like to thank you young lady for looking after my boys." The judge said as he turned and shot Kerra a smile.

"Your very welcome sir." Kerra said smiling back at him.

Zander walked over to Vallerus and handed him Vallus' sword. "I wanted to bring Ebony to you so you could give it to Vallus when he returns. I know that this is the safest place to keep it for him" Zander said.

"Why that's very thoughtful of the both of you thank you." The judge said smiling. Suddenly there was another knock at the door, "You may come in."

The door opened slowly and the three of them stared in amazement as Vallus walked into the office. Zander had noticed something different about him aside from his new clothes. He hadn't looked very happy to see them.

"Good evening everyone." Vallus said.

"Vallus, it's good to see that you're finally awake." His father said overjoyed at seeing his son alive and well and out of the hospital.

"How are you feeling Vallus?" Kerra asked.

Vallus walked over to them but he wasn't smiling like usual, he had a blank expression. "Never better." He said. The closer that he had gotten to them the more uncomfortable Zander became.

Vallerus removed Ebony from the top of his desk and handed it to Zander, "Zander and Kerra had brought your sword to me for safe keeping until you were released from the hospital." His father explained.

Zander walked over and handed Ebony to him, and Vallus gladly accepted it. "Zander, where is Ivory?" Vallus asked. The question was a strange one for Vallus to ask after all Vallus had given the sword to Zander as a gift.

"Why are you asking for it?" his father asked, his son's strange behavior struck an uncomfortable cord in him as well.

"This doesn't concern you father." Vallus said. "I was talking to Zander."

The judge became angry, "How dare you speak to me that way!" he shouted. Vallus ignored his father's ramblings and focused all of his attention on Zander.

"Where is it Zander?" Vallus asked. "It is important that I get it from you."

Zander shook his head, "I won't tell you."

"You won't tell me?" Vallus asked.

"No, something is different about you." Zander said feeling as if he was going to vomit. Vallus' very presence and behavior was making him sick to his stomach.

Vallus laughed, "Well if you won't hand it over I guess I'll just have to take it from you." He said.

"Vallus he doesn't have it with him!" Kerra shouted.

Vallerus walked out from behind Zander and Kerra and threw up his arms barring Vallus' path. "You will do no such thing." He said. "Ivory doesn't belong to you."

Vallus held his hand out with his palm facing them and the three of them had noticed a strange purple aura appear at his fingertips. He placed his hand on the ground. "Demonic Art: Hellhounds!" he shouted. Out of nowhere five black beasts with red eyes and razor sharp teeth materialized from the floor.

"He just conjured those beasts." Zander said. "That's demonic magick."

"Isn't it forbidden?" Kerra asked with a look of terror on her face.

Vallus whistled and the beasts disappeared. "They will tear the city apart; every last man, woman and child." He said. "Now tell me where the sword is hidden."

"No, I won't tell you!" Zander shouted.

They stared at the monster before them; this wasn't Vallus at all. It was something else, something not human. He was darker and menacing; his very presence in the room had made their skin crawl. Vallus drew his blade and pointed it at them, "I'm going to enjoy tearing you to pieces." He said laughing manically.

In that moment Zander and Kerra were more afraid than they had ever been; their best friend who they had loved had meant to kill them. Even if it was a monster possessing Vallus, it was still their friend. In that very moment they had felt helpless, and most of all hopeless.

CHAPTER IV

Vallus' group of Hellhounds had entered the city and began to track down anyone in sight that they could sink their teeth into. Zander had remembered reading about them at the academy. Their hunger was never satisfied no matter how much flesh they had consumed. They were unlike any creature that he had read about, they were supernatural beings from the underworld. Zander still couldn't wrap his head around the idea of Vallus conjuring demonic beasts. Conjuring them was one thing but setting them loose on the citizens of the Capital was insane. The Capital had always been his home and the place he had loved most.

"Well father are you prepared to step down?" Vallus asked.

"I beg your pardon?" Vallerus asked. "Step down from my position?"

"V'nairia doesn't need you anymore." Vallus said leering at his father. "It needs a stronger leader, one that will lead it into the future."

"Vallus, please stop this!" Kerra shouted. "This isn't you at all!

This hadn't been Vallus at all; it was as if their friend had been replaced with some kind of demon. They had never seen their friend with such lust for blood in his eyes. They couldn't fathom why these feelings that Vallus had felt at that very moment could have risen so suddenly to the surface. Zander knew deep down in his heart that this was his friend in bodily form, but his mind had been under the influence of some kind of evil essence. His mind kept wandering back to Kerra and her safety. He knew that he had to get them out of the office quickly before Vallus could act.

Vallus' focus was destroying his father and retrieving Ivory from Zander, which was all that mattered at this point. It was strange; Vallus had never mentioned anything about this before. He had never questioned the way his father ran the kingdom at least not out loud. He would do anything necessary to meet his goals. "Zander, Kerra go down and help the guard." The judge said moving his cape to reveal his sword. "I'll handle my son."

Without hesitation Zander had grabbed Kerra's hand and they both ran right past Vallus and out of the room. "I'm surprised you didn't run after them." Vallerus said.

"I have a mess to clean up here first." Vallus said menacingly. "Don't worry Ivory will be mine soon."

"I don't know what demon has possessed you, but I will drive it out" his father said as he drew his sword.

"You can try father, but you will never change your fate." Vallus said.

They ran at each other and exchanged multiple blows. Sparks flew from their steel as they collided with one another. "You're in way over your head Vallus. I am the Supreme Judge of V'nairia." Vallerus explained.

Vallus chuckled, "Its time someone else took over." He said.

The judge hurled a wave of flames at Vallus who easily blocked it with his sword. "Demonic Art: Shadow Claw." Vallus said as his shadow extended and from it came a large black claw that grabbed Vallerus. It lifted him up off the ground and threw him out the office window.

"Flame Art: Fire Stream." Vallus said engulfing his father in his fire spell. The office was five stories up it would have killed any normal person, but he knew his father wouldn't be killed so easily.

***

Zander and Kerra had already made their way to Kerra's house and retrieved Ivory. Zander had strapped his sword to his side and they ran out the door. "My mom was off today, she was home when I left." Kerra said. "We should try to find her."

"Alright we will look for her." Zander nodded "We need to track one of those things down in the mean time."

"What are we going to do? That can't be Vallus he would never attack the city." Kerra asked.

"For now I'm not sure, we have to find your mother and protect the city." Zander said looking over at her. She could tell he was just as scared as she had been.

"Zander I'm terrified." Kerra said shaking with fear.

He grabbed her hand, "I will protect you with my life Kerra." He said smiling at her. Suddenly most of the fear had subsided for the moment. She had felt safer than she had ever felt before.

"Zander, behind you!" Kerra shouted suddenly pointing to a hellhound running towards them.

Zander drew Ivory from its scabbard and waited for the beast to come closer. "Lightning Art: Thunder Crash!" a voice shouted summoning a bolt of lightning that struck the beast paralyzing it. The beast fell to its knees smoke coming from its body.

"Mother, you're here." Kerra said looking across from them to find her mother standing there.

The Fated Swords

Kiarra came running towards them. Growing up Kerra was always frightened when her mother became angry; she always said her mother shouting sounded like thunder crashing down from the heavens. "Are you two alright?" she asked hugging Kerra.

Zander walked over to the hellhound and thrust his sword into its skull and watched as it turned to ash and was swept away by the wind.

"Yes were fine." Zander said sheathing his sword.

"Where is Vallus? Where did these demons come from?" Kerra's mother asked. It was hard for them to even think about let alone even say it out loud.

"The beasts were summoned by Vallus; he's at the Capital building fighting his father. We don't know what's going on." Kerra explained.

"It must have started with the coma, something just isn't right." Zander said. "He actually performed demonic magick."

"Something definitely isn't right, Vallus is only a half mystic." Kiarra said. "He couldn't have learned that type of magick."

"Tell that to him when you see him." Kerra said.

Kiarra thought for a moment on what they should do, "We will go to the square, leave the rest of the hounds to the guard." She said. They ran off toward the square to find Vallus and his father. They had hoped they weren't too late.

***

Vallus had jumped out of the office window and met his father on the ground below, Vallerus' clothes were burned but he had received no damage from the flames or the fall. He was a master of flame magicks and was impervious to them, Vallus had foolishly forgotten that fact but it hadn't mattered to him in the slightest.

"Well I knew that wouldn't have finished you, being your son I know you have quite a few tricks up your sleeve." Vallus laughed.

"For the good of my kingdom Vallus I swear upon my life I will kill you if I must. Do not make me do this." His father said.

Vallus rubbed the handle of his sword against his head, "Well if you want to go ahead and offer up your life so easily I won't turn you away." Vallus said.

Vallerus needed to think of a solution quickly, he didn't want to kill his own flesh and blood but also didn't want to see the people of his kingdom slaughtered. This was his kingdom; his responsibility was to protect it no matter what the cost. "Then there is no stopping you, I will just have to put an end to you here." He told his son.

"Then I shall give you a parting gift?" Vallus asked. "Demonic Art: Greater Demon!" Vallus shouted.

It was the same summoning style as before, except for this time Vallus had summoned a giant demon with fangs, giant horns, and a razor-sharp tail. "Kill him" Vallus commanded the beast.

It charged at the judge, extending its long claws attempting to strike him. Luckily for Vallerus the beast was slower than he was; all except for the tail which came at him so fast he didn't have time to block it. The barbs on the tail had dug deep into his skin and ripped across his side. He regained his composure, leapt into the air and with one swift motion severed the demon's left arm.

"You won't defeat my friend here with such normal tactics." Vallus said smiling. Vallerus looked back to the beast whose arm had grown back almost instantly.

"It can regenerate parts of its body; it looks like I'm going to have to use that technique to finish this" He thought to himself.

He held two fingers in front of his face, and watched as his sword had suddenly vanished. "Enough games, I will finish this now!" he shouted. Vallus' expression had not changed, he was hell bent on destroying his father.

Zander along with Kerra and Kiarra had finally made their way into the square just in time to see the large beast that Vallerus had been fighting.

"What the hell is that thing?" Zander asked.

"It's a greater demon, far more powerful than the hellhounds." Kerra said. She had learned all about different types of demons and other creatures from the many books in the Capital's library. Her mother had taught her everything she knew, she had even taught her in the same arts as her ancestors.

Kiarra had looked over and saw the sign that Vallerus was making and instantly she knew what was coming next. "It's over, in just a few short moments." She said. Zander looked over at her,

"What do you mean?" he asked.

"Judge Vallerus is gathering magickal energy for his signature move; it's his trump card that has never failed him." Kiarra said.

"A signature move?" Zander asked.

"Yes, every mystic or half mystic eventually creates their own original spell. Judge Vallerus had created his own just as our family has passed down the same signature spell for generations." Kiarra Explained. "This type of spell normally depletes well over half of the caster's remaining magickal energy. It is a formidable but dangerous spell."

"I see." Zander said and turned his attention back to Vallerus and the demon.

"Sacred Art: Dance of a Thousand Blades!" Vallerus shouted snapping his fingers together. The beast had suddenly stopped moving. Its body had begun to deteriorate; it was cut to ribbons by Vallerus' spell. The ashes of the beast were spread all along the square. Zander and the others rushed over to see if Vallerus was injured.

"Lord Vallerus, are you alright?" Kiarra asked.

"I'm fine Kiarra it's just a scratch." he said tying a piece of cloth around his arm and tightened it to stop the bleeding. "What of the hellhounds?"

"I had destroyed one just before we arrived in the square, we believe that the guard has taken the rest down as well." Zander reported.

Vallerus was indeed relieved the people were safe, "Kiarra I need you to give word to Lieutenant Omak immediately." Vallerus said to Kerra's mother. "Have him rally a group of Militia soldiers and send them out to search for Vallus."

Kiarra saluted him, "And what should they do once they track him down sir?" she asked. Vallerus turned back toward the Capital building before falling silent.

"He is a traitor to not only his kingdom, but to his family as well." He said walking away. "They are to eliminate him on sight."

"Your grace! He is your son and our friend. Please reconsider." Zander shouted. "We have to find out what has caused this change in him."

"Zander, I don't expect you to understand. You are still too young." Vallerus said not even turning to face them. "This is my order and I will see that it is carried out."

"Lord Vallerus please." Kerra said begging tears running down her face. Zander hated seeing her in so much pain, but he hated the fact that his best friend was now a wanted criminal even more.

"I am sorry." Vallerus said continuing to walking toward the Capital building.

This news hit Zander and Kerra hard, this was their best friend and now he was a traitor with a price on his head.

They just didn't know what to do. Going against the Supreme Judge's orders would mean being named traitors themselves. They were caught between the love of their friend and the home that Zander had sworn to protect, no matter what the cost. It was one of the hardest decisions he knew he would ever have to make.

***

The next day Zander had requested a meeting with the High Court and decided to take Kerra with him. They walked into the large round room, where the judges presided. There were six judges total including the Supreme Judge. They stood before them in fear, for these were the strongest warriors in all of V'nairia gathered together in the same room. Zander had known that the request he was about to make was a ridiculous one but he had to try something, anything to get his friend back home safely.

"Zander, you come before this court today on the matter of my son Vallus?" Judge Vallerus asked.

Zander stepped forward, "Yes your honor we have a plan to bring Vallus back to the city." He said.

Judge Terrian cleared his throat, "Impossible, Vallus was branded a traitor and must be eliminated." He explained. Terrian was the member of the High Court who had specialized in earth magick. The rest of the court agreed with Vallerus and Terrian, even Kerra's mother only because she knew she had no other choice.

"Then allow me to take responsibility for this task and eliminate the traitor myself." Zander said bravely. "Allow me to fulfill my oath to protect V'nairia and its people."

"You would kill your closest friend to protect your kingdom?" Judge Durga asked leaning in closer to have a look at Zander.

"Yes if that is what I must do." Zander said without hesitation.

Things were quiet for a moment before Judge Vallerus spoke up, "Zander I do hereby grant you the task of eliminating the traitor." He said.

"This is madness!" Kiarra shouted slamming her fist down on her podium.

"You disagree Kiarra?" Judge Vallerus asked her.

"He is a sixteen year old boy who has only just graduated from the academy." She said. "You really think he is a match for Vallus?"

"She is right Vallerus. The boy cannot defeat Vallus alone." Judge Aronei said twirling her green hair around her fingers looking as though the meeting had bored her.

"If I recall Lord Vallerus, your son had given even you a run for your money." Kiarra said.

"Silence Judge Kiarra!" Vallerus shouted. "You will not speak to me in my court room with such disrespect."

"Kiarra's anger had quickly subsided, "I apologize. I don't know what came over me sir." She said looking down at her feet.

"Your grace, I will be accompanying Zander and making sure that the task is carried out." Kerra chimed in.

Kiarra had suddenly felt five inches tall, she knew that Kerra would go with Zander. The three of them had always been inseparable. Kerra was her only child and she couldn't stand the thought of losing her, but when it came to Zander and Vallus there was no changing her mind.

"Your honor, I do have another request." Zander said.

Vallerus raised an eyebrow, "Go on." He said.

"Well with more manpower, it would make this task much easier. So with your permission we would like to take the mystic prisoner with us to find Vallus." Zander said.

The court began to laugh, "Are you out of your minds? That man is a criminal who deserves to rot behind bars." Judge Durga said.

"Not to mention a mystic." Judge Terrian said.

"He deserves to be killed if you ask me, for all we know it could have been a spell he cast on Vallus that created this mess in the first place." Judge Oran suggested.

Vallerus raised his hand to silence the court,

"Request denied. You may take a group of soldiers with you to command but the prisoner stays behind." Judge Vallerus said.

"Please reconsider! I beg of you!" Zander shouted.

"Enough!" Vallerus shouted. "You will leave at daybreak tomorrow, you are dismissed."

That was what Zander had thought they were going to say, it was up to the two of them to bring Vallus back and without any help they didn't know how they were going to do it. They gathered what was left of themselves and left the chamber.

"Want me to walk you home?" Zander asked.

"Well now, quite the gentlemen aren't we?" Kerra asked smiling.

Zander began to laugh, "Aren't I always?" he said smiling at her.

"I guess so." She agreed.

"Don't worry Kerra, we will get him back. Vallus will not die." Zander said trying to reassure her.

She grabbed his hand and held it, "I know we will, I believe in you Mr. Gentleman." Kerra said. "I just don't understand why they just couldn't let us take the mystic with us."

Zander looked over at her and smiled, "Who said we couldn't break him out ourselves?" he asked grinning from ear to ear.

Kerra was shocked; he had just proposed they break the law. "Are you crazy? They will kill us." She asked.

"No he isn't crazy, he's determined" Kiarra said sneaking up behind them. Zander and Kerra both jumped out of their skin.

"Mom how long have you been there?" Kerra asked.

Kiarra laughed, "Long enough, and Zander's plan isn't crazy you'll just have to have a way into the underground holding cell." Kiarra explained.

"But we don't have a cardkey to access the door." Zander sighed.

Kiarra placed a cardkey into Zander's hand, "Now you do." She said.

The two of them were confused as to why Kerra's mother was helping them.

"If they find out that your helping us they will kill you?" Zander said. "Why are you doing this?"

"Because I know what Vallus means to you both and that's a friendship you should fight for. Kiarra said smiling at them. "Get in and get out, don't stay a moment longer."

She had pulled out a scroll and handed it to Kerra. "Never forget how strong you are Kerra." Kiarra said.

"Mom are you sure I should take this?" Kerra asked looking down at the scroll.

"Yes, you may need it along your journey." She said. "Use it wisely; you only get one use out of this scroll."

"Of course. Thank you mother." Kerra said hugging her mother tightly.

Zander's eyes met Kiarra's and he watched as a single tear ran down the side of her face. "Kiarra I will protect her with my life." He said.

"I have all the faith in the world in you Zander. I'm sure if your parents were here they would be very proud." Kiarra said wiping her eyes.

"You're the closest thing I've ever had to a mother; I just want you to know that I appreciate all you have done for me." Zander said trying to hide his emotions.

Kiarra kissed him on the forehead, "Now go, hurry to the holding cell." She said. Zander and Kerra turned and ran down the street in the direction of the underground holding cell. Kiarra watched the two things in the world that she had cared about most appear into the darkness of the night unsure of when she would see them again.

***

There was at knock at the Supreme Judge's door, "Come in." he said. The door had opened slowly and Lieutenant Omak had walked inside.

"You wanted to see me sir?" Omak asked.

"Yes Lieutenant, please have a seat." Vallerus said motioning him to a chair in front of his desk.

"I'm surprised you had called for me this late, it must be urgent." The Lieutenant said taking a cigar from his front pocket and lighting it.

"You could say that." The judge said. "Zander Kyre had met with the High Court today; he has agreed to take on the task of eliminating Vallus."

Omak had taken a long drag from his cigar and exhaled, "You might as well be sending the boy on a suicide mission. He said. "Vallus is too strong for him."

"Maybe your right but I can't shake the feeling that there is something different about this boy." Judge Vallerus explained. "It is possible that he could be more powerful than Vallus even as a human."

"If you say so, but my bet is still on that boy of yours." The Lieutenant said flicking the ashes of his cigar in the nearby ashtray on the judge's desk. "Why the sudden interest in this boy anyway?"

Vallerus stood up from his desk and walked over to the office window which had been replaced after his fight with Vallus only the day before. "It was a curious request he had made to the court that sparked my interest." Vallerus said. "He asked that the mystic in the holding cell be released to help them eliminate Vallus."

Omak laughed, "What the hell kind of plan is that, a militia soldier asking for the help of a rogue mystic?" Omak asked. "A dangerous one at that."

Vallerus nodded, "Yes and after being denied I get the feeling that he will disobey orders and try and get the mystic's help anyway." He said.

"How do you suppose he will do that?" Omak asked.

"Breaking into the underground holding cell of course." The judge said.

"Lord Vallerus, they are only sixteen. They can't get in without a keycard." The Lieutenant said trying to reassure him.

"You're forgetting that he has grown up around Vallus. He is just as stubborn at times." Vallerus explained. "Besides I suspect he will have help."

"So you want me to stop him and bring him back here to you?" Omak asked taking another drag of his cigar.

"Precisely." The judge said. "I will deal with his helping hand when the time comes."

"Alright sir I will head to the holding cell now." Omak said getting up out of his seat and walking towards the door. He opened it, walked outside and closed the door behind him.

"*This has turned into quite the little game hasn't it Vallus?*" Vallerus asked himself still gazing out at the city from the office window.

***

Zander and Kerra had made their way across the city to the entrance of the underground holding cell. "Finally were here." Zander said swiping the card key in the door of the holding cell. The screen lit up green with the words *Access Granted* flashing across it. They quickly slipped inside undetected, but they had noticed there were no guards at the entrance or anywhere inside. They rode the elevator to the bottom floor which was where the Militia had kept the most dangerous of the mystics until their day of execution.

"This is kind of strange; I haven't seen a single guard." Kerra said stating the obvious. Zander had thought the same as they stepped out of the elevator.

"Maybe they keep minimal security down here, after all it is pretty hard to get in here normally." Zander said.

He was right only a judge or high ranking officer had clearance to enter. That is why Kiarra had given them her cardkey to get inside. They walked inside the large circular holding cell. All of the cells were empty except for one.

"They couldn't have made it any easier in finding him." Kerra said pointing to his cell door.

"Okay let's get him out." Zander said walking over to the door.

Suddenly there was an alarm that blared and the room flashed red. "*How did we trip the alarm?*" Zander asked himself. "*Was this a trap?*"

"Well, look what we've got here." A voice said. Zander didn't have to turn around to know who had entered the room behind them. He knew that voice well; it was a voice he had hated. He swallowed hard and grabbed Kerra's hand tightly, it was Lieutenant Omak.

CHAPTER V

"Supreme Judge Vallerus had a feeling you would defy orders." Omak said. "You teenagers are so predictable with your rebellion and crap."

Zander stood in front of Kerra, shielding her, "So you're here to stop us, is that it?" he asked angrily.

"Don't make me take you back by force boy. Don't make this harder on yourselves." Omak said trying to reason with Zander.

Zander thought about Vallus, they needed to find him and they couldn't turn their backs on their mission now. They were prepared to face the consequences. The court, Vallus' father nor the Militia understood that this was their friend. Vallus was like family to them they could not just leave him in this state of hatred.

Zander knew that in order to stop them the Lieutenant would have to use deadly force, then he thought of Kerra and how he had wished she hadn't gotten caught up in everything. She was the only one that he could trust and she had trusted him to the same degree.

"Well son, what's your decision?" he asked.

Zander clenched his fist, "No! We won't go back; I'm taking Heiro right now!" He shouted.

The Lieutenant shook his head and sighed, "Alright, then you leave me no choice." Omak said as he drew his sword.

Zander drew Ivory and stepped out in front of Kerra, "Kerra stay here, I'll handle this." He said.

"Please be careful Zander." She begged him.

Zander ran towards the Lieutenant and locked swords with him. Zander's sword skills were not as good as Vallus' however he could hold his own at the academy when it came to sparring. He knew that this couldn't be like the fight with Heiro in Oaba desert. Kerra was with him and he would be damned if someone was going to hurt another one of his friends.

"Zander came down with an overhead blow but the Lieutenant had side stepped away from the strike.

Omak had quickly grabbed Zander by the shoulders and thrusted his knee into Zander's stomach. Just before the Lieutenant could punch Zander across the face, Zander grabbed Omak's hand and twisted it delivering a kick to his side that had pushed him away. "You have some spunk kid; I knew you would be a great addition to the Militia." The lieutenant said.

"Screw you and your squad! I quit." Zander said as he took Ivory's scabbard and thrust it into the lieutenant's ribs. He seemed unaffected by the force of the blow.

Omak pulled out his rocket launcher, "I'm supposed to bring you in unharmed but you're not leaving me with much choice." He said before firing a rocket towards Zander; who wasn't fast enough to out run it.

"Lightning Art: Thunder Crash!" Kerra shouted firing bolts of lightning magick. The magick connected with the rocket and exploded.

Zander looked over and saw her smiling, "I owe you one Kerra." He said.

"I can't let you have all the fun now can I?" Kerra asked. Zander stopped to take a breath, if it hadn't been for

Kerra's spell he would have been blown to a million tiny pieces and splattered along the holding cell walls.

The Lieutenant began to reload his weapon, "You two sure are a hell of a lot of trouble." He said.

Zander ran at him to strike him with Ivory but was blocked by the body of the launcher. They both pushed against one another, trying to gain the upper hand. Omak saw Zander's eyes flash red it was unusual he had never seen such an occurrence before. Suddenly a light emanated from Zander's sword and with a powerful swing he sliced right through the rocket launcher and threw the Lieutenant into the wall of the holding cell. He hit the wall hard and fell to the ground, he was knocked unconscious. Kerra looked over at Zander and couldn't believe her eyes.

"*Was that magick?*" She asked herself.

"Kerra come on let's get him out." Zander said pointing to Heiro's cell that he had opened with the card key from her mother.

Heiro began to cough, "What the hell do you want? Didn't I kill you?" he asked recognizing Zander from their previous fight.

Zander and Kerra walked inside and saw him bound by anti-magick chains. These had been used to restrain mystics from using their powers against the Militia while in custody.

"I need your assistance in exchange for your freedom." Zander said.

"Well now I'm listening please go on." Heiro said.

Zander knelt down to face him, "Our friend Vallus, something has happened to him and he fled the city. We need your help to bring him back." Zander explained.

Heiro began to laugh hysterically, "You want me to go on some boring little adventure with you two, and bring your friend back?" He asked. "You've got to be kidding me."

Kerra tapped Zander's shoulder, "Come on let's just go, we don't need his help Zander." She said.

Zander got up and they began to walk out of the cell, "Make me a better offer." Heiro said.

Zander froze he didn't know what to offer a criminal; he said the first thing that had come to his mind. "Fine, I'll make sure you're well compensated." Zander lied.

"Then I am at your service, young swordsman the name's Heiro." He said. "I'll do anything for a big bag of Yol."

Zander pulled out Ivory and cut the chains off him, "I'm Zander and this is Kerra." He said pointing to her.

Heiro bowed before her, "Pleased to meet you my lady." Heiro said in a polite tone. She turned her head and stuck her nose in the air in disgust.

"Okay let's get out of here before the soldiers arrive." Zander said as they left Heiro's cell.

"You'd better take his keycard so he can't follow us." Heiro suggested pointing to Omak who was unconscious lying on the floor across the room.

"Good point." Zander said as he walked over and grabbed the Lieutenant's cardkey and removed it from the keys that hung from his belt. They made their way to the elevator and rode it to the top. They could hear a group of soldiers making their way towards them from up the street.

"They must have been notified by Omak somehow." Kerra said.

"We need to make a run for the front gate; the guards should be changing soon. We can slip through." Zander said. Without hesitation they had ran down the street and towards the large front gates of the city.

Zander was right, there were no guards watching the gates. They quickly pushed the large doors opened and slipped through to the other side.

The three of them had made their way into the Durean Forest behind the city walls, it was pretty old but it was still beautiful. After walking a couple of hours they had stopped to set up camp, after battling the Lieutenant, Zander had been exhausted. Kerra looked over at Zander and saw a strange marking on his hand.

"What is that?" she asked pointing to his arm. Zander looked down and saw the same marking,

"I'm not sure; I've never seen it before." He said.

"It's the sign of a mystic; it only appears when your powers awaken." Heiro spoke up attempting to light a fire by hand.

Zander thought back to the battle when the energy surged from his body and knocked Omak into the wall of the cell. *"So that's what that was, my powers had awakened?"* Zander asked himself.

"I also have one." Heiro said pointing to his on his right forearm, except his was different he only had two marks. Zander however had had four marks appear on his hand.

"Why is my mark different?" Zander asked.

"Each line represents an element of magick you can control; the lines are color coded depending on what the elements are." Heiro explained. "I have two lines, one red and the other brown for my fire and earth magicks."

"So they are like tattoos?" Zander asked.

"Something like that." Heiro said laughing at him.

Zander looked down and examined his mark again, "So I can use four elements?" he asked. Heiro nodded and popped some berries into his mouth.

"So why don't I have a mark, I can use lightning magick?" Kerra asked.

"Only those whose mystic heritage is pure can have the mark, meaning both your parents had to be mystics." He said.

"So then I'm not a mystic?" Kerra asked.

"No you're what they call a half-mystic." Heiro explained.

Zander was shocked by what was said, his parents couldn't have been mystics his father was a war hero for the Militia. Nothing was making any sense to him that would mean his parents were killed in the mystic genocide. "So how do I learn to control my powers?" Zander asked.

Heiro looked over at him and grinned, "I guess I could teach you, you'll need to get stronger physically and mentally in order to control your magick." He said

There was definitely no denying what he was saying, Vallus could use demonic magick and has one of the cursed swords. He was a deadly advisory almost on his father's level.

"Thank you Heiro, we would appreciate that." Kerra said.

"Don't mention it hot stuff, it's the least I can do." Heiro winked at her which made her blush even though she had hated him already.

This angered Zander he never liked Heiro from the beginning, let alone trust him. He loved Kerra and was sure that he was destined to be with her and the thought of Heiro sweet talking her infuriated him.

"I think we should get some rest, we will need our strength tomorrow." Zander said. Each one took turns keeping watch while the others slept through the night peacefully. Tomorrow they would begin their long journey through the kingdom in search of Vallus to bring him safely back home.

***

The next morning Zander awoke to the sound of birds chirping, he immediately rubbed his eyes and looked around. He saw Kerra lying across from him sound asleep but he didn't see Heiro anywhere. He walked over and nudged Kerra awake, "Kerra wake up he's gone." He said.

Kerra rose up slowly and then realized what Zander had said and jumped up. "Where could he have gone?" she asked.

"He probably took off in the middle of the night." Zander said angrily. "I knew that he wouldn't help us."

Suddenly they heard footsteps and rustling in the bushes. Zander grabbed Ivory and motioned Kerra to remain quiet. Heiro appeared from behind the bushes carrying fish he had caught from the river. "Good morning sleepyheads, you hungry?" he asked.

"We thought you fled for the next town!" she shouted.

"Whoa calm down guys, you think I'd leave without collecting my reward for helping you?" Heiro explained.

"I guess you're right." Zander said already annoyed with Heiro and he'd only been awake for five minutes. "Where are we headed?"

Kerra began to pack her things and put out the fire, "All I know is that we need to get to the next town before the Militia reaches us, who knows how many soldiers they will send after us." She said.

Heiro pointed to a small path through the woods, "We will take that path to the town of Durea we can find shelter for the night there." He said.

"You're sure it's safe to travel into town?" Zander asked.

"Of course Durea is a quiet little town." Heiro said. "No one will find us."

Zander looked over at Kerra who had just finished packing her belongings, "What do you think?" he asked her.

"It doesn't look like we have much choice." Kerra said.

"Alright lead the way Heiro." Zander said hesitantly.

Together the three of them had taken the path through the Durean Forest toward the small town of Durea.

***

A few hours later, they had finally made it to the entrance Durea; it was a fairly quiet place all except for the local bar called "*The Howling Wolf*" which most of the bandits and drunks spend most of their time brawling outback behind the building.

"I've been here once or twice selling some things, it's an okay place." Heiro said.

"Yeah, stolen things." Zander said.

Heiro turned to look at him and waved a finger in disapproval of his comment. "Hey you shouldn't judge other people." He said.

"They were stolen weren't they?" Kerra asked.

Heiro chuckled, "That's beside the point."

They walked across the street to the inn and walked inside. They went over to the counter and rung the bell. A short older woman walked over to greet them. "Good evening dears, how many rooms will you need?" she asked.

"Two madam if you please." Heiro said grinning.

Zander was disgusted by him even in his eighteen years Heiro would still sweet talk someone twice or even three times his age. "Right this way dear." The woman said showing them to their rooms.

"Goodnight." Kerra said opening the door to her room and walking inside. The boys waved goodnight and also retired to their room for the evening.

That night Zander laid in bed restlessly as Heiro snored like a wild beast. It was ridiculous to think about the mess that he had gotten himself and Kerra in. They were no w wanted fugitives and to beat it all Kerra's mother had helped them. In just one day the three of them had committed treasonous acts against the kingdom. He knew the Militia would be looking for them soon so they had to lay low for awhile and not draw attention to themselves. Zander knew that he had to get stronger, finding out that he had this newfound power had shocked him at first but then he had realized that it could really help him to bring his friend back home. He would train as much as he could until they had found Vallus. He knew that there was a possibility that he may have to use force to bring him back. He knew if it came to that he had to be ready, they all had too.

***

Vallerus pushed open the large double doors to the High Courts' chambers and found that the other four judges were already waiting for him. The only judge not present had been Kiarra. "Good evening." He said greeting them.

"Vallerus, what was so important that you have summoned us at this hour?" Judge Oran asked. Judge Oran had always been the impatient type; he had never liked to be kept waiting. He glared across the room at Vallerus while stroking his white mustache.

"Forgive me, I realize that it is rather late but we have an urgent matter to discuss." Vallerus said.

"Go on." Judge Durga said.

"It is Zander Kyre and Kerra Lyale; they had broken into the underground holding cell and released the rogue mystic." Judge Vallerus explained.

Vallerus had been shot skeptical look from around the room, "You're sure of this?" Judge Terrian asked. "Two sixteen year olds broke into the holding cell?"

"Yes I have already spoken with Lieutenant Omak who had tried to subdue them. They had overpowered him and released the prisoner." Vallerus said.

Suddenly the room was in frenzy, the judges shouting questions back and forth it was if they had all lost their minds. This news had caused them to panic.

"Silence!" Vallerus shouted.

The shouting and arguing had quickly ceased. Everyone in the room turned their attention to the Supreme Judge. "It has also come to my attention that Zander Kyre's mystic powers have awakened." Vallerus said.

This certainly had been surprising news no one in the entire kingdom would have guessed that Zander would have become a mystic. After all he had bared no marking of a mystic or hadn't showed any sign of magickal potential.

"I have taken the liberty of preparing for this newfound threat." Vallerus said reassuring them. Zander, Kerra, and Vallus will be eliminated on sight. It is for the good of the kingdom."

Some of the judges gasped, "What does Kiarra have to say about this?" Judge Durga asked. "After all; one of the traitors is her own daughter."

"Do not worry about such things. She will be told in time, which is why I did not call her to this meeting." Vallerus explained.

"What preparations have you made Vallerus?" Judge Oran asked curiously once again stroking his mustache.

Judge Vallerus had suddenly snapped his fingers and the double doors to the chamber had opened. "I'm glad you asked." He said smiling.

Two figures had passed through the doors and slowly made their way into the middle of the chamber. One of the figures had been tall, the other was much shorter. Each wore a demonic mask that had hidden their identity, one red and the other blue. The taller man had carried a sword while the shorter one carried an axe.

"These warriors are the answer to our problem?" Judge Terrian asked skeptically.

"Yes they hardly seem worthy of such an important task." Judge Oran agreed.

"Ladies and Gentlemen of the court, I give you Taru and Tora. You probably know them as The Slaughter Twins." Vallerus grinned devilishly.

The Slaughter Twins had been the most talked about bounty hunters in all of V'nairia. They are infamous for ripping their enemies to shreds and leaving them unrecognizable. They reveled in the very sight of blood and gore. To them killing was not just a sport or a job, to them it was enjoyable.

"So I see, well perhaps we were hasty in our judgments." Judge Durga said.

"I assure each and every member of the court that we are good at what we do." Taru said in a deep menacing voice. "There will nothing left of them."

"Right, nothing left at all." Tora agreed. The twins turned and walked back across the room to the double doors and opened them making their exit. As they began to walk down the hall, Taru turned his head and peered into the darkness near the doors to the chambers.

"It's very impolite to eavesdrop, it could get you killed." He said glaring devilishly his eyes glowing red in the dark hallway like that of a demon.

Kiarra had taken a deep sigh of relief as she watched them continue down the hall and into the elevator. She had been standing outside the door and listening the whole time. She was shocked by everything she had heard. The only thing she could think about was Taru's eyes. She could see his thirst for blood staring back at her. It had sent a cold chill down her spine. She didn't know what she should do, but she had to think of something fast.

CHAPTER VI

Zander and Heiro awoke the next morning feeling well-rested. They had gotten dressed and walked down the hall past Kerra's room and knocked on the door,

"Kerra, Heiro and I are going out to train for a bit. Would you like to come?" Zander asked.

There was no response, "Maybe she's still sleeping, it had taken a lot out of us to get here." Heiro said.

"Yeah I guess you're right, we can let her rest." Zander agreed as they walked down the stairs and out of the inn.

Outside they walked by the small shops and stands, taking a few moments to take in the smell of delicious food that had been prepared. Zander hadn't had a decent meal since the day before he and Vallus set out on their mission to Oaba Village. His stomach had been growling; he was famished. He looked over at Heiro and immediately noticed his manliness. Heiro definitely wasn't complaining about not eating so why should he. He thought it best to not complain about his hunger and train first before mentioning that they pick up food.

"Where are we going?" Zander asked.

"There is a small river just down the hill from the town." Heiro said.

A few moments later they had arrived at the river that Heiro had been talking about. "Why are we training down here?" Zander asked.

"This river is on the outside of town and it is secluded, no one will spot us here." Heiro explained.

"Good idea, the last thing we need is a militia soldier spotting us." Zander said.

Heiro laughed, "You don't think I can handle one militia soldier?" he asked so sure of himself.

Even though he was a bit of a smartass and full of himself, Zander knew that he was right. He had had a lot more training not just in magick but combat in general. Zander looked up at him and nodded in agreement.

It was definitely the prime place to train; they knew that the Militia would be looking for them. The river would be the last place anyone would think to look. "Today we're going to learn a few simple spells." Heiro said walking out into the middle of the river, "I can normally only use earth and fire magick, but I happened to learn a couple of other spells from an old mystic I met a while back." He went on to say.

"So I take it since we're at the river I'm going to learn water magick?" Zander asked.

Heiro began to laugh, "Nothing gets past you. Yes I'm going to teach you a defensive water spell." Heiro replied.

"So if you're only a fire and earth wielding mystic, then how can you perform any of the other elements?" Zander asked curiously.

"You make a good point, see the thing is I can learn to bend the will of water and wind natured magick but I would never use them in combat." Heiro said.

"So what's the point in learning them then?" Zander asked.

"So I can train little assholes like you that ask a dozen questions." Heiro replied starkly. "I can use them but they aren't powerful enough for shit."

Zander stood and watched carefully as Heiro proceeded with his demonstration. He had begun to focus and gather his energy, "You have to take in all the energy you can and release it down into the water through your feet like so" Heiro said as the water below him had begun to bubble. "Water Art: Water Wall!"

Suddenly the water sprang up and formed a wall. "Normally water can be sliced through easily, but when you infuse it with magick it is strengthened, making it harder to penetrate." Heiro explained.

Zander removed Ivory from its scabbard and tried to cut through the water, the blade had bounced back unable to make its way through.

"See how useful it can be?" Heiro asked. "Now its your turn to try."

Zander walked out to the water and joined him. He had begun focusing his mind on gathering the energy he needed to perform the technique. He had tried for several minutes but had felt nothing.

"Nothing is happening." Zander said sighing heavily.

"You have to clear your head, stop thinking about everything and only focus on what you're doing." Heiro instructed.

Zander had cleared his head and tried once more, after a moment he had felt warmth throughout his body. It was his magick, he could finally feel it. He had gathered it up and forced it out through the bottom of his feet into the water, "Water Art: Water Wall!" Zander shouted as the wall formed from the river, it wasn't as large or as strong as Heiro's spell but it would have to do for now.

"Looks like you're a natural when it comes to spell casting, that's good." Heiro said.

"So do I have to be near a water source to use water spells?" Zander asked.

"Nope not at all, you can use the water deep within the ground. Your magick essence is stronger than you may think." Heiro explained. "It takes less magick to control if you're near one though."

"Now I understand how defensive spells are useful but what about offensive spells?" Zander asked him.

"That's your next lesson, wind magick." Heiro said pointing to a tree across the river. "This time you will be using your sword instead of your body. You must channel your magick through the blade of your sword, Wind Art: Slicing Gale." Heiro said as he released his sword and sent gusts of air towards the tree slicing off several of its branches.

"See?" Heiro asked. "No sweat kid."

Zander faced the tree and released his sword, he gathered the energy he needed and just as Heiro instructed he channeled the magick through the blade. With one quick motion he released it but instead the blades were so powerful they sliced the tree itself in half. "I figured as much, Ivory amplifies all magick that is passed through it. That will be a valuable asset later on." Heiro explained.

Zander had no idea he was this powerful, and by his parents no less. He thought back to when they had fought Heiro before, if he had known he had this much power and used it then Vallus wouldn't have went into a coma. They wouldn't be here in Durea right now trying to find him and bring him back. He was no longer angry with Heiro, they know now that it was a dark essence that had consumed him. He no longer cared whether they were mystics or not he was glad he was born with the power to bring his friend home. That was his main focus; he would bring Vallus back to the Capital and nothing else mattered.

"Alright, I think that's enough training for today." Heiro said. "How about we go get some lunch, I think I smelled some delicious chicken back in town?"

"I'm starved! Let's go!" Zander shouted racing Heiro to the nearest restaurant in town.

***

Later that evening the boys had made their way back to the inn. As they walked past Kerra's door and knocked, there was still no reply.

"Something's wrong, we should check on her." Zander said.

Heiro nodded as they slowly opened the door, "Kerra, were coming in!" Zander shouted but there was no answer. Inside the room there was no sign of Kerra. Her window was open and a breeze blew in through the curtains.

"Where could she have gone?" Zander asked himself.

Heiro spotted a note on the bed out of the corner of his eye. He picked it up, examined it and was in immediate shock. "Zander she was kidnapped!" Heiro shouted.

"What does it say?" Zander asked snatching it from his hand. It read:

If you want the girl, meet us at the shack outside of town.
We're asking 100,000 Yol in exchange.
Come alone at midnight or she dies.

"Damn bandits, sadly this is a common occurrence in Durea." Heiro said.

Zander noticed an odd symbol on the bottom of the letter, it looked like a claw. "What does this mean?" he asked Heiro.

"That is the symbol for the Iron Claw Bandits, their leader Jackus is a ruthless killer." He said.

"What the hell are we supposed to do? We don't have that kind of money" Zander asked.

"We're going to have to fight them and get her back." Heiro explained. Heiro was right there was no alternative; a few bandits couldn't be that much to handle for the two of them. "I failed to mention that Jackus is also a mystic and I'm unaware of what powers he possesses, so we must be careful." He added.

"We don't have time to waste we have to hurry." Zander said running out the door to Kerra's room with Heiro following behind him.

They rushed out of the inn and down the street; it was already a few minutes after ten they didn't have much time left to spare. Kerra's life was at stake and Zander would be damned if they were going to kill her. He regretted even letting her tag along but she wouldn't back down, Vallus was her friend too and she wanted to see this through just as much as he did.

Zander and Heiro had made their way to the old shack on the outskirts of town. They looked around and had seen no sign of Kerra or the bandits that had left the note behind.

"Something isn't right, it's after midnight." Heiro said. They had plainly told them to bring the money to the old shack at midnight; Zander definitely had a bad feeling in his gut.

"Well, you did decide to show after all." A voice said.

They looked around and didn't see anyone, it had been too dark. A shadowy figure emerged from behind the old shack. The man was bald and had a beard and looked as though his face had been badly scarred. Zander didn't even have to guess who it was, it was Jackus.

"Where is she?" Zander asked clenching his fist tightly.

"She's safe for now, her continued safety depends on you two upholding your end of the bargain." Jackus said.

Zander saw the large curved blade that Jackus was carrying and he immediately remembered Heiro telling him that Jackus was a mystic. For now neither of them knew what to expect from him. They had to be cautious in this fight if they wanted to make it out alive.

"We don't have that kind of money." Heiro said.

This had angered Jackus but soon after he found it mildly humorous, "You come to this place without the requested funds? How foolish could you be?" Jackus asked.

"Where is Kerra!?" Zander shouted angrily

Jackus raised his curved blade so that it met Zander at eye level, "Shut your fucking mouth or I'll kill her right now." He said.

Jackus snapped his fingers and they watched as the other members of the clan began to appear. They wore masks and had long bladed claws attached to their arms. Two bandits walked out of the shack holding Kerra by her arms.

"Zander help me." She said frightened.

"Be quiet you little slut!" one bandit said, slapping her across the face.

Zander stepped forward in a rage, "Touch her again you son of a bitch and I'll kill every last one of you," he said.

His blood pressure had spiked and the veins could be seen in his neck, when it came to Kerra he would rip them all to pieces.

"I'm done with these idiots, kill them both." Jackus commanded.

The bandits had begun to run in for the attack, there were more men than they had anticipated. Zander and Heiro readied their weapons and prepared to defend themselves.

"I think it's about time we seen your magick in action." Heiro said.

Zander nodded, "Wind Art: Slicing Gale!" he screamed, as the blades of wind flew through the air toward the bandit army, the spell split one of the bandits in half.

"Zander we can take out the small fry with one move focus your wind spell and combine it with my fire spell." Heiro explained.

"Alright let's do it." Zander said in agreement.

"Flame Art: Fire Stream." Heiro said spewing the fire from his lips.

"Wind Art: Slicing Gale!" Zander shouted releasing his wind spell once more.

The two spells had combined, increasing the speed and strength of the attack. "Combination Art: Flame Vortex!" Both of them shouted as the whirlwind of flame raged through the crowd engulfing every last bandit in its path. Jackus and the bandits holding Kerra had quickly moved out of the way before the spell had set the old shack on fire. Zander and Heiro watched as it had burned to the ground.

"Combining fire and wind magicks, they are very impressive." Jackus thought to himself.

"Is that all you have Jackus? Hiding behind your pawns?" Heiro asked.

Jackus began to walk toward them, "On the contrary my friend, I'm just getting started." He said. Zander had seen a shadow appear behind him, it was like a mirror image. There were two of Jackus,

"Are you seeing this Heiro?" Zander asked.

There was no response, Heiro had also been rendered speechless. "This is my ability; it's my body double technique. My copy has all the strength that I do." Jackus explained.

Zander cast his wind spell again but the second body blocked the attack with its blade. "It is no use, the double automatically blocks any incoming attacks aimed at the original." Jackus said.

The Fated Swords

"We could try the combination again" Zander said looking to Heiro for an idea.

Jackus laughed, "Don't even bother with your little fire show; it won't take me down that easily." He said.

He was right the combination attack took a lot of magick to perform in the first place and it would certainly tire them out a lot faster. They had to think of another plan, they were going to have to resort to physical attacks for now.

Each of them ran towards one of the Jackus bodies and tried to strike them but was blocked immediately by their weapons. Jackus and his double had incredible speed as well as strength; it wasn't going to be an easy fight for the two of them.

"Cross Cleaver!" Jackus shouted as the bodies crossed their blades in an X shape sending out a wave of energy damaging Zander and Heiro and sent them flying backwards

"He is toying with us." Heiro said as he quickly examined their wounds.

They tried to separate the bodies by each taking one but it was no use, Jackus didn't allow his double to separate from him for he knew that was his only weakness. They exchanged blow after blow getting nowhere, they were beginning to feel exhausted. "What if I used my blood sword technique?" Heiro asked.

"You don't have enough magick left for such a strong technique, besides you won't be able to maintain it for long." Zander said.

Zander was right, after Ivory struck Heiro during their battle and destroyed the evil essence within him Heiro had lost the power to maintain his blood sword technique for long. If he tried to use it now, it would surely kill him.

"Are we going to finish this or not? I'm bored." Jackus asked. They hadn't even put a dent into the original nor the double; they were a very formidable team.

"Cross Cleaver." Jackus said attacking them again, this time it was more powerful than before and once again sent the two of the flying backwards.

"I think I have an idea, focus on the body double and I'll handle the original." Heiro said trying to stand.

Zander knew now more than ever he had to trust him, if he didn't neither of them weren't going to make it.

"Earth Art: Stone Bindings." Heiro said as the earth covered the double's legs and had begun to harden. The body tried to break itself free but couldn't move, "Now Zander!" Heiro shouted as he jumped in front of Jackus, grabbing his arms and trying to restrain him.

Zander ran up behind the second Jackus and pierced its chest and right through its heart. The attack had no effect, the double had gotten free. The double grabbed Zander by his neck struck him with his blade and threw him across the field.

Zander struggled to get to his feet, "How is he alive?" Zander asked wincing at the pain from the deep cut along his side.

Heiro thought for sure that attack would have finished the double off, and then it hit him. He knew why the double hadn't died; now he knew how to beat them. He used his earth binding spell once more, and this time on both Jackus bodies. They were both almost out of magick, this was their last chance.

"You can't defeat us with mere physical attacks." Jackus said.

"Who said anything about physical attacks?" Heiro asked. "Earth Art: Stone Prison."

Stones came from the ground one by one surrounding them and blocking them in. "Zander aim your wind spell for the center of the prison." Heiro instructed.

Zander used the spell to create an opening in the wall, "Okay go for it." He said.

"Flame Art: Great Fire Stream!" Heiro shouted spitting the fire into the hole. They could hear Jackus' screams from outside; the prison of earth was melting from the inside out and the scorched bodies were trying to escape.

"I'll finish this." Zander said running up and thrusting his sword into the middle of the prison and as fast as he could he ran around the prison dragging his sword in a circle slicing the prison and the Jackus bodies in half.

"Good thinking Zander!" Heiro shouted over to him.

Zander rushed over to Kerra who was still being held by her captors. They saw him running towards them and dropped Kerra, they both ran as fast as they could away from them frightened out of their minds. Zander picked up Kerra and held her. "I knew you would come for me." She said weakly smiling up at him.

"Of course I did." He said smiling. He picked her up and carried her as they had begun to walk back toward town. "So you had to end up defeating them both at the same time?" Zander asked.

"That seemed to be the deal; of course I wasn't exactly sure." Heiro said.

"What? You could have gotten our asses killed." Zander said scolding him.

"Hey now let's just savor the victory, were still alive." Heiro said.

They both had begun to laugh, Zander was grateful to him. Maybe he wasn't as bad as he had thought he was in the beginning. Sometimes certain situations bring a person's true self to the surface, and that's exactly what Zander had hoped for Vallus when they next met.

CHAPTER VII

Vallus sat under an old oak tree in the middle of the forest; he had stayed there for several days planning his next move sitting in the silence of the forest. The only things that could be heard were the wind blowing through the trees and the sounds of chirping crickets in the middle of the night. It had been the best spot for clear thinking.

The battle with his father had been a close call; he hadn't been ready to face him just yet. Vallus hadn't taken into account his father's deadly signature technique, but he wouldn't make the same mistake twice. He needed to learn to control his newfound powers first. His father had been poisoning everyone's mind all along; they were hypocrites for using magick while everyone else feared the mystics and wanted them eliminated. It was his goal to bring peace to the world, and he wanted it all for himself. He never did agree with the way his father governed his people and one day he knew he would put an end to it all.

"You have sat in that spot for days, shouldn't you get moving?" a voice said.

Suddenly a figure appeared before him, Vallus recognized him as the man from the hospital. "Following me I see." Vallus said reaching over and grabbing Ebony just in case he needed it. "Don't you have anything better to do?"

"Weren't you ever taught any manners?" the man asked.

"I don't make it a point in my daily schedule to make small talk with mysterious strangers." Vallus said.

"I guess you're right, forgive me for not introducing myself before. My name is Raphael." He said taking off his shroud. He wore a black t-shirt and pants and had short black hair. He had also worn a white mask that covered half of his face.

"Why the mask? Have something to hide?" Vallus asked.

"No, the left side of my face was burned in a fire" Raphael said.

"Are you human?" Vallus asked, "Or are you a mystic?"

"I am neither I am a voidshade." Raphael said sighing from annoyance.

Vallus had remembered hearing that word once before in a lesson with his father when he was young. "So you're from the Foreignlands. Voidshade are one of two races from the Foreignlands." Vallus said.

Raphael was surprised, "So you know about things other than your own people. I'm shocked." He said sarcastically."

Vallus quickly released his sword and held it only an inch from Raphael's face. "Enough of your arrogance." He said.

The voidshade took his index finger and pushed the blade aside unafraid of Vallus or his weapon. "Put your toy away before you hurt yourself, apparently you hadn't learned that voidshades can't be harmed by physical means." Raphael explained. "Weapons are useless."

"Why the hell are you here!?" Vallus shouted angrily sheathing his sword.

"As I told you before, I need you to bring the cursed swords to the shrine in the cave within the northern mountains." The voidshade said.

"I get that part, but why do I need to bring them there?" Vallus asked.

"What is with all of the damn questions?" Raphael asked, he was even more annoyed than before. "I need them to awaken the Demon King, Diaboro."

"Why would I awaken some Demon King who would just enslave me like every other being in this world?" Vallus asked.

"Diaboro will destroy this world and rebuild it. He could rebuild it to your liking for you to rule all of V'nairia." Raphael said.

Vallus was skeptical, "Why would he give me V'nairia?" he asked.

"You're the one helping revive him of course, he will be in your debt." The voidshade said convincingly. "He will rule the Foreignlands and you will rule V'nairia."

"That seems like a reasonable agreement." Vallus said.

"Good then it is settled." Raphael said delighted. "What will you do about Zander?"

"I will find him and retrieve Ivory." Vallus said simply.

"And if you have to kill him to get it?" the voidshade asked.

Vallus had sat and thought for a moment; even with the darkness taking over his heart he had still had feelings for Zander and Kerra. They were his best friends and aside from the revenge on his father he still cared about him. He had also felt the overwhelming thirst for power which was squeezing all of the goodness out of him.

"If it comes to killing him then that is what I must do." Vallus said.

Raphael's devilish grin had widened, "It is for the good of the new V'nairia." He said. He was already inside Vallus' head and now his heart was tainted by darkness, he was far beyond the reach of the light.

"Is Kerra with him?" Vallus asked.

"Yes and they also have a third in their group." The voidshade said.

"A third? Who is it?" Vallus asked surprised at the news.

"It is the rogue mystic Heiro, the one you fought in Oaba desert." Raphael said.

"Killing him will be a lot of fun; he had bested me before but never again." Vallus said clenching his fist.

"Vallus I have an idea." Raphael said. "Why don't you just let the boy follow you to the cave in the north, cut him down and take the sword there?"

Vallus sat and thought about it for a moment, it had definitely made more since to lure him to the shrine. It would makes things easier not to mention save him time. "Alright that's a fine idea." Vallus agreed.

"There's just one problem, your father has sent out the Slaughter twins to eliminate the three of them before the rest of the kingdom can find out what they are up to." Raphael said.

"Then I expect you to handle the situation, Zander and the others cannot be harmed until I get that sword." Vallus said.

"As you command Lord Vallus." Raphael said before disappearing into the forest.

"You had better stay alive Zander." Vallus said staring at the cold steel that was Ebony's blade.

***

The next day Zander and the others had left the small town of Durea and were back on their path through the forest.

"Are there plenty of other mystics as powerful as Jackus out there?" Kerra asked.

"Probably even more powerful, were going to have to watch you real close missy." Heiro chuckled.

Kerra became angry, "Hey! Don't act like I'm some weakling; I was asleep when I was kidnapped." She said raising a fist to him.

Zander turned to her and placed his hand on her shoulder, "You know Heiro in her defense, and she did save me from the Lieutenant back in the holding cell." Zander said as he winked at her.

She began to blush; Zander always knew how to make her feel better. "Thank you Zander." She said smiling at him.

As they walked through the forest Heiro got an uneasy feeling, he heard footsteps behind the bushes. "I feel like we're being followed." He said.

"Maybe someone followed us from town?" Kerra asked fearing it had been someone from the Militia tailing them.

Two figures leapt out from the bushes, they had been spying on them. One was tall and wore a red mask and carried a sword, the other was shorter and wore a blue mask and carried an axe.

"Who the hell are you two?" Heiro asked.

"Brother how did they sense us?" the shorter one asked the taller one.

"Well neither of you are mystics or I would be able to sense your magick, and you're not the best at stealth either. I heard your footsteps." Heiro said.

"Brother I'm tired of his smart mouth, let's kill him already." The short one said. The taller man motioned for him to be silent.

The Fated Swords

Zander had quickly realized who they were; these were no ordinary thieves or bounty hunters. "You're the Slaughter Twins, Taru and Tora." Zander said.

"So you do know who we are, I was beginning to think I would have to give you some kind of ridiculous introduction." Taru said.

Zander stood in front of Kerra, "Stay back Kerra, they may not be mystics but these guys are deadly." He said. He had remembered hearing about their murders back at the academy. They were the most feared out of all the bounty hunters in V'nairia.

Heiro pulled out his sword, "It looks like the judge spares no expense in finding us." He said.

"When were through with you, no one will be able to identify your bodies." Taru said.

Suddenly a man jumped out from a nearby tree landing in between both parties. "I think you two should leave, these people have done no harm to you." The man said.

The brothers looked at each other and back at the man standing before them. "Who is this guy? They never mentioned a fourth person." Tora asked.

"I guess killing him will cost the judge extra." Taru said as they readied their weapons.

The man pulled out a rapier, "I can dance all night if you wish." He said confidently. He was tall with short blonde hair, and had piercing blue eyes. He was certainly awkward and talked funny. Zander didn't know how someone like him was ever going to be able to take down bounty hunters as ruthless as the slaughter twins.

"Who are you?" Heiro asked.

The man turned to them, "There's no time for questions, I'll hold them off. Take that path into the woods." He said pointing just to the left of them.

They took off down the path the man instructed, they could hear the collision of steel coming from behind them. Whoever the guy was he could hold his own against two renowned bounty hunters. They were still exhausted from their last fight with Jackus and were grateful that he had helped them escape.

They ran for a good fifteen minutes before they finally stopped. "How much farther do we go?" Kerra asked.

"I don't know he just said to keep going." Zander said trying to catch his breath.

"It's a good thing I came along in time." A voice said.

The man from before had emerged from the bushes, "Who are you?" Zander asked him.

"I do believe it's rude to question one's identity before revealing your own." The man said.

"We apologize sir, I'm Kerra and this is Zander and Heiro." She said.

He bowed courteously, "I am Ryder from the city of Talias." He said.

"Is Talias far from here?" Zander asked as they proceeded down the path.

"No not at all, it's just down the mountain, about half a day's journey from here." Ryder explained.

They were relieved; they felt as though they had been walking forever. "So what brings you three all the way out here? Judging by your clothes you're from the Capital." He asked.

The three of them didn't know exactly what story to go by. "Well you see, being from the Capital and all we have never really seen the countryside; so were sightseeing." Heiro said.

Ryder looked confused, "So why are two very well-known bounty hunters chasing three sight seekers from the Capital?" he asked. They were silent they feared that he was onto them or that the judge also sent him to bring them back. "How rude of me, that's none of my business, my apologies." He said.

"You sure do ask a lot of questions, didn't you save us? What's with the third degree?" Heiro asked, there was anger in his voice.

"I meant no disrespect I feared that the three of you were in some kind of trouble that's all." Ryder said sympathetically. The three of them were grateful to him, so much had happened lately they didn't know what to do or who to trust.

"We apologize for our rudeness Ryder." Zander said.

Ryder looked back at him and smiled, "Think nothing of it my friend." He said. It was odd, he smiled at him with the same smile that Vallus always gave him; Zander hated that smile.

They had finally made it out of the forest and at the top of the mountain path just as Ryder said. "So the city is at the bottom of this mountain?" Heiro asked.

Ryder stopped and fell silent, "What is it?" Zander asked.

"Above us, Move!" Ryder shouted.

They had jumped out of the way just as Ryder was struck. It was the slaughter twins; they had come back for more. As they smoke cleared they could see Ryder had blocked both brothers' weapons with his one sword. Ryder overpowered them and threw them off balance as he leapt away. "I thought I had taken care of you two earlier." Ryder said.

"We won't go down so easily." Taro said. Ryder held out his sword as it began to glow a bright blue.

"Damn these guys are persistent." Heiro said.

"We simply do not have time for this, Soul Cutter!" he shouted. Within the blink of an eye he appeared behind the twins and lowered his sword. The brothers fell to the ground; they were no more than hollow shells. Ryder had extracted their souls and absorbed them into his blade.

"What kind of technique was that?" Heiro asked leaning over to Zander and whispering in his ear.

"I have no idea but just be glad that you weren't on the receiving end of it." Zander said mesmerized.

Zander looked over at Ryder in amazement, "You just defeated two of the strongest bounty hunters in V'nairia with a single technique." Zander said.

"They didn't seem like a threat at all, for such renowned bounty hunters I had never heard of them." Ryder said.

"Have you lived under a rock all of your life?" Heiro asked.

Ryder had found the question puzzling, "Heiro I don't believe it's possible that someone live under a rock." Ryder said. "It would crush them."

Heiro began to laugh uncontrollably, "I don't believe this guy."

Zander and Kerra had fought the urge to laugh as well, Ryder had certainly been a strange character to encounter under the circumstances but they were happy with his appearance all the same.

Ryder walked back over to them and smiled, "Now, shall we move on." He said.

"Yes, please lead the way." Kerra said.

The three of them followed him down the mountainside to the city of Talias. They hadn't known much about Ryder or why he was in the forest at the right place at the right time, but they certainly welcomed his help.

CHAPTER VIII

    Ryder had Zander and his group down the side of the mountain to the entrance of the city of Talias. Talias was the second largest city in V'nairia, the Capital being the first. Each of the towns and cities in the kingdom were governed by a nobleman or woman except for the Capital, which was governed by the High Court itself. Just like the Capital, Talias was one of the biggest tourist spots in all of V'nairia with a wide assortment of shops and restaurants.

    "So Ryder, you said before that you were from Talias?" Kerra asked.

    "Yes I grew up here; but sadly I haven't been back inside the city in over fifteen years." Ryder said.

    "Why did you leave?" Kerra asked.

    Ryder fell silent and kept walking, after a moment or two he stopped. "I would rather not discuss my past if that's okay." He said.

    "My apologies I didn't mean to pry." She said.

    "It is alright no harm done." Ryder said and continued walking toward the city.

    Talias was a very large and beautiful city, although it wasn't as grand as the city they were from but it had seemed like it would be a decent place to make a living.

    "Talias look like a very nice place to live." Heiro said looking up at the tall buildings.

"Yes it is." Ryder agreed. He seemed rather offended by them even mentioning anything about Talias whether it was related to him or not. From the moment they had met him, Zander had a strange feeling about Ryder. He had felt like he had been hiding something. For now Zander simply wrote it off as paranoia and ignored it.

"We need to find the inn, I'm feeling a bit tired." Kerra said.

"It's over there." Ryder said pointing to the tall building across the street from them. They had walked over to the inn and Zander looked up at the large neon sign above them. Most shops or inns had names but this one was simply called *Inn*.

"*That's original.*" Zander thought. Before they could walk inside the building they were approached by a couple of the city's guards.

"Good evening folks are you all new to the city?" one guard asked.

"Yes sir, that's right." Heiro said.

The other guard held up a sheet of paper with their pictures on it. Zander noticed that the word "Wanted" had been printed at the bottom of the paper just below the pictures. There had also been a large denomination of Yol printed on the poster.

"It looks to me like you're the ones from this wanted poster." One of the men said.

"I don't understand what's going on, we aren't criminals." Zander spoke up.

"Quiet you!" a guard said.

"The three of you are coming with us; the Baroness wants to meet with you." The other guard explained.

They grabbed the three of them and walked them down the street toward the Baroness' estate, leaving Ryder behind in bewilderment. Zander had found it quite strange that

Ryder had helped them before but now stood idly by and watched as they were taken away. Maybe he had been the reason why the guards found them. Maybe that had been his plan all along.

As they continued walking down the streets of Talias with the guards, they could finally see the Baroness' mansion in the distance.

The guards had walked them up the stairs of the entrance and inside the large double doors of the mansion. Inside, the walls were painted white and red; there were bouquets of red roses perfectly placed upon the walls in each room. There was also a large staircase that had spiraled up into the higher floors. The guards had begun to unshackle them, "Wait here." One guard said as he opened the front doors and both men walked outside and closed the doors behind them.

Zander thought it was strange, why take them to see the Baroness? Why not just throw them in a cell to rot? The law certainly didn't discriminate against anyone, in V'nairia anyone over fifteen was considered an adult and had been tried as such.

"Sorry to keep you waiting." A voice said. It was the voice of a beautiful young woman.

At the top of the staircase, there had been a woman in a long blue dress; she had long curly brown hair. She had to be in her early thirties Zander thought, staring at her beauty. When she made her way down to the entranceway she greeted them with a warm smile. "I am Thesia, Baroness of Talias. Welcome to our city" She said. The three of them knelt before in respect.

"It is an honor to meet you my lady." Kerra said.

"Please rise there is no need for formalities." The Baroness said. Her kindness somehow put Zander and the others at ease.

"If you don't mind me asking your highness, why have you brought us here?" Zander asked.

The Baroness began to laugh, "You are just as curious as your father was." She said. "I hope the guards hadn't startled you."

"They had shackled us." Heiro said.

"Oh those brutes, I'll just have to talk to them about that later, I apologize." Thesia said.

Zander was in shock, "*How did she know my parents?*" He asked himself

"How did you know my parents?" he asked the Baroness.

"Oh I knew Lillian and Zephyr quite well." Thesia said. Zander finally knew their names, at this moment he couldn't have been happier. He could finally get some answers about his past and his parents.

"As for the reason as to why you're here, you will need to follow me to discuss that." She said. She was a very elegant and gracious host. She had a certain charm about her that the three of them had liked. They didn't see anything wrong with following her and getting some answers.

They had followed her up the long winding staircase until they had finally reached a large portrait at the top; it was a painting of a group of warriors battling a large demon. It had been an interesting piece especially for someone like the Baroness to have in her home. Thesia had pressed a button behind the painting, revealing a secret passage in another room. They walked down the narrow passage into a room that had been filled with many books. It looked as though it had been the Baroness' personal library but they didn't understand why she had hid it in a secret room.

"What is this place?" Heiro asked.

"This is the hall of the Order of the Cursed Blades." She said.

Zander looked down at his sword, "You mean the cursed blades Ebony and Ivory?" he asked.

"Yes Ebony the demon blade and Ivory the holy blade." The Baroness said.

Kerra looked around at the many books that lined the shelves, there were thousands waiting to be read. "There's a book for everything in here." She said. Kerra and Zander both loved to read, that was one of the things that had made them so close growing up.

"What exactly is the Order of the Blades? What do they do?" Zander asked.

"The Order protects V'nairia from all menacing outside threats and we also relay information back to the Capital about any and all dark activity." She said.

"So then you've heard about Vallus, son of the Supreme Judge." Zander asked.

Thesia motioned for them to have a seat. The three of them sat down at the large table in the middle of the room. "Yes we know all about your friend Zander but I think there are some details you may not be aware of." The Baroness said.

This had definitely gotten their attention, they hadn't really known why Vallus left the city and they needed to know the truth. "Vallus is making his way to the shrine just below the northern mountains outside of Rygoth; there he is going to resurrect the Demon King Diaboro." Thesia explained.

Zander began to laugh, "That's ridiculous, and Vallus isn't evil. Why would he resurrect some ancient demon?" he asked.

"I can assure you young man, this is a very serious matter, and the fate of our kingdom depends on it." Thesia said, Zander had noticed her tone and demeanor had changed.

"My apologies, my lady." Zander said. It all just seems a little absurd."

"It is alright, I know it must be hard on you and Kerra to have to deal with this kind of situation." Thesia said.

Heiro stood up and took a nearby book off of the shelf behind him and examined it, "Isn't it true that the Demon King was sealed away by the order?" he asked.

Thesia nodded, "Yes the instruments used to seal his power away were the cursed blades." She said.

"So that's why he had tried to take Ivory from me back at the Capital?" Zander asked. All of the pieces of the puzzle were starting to come together; her story had to be true.

"Precisely." The Baroness agreed.

"Legend says that the shrine is in a cave below the northern mountains and is protected by a door that can only be unlocked with a certain key." Heiro read from the book.

Thesia pulled something silver out of her pocket, "It's referring to this key." She said holding up a silver key with an onyx stone placed in the top of it.

"You have the key to the door!? When he finds this out he will find you and kill you." Heiro said surprised.

"I do not fear death." Thesia said. She turned to Zander and grabbed him by the hand, "Zander as leader of the Order I ask that you and your friends join the Order and help us prevent the reawakening." She said.

"Of course we will help, this is our home." Zander said. This had relieved her knowing they would help.

"You would each make your parents proud, each of them were also members of the order. Well more or less" Thesia chuckled slightly.

"Each of our parents?" Kerra asked. "What do you mean?"

"Yes, that is why I believe it was fate you were brought together." Thesia explained.

A soldier walked into the room and gave a salute to the Baroness and her guests, "Your highness the Fire Drake's squad is returning from their mission they should be here in a day's time." He reported. "We just received the letter."

"Thank you Captain, you are dismissed." She said.

"So who is this Fire Drake?" Zander asked.

"The Fire Drake is the title we have given to our strongest warrior, for they are a master of fire magicks." The Baroness said.

"A master of fire magick sounds pretty interesting; I hope to meet him soon." Heiro said.

Thesia began to laugh, "I believe you will, but for now you may go." Thesia said.

"Of course." Heiro said as Kerra and Zander rose from the seats and the three of them proceeded towards the passage.

"Zander if I could ask a favor of the three of you?" she asked.

Zander had stopped and turned to look at the Baroness, "Of course." He said.

"Could you come back to the mansion tomorrow about midday? I would say the three of you have a few questions." Thesia asked.

"That would be great thank you." He said smiling just before turning and walking through the secret passage back into the mansion. They would definitely be back; they had so many questions that needed answering. They walked down the stairs and out the door of the mansion. As they left the estate they waved goodbye to the Baroness and headed back to the inn.

"Zander are you okay with this? What if he doesn't come back?" Kerra asked.

"He will come back I swear he will." He said determined to bring his friend back home.

She knew from the look in his eyes he was determined, that had been one of the things she loved most about him. He never gave up. They were finally getting closer to bringing their friend home and one step closer to saving all of V'nairia.

CHAPTER IX

Zander and the others had gotten up early the next morning anxious to meet with the Baroness again. They had so many questions that needed to be answered. There had been no sign of Ryder that morning, so they concluded that he must have gotten up earlier and left to run errands. They still had no idea what Ryder's place was in the group, he was only supposed to guide them to the city. But they weren't too worried about that for now. They knew they had to get to the mansion as soon as possible to meet Lady Thesia.

They walked by Kerra's room and tapped on the door. The door opened slowly as she walked out to greet them,

"Are you ready?" Zander asked her.

"Yes." She said smiling at him. The three of them walked out of the inn and began to walk down the street towards Thesia's estate. Along the path leading to the mansion were large apple trees that covered the fields on both sides of the dirt road. They could smell the flowers that were growing in the garden on the side of the mansion as well. The Baroness did like to be surrounded by a lot of color and sweet smells.

As they arrived the Baroness greeted them outside, "Good morning." She said.

The three of them bowed courteously and greeted her. She motioned the three of them to come inside; upon entering her home they had followed her up the staircase to the portrait on the top floor once again. Inside the secret room she had tea and fresh muffins waiting for them. The smell was heavenly; she had prepared fresh blueberry muffins and piping hot tea with lemon. It had been a perfect start to their day.

"Thank you for your kindness my lady." Zander said.

"Do not thank me; I should be thanking you for helping me." Thesia said.

Heiro took a bite of muffin and instantly melted, "Did you bake these yourself?" he asked.

"Yes of course baking is one of my passions." Thesia said.

"Well they are amazing." Heiro said smiling at here.

"Thank you very much Heiro." She said.

"You wanted to meet with us today milady?" Kerra asked.

The Baroness sipped her tea and gently placed the cup back on the table, "Yes we need to form a plan of action and figure out where to send you next." She said.

"What do you suggest?" Kerra asked.

"Well we have been watching you three ever since you left the Capital, and I must say you are all quite skilled." Thesia said praising them. "Especially you Zander, your skills are rapidly growing. You will definitely be as strong as your father if not stronger."

"I am still a bit new when it comes to spell casting but I've been learning quickly thanks to Heiro." Zander said.

"You have natural talent inside of you, besides you have a splendid teacher. You all will grow much more powerful in time." Thesia said.

Suddenly they heard screams coming from inside the mansion, a guard busted through the door. "Milady, it's the Militia they're attacking the city." He said out of breath.

"He's found us." Zander said.

"We were careful, I don't understand." Thesia said confused as to what was going on.

"We have to get you out of here Lady Thesia." Kerra said frantically.

"That right everyone let's get downstairs." Heiro said.

None of this made any sense to the Baroness; their location had been kept secret. There was an informant somewhere either in the mansion or in the city itself, but they had no time to worry about it now. "How many men are there?" Thesia asked the man.

"There is at least a few hundred. There are infantry men as well as archers" He said.

The four of them got up from their chairs and made their way back through the passage. "Get every available soldier you can find in the area to help outside, meanwhile send a few men to evacuate the civilians." She explained to the guard. He nodded and ran as fast as he could down the stairs and out the door.

"What should we do?" Heiro asked.

"You three will guard me, I am merely a diplomat and leader of the organization I have no battle skills or experience." The Baroness said.

"Who will lead the men outside?" Kerra asked.

"I'm sure the Fire Drake already has that covered." Thesia said.

They finally made it down to the entrance and looked out the windows; they saw the soldiers from the Militia battling the soldiers from the city. "There are so many of them." Zander said.

"Zander you and Heiro help outside, I can protect the Baroness." Kerra spoke up. Zander turned to look at her, he was frightened.

"You can't protect her alone." He said.

"I'm not helpless; I can handle this." Kerra said.

"Absolutely not, you'll both get killed." Heiro said.

Zander could see the determination in her eyes, if she believed she could do it then he had to believe in her too. "Alright, but if it gets too bad take the back exit and get the hell out of here." Zander said as he and Heiro opened the door and ran out.

"Is there a room in the back of the mansion we can go and wait?" Kerra asked grabbing her hand and leading her away from the entrance.

"Yes we can go to the ballroom." Thesia said.

***

Outside Zander and Heiro joined the battle; they readied their weapons as a pair of soldiers ran at them with their blades drawn. They exchanged blow and with two quick swipes of their blades the soldiers went down.

"Wind Art: Slicing Gale!" Zander shouted using his wind spell to take out a group of soldiers to the east. Heiro used his fire magick to hit the group in the west.

The soldiers had kept coming, "There seems to be no end to them." Heiro said.

"Water Art: Water Wall!" Zander shouted as a wall of water appeared before them, protecting them from enemy gunfire. They split up to take separate groups, when they saw another warrior enter the fray.

The warrior wore a red helmet, and was clad in armor. He ran towards the enemy, "Flame Art: Flare Burst." The warrior shouted throwing a ball of fire into the mass of soldiers.

The fire ball expanded engulfing the men in the flames. The warrior pulled out a bow with three flaming arrows drawn and pointed it upward into the air. He shot the arrows into the air, "Flame Art: Scattered Fire Shower." The warrior said as the small flames burst into streams of fire raining down from the sky. Many of the Militia's soldiers were set ablaze, screaming and writhing in pain.

Zander and Heiro walked up to the mysterious man, "Who are you? That was incredible." Zander asked.

"Stay out of my way." The man said walking past them.

More soldiers were rushing in, Zander and Heiro took the chance to show off their skills. They cast their wind and fire spells together just like in their battle with Jackus and the bandits, "Combination Art: Flame Vortex!" they shouted. The whirlwind of flame swept through the soldiers lifting them into the air. The warrior didn't seem impressed at all and had ignored their efforts. The enemies ranks had quickly begun to decline, they were finally getting somewhere.

***

Inside the mansion, Kerra and Thesia had heard the glass from the front windows shatter and hit the floor. Kerra motioned the Baroness to remain silent. "Whatever happens to me I want you to run." Kerra said to the Baroness.

Kerra left her in the ballroom and walked out into the entrance, there were a couple of soldiers waiting for her. Kerra wasn't the type to use weapons, in fact she despised them. She was a master of hand to hand combat, as well as a lightning magick user like her mother. One soldier ran at her and tried to strike her with their blade, but she caught it in her hands and kicked the man in the stomach. The two others came at her with fists this time, trying to overwhelm her. It hadn't been a very successful attempt; she gave a roundhouse kick to one soldier's head knocking him out. The last soldier stood in front of her with his weapon drawn, trying to carefully determine how to act.

"Lightning Art: Thunder Crash!" she shouted as the bolt of lightning struck the soldier and threw him backwards against the wall. She ran back into the ballroom to meet back with the Baroness.

"Are they gone?" she asked.

"They definitely aren't getting up for a while." Kerra said smiling.

"You have your mother's fire, there's no denying that." Thesia said smiling back at her.

The soldiers outside began to fire on the mansion with their guns and arrows. "We need to get out of here." Kerra said as she grabbed Thesia's hand and led here out of the room.

They began to fire flaming arrows which caught the mansion on fire. Zander and Heiro had saw the flames and rushed inside. The Baroness and Kerra were lying in the entrance unconscious from smoke inhalation. Each of them had grabbed one of the women and rushed outside, a safe distance from the collapsing building. The mysterious warrior had defeated most of the soldiers and watched as the rest had slowly started to retreat.

"Kerra are you okay?" Zander called out to her stroking her cheek.

Her eyes opened and she looked up at him, "Took you long enough, we have to stop meeting like this." She said trying to laugh but only began to cough. The Baroness also opened her eyes and slowly rose up.

The warrior came over and joined them; Zander and Heiro were staring and admiring his armor. "You're pretty powerful; I'm Zander from the Capital." He said holding out his hand, only to get it slapped away.

"Ashe, you mustn't be so rude they helped you did they not?" Thesia asked.

"Did she just say Ashe?" Heiro asked.

The warrior took off their helmet; it was a girl with long red hair and glowing red eyes.

"Yes mother, but it's not like I needed it." Ashe said.

"Mother?" Zander asked looking at the Baroness.

Thesia stood slowly; she was still feeling the effects of the smoke. "Yes Ashe is my daughter, she is our champion known as the Fire Drake." She said. They were all very confused by what the Baroness had said; she never told them she had a daughter. "I know you must have a lot of questions, but here is not the place to discuss it. We will meet back at the inn." She said as Ashe helped her up and walked her down the street to the inn.

"Are you guys alright?" Kerra asked. She was still weak; Zander had seen the three soldiers enter the mansion earlier so he knew she must have taken them out.

"Yes we're fine." Heiro said. "So I assume that you had your fair share of the fight as well?" he asked her.

She raised two fingers indicating that it was only a small fight. Zander picked her up and carried her to the inn, she knew that it somehow always ended up her being carried by him; but she didn't mind it at all he made her feel safe. Her feelings for him were definitely beginning to grow, though she never knew how to deal with it. The three of them followed Ashe and Thesia to the inn hopeful in getting some answers.

Back at the inn they had freshened up with a nice hot bath and they waited in the boy's room for Ashe and the Baroness to join them to discuss the matters at hand.

There was a knock at the door, "Come in." Zander said.

Ashe and Thesia walked through the door; the Baroness found a chair and sat down while Ashe stood against the door. This time Ashe wasn't wearing her armor, she wore a black buttoned top that was obviously snug considering the size of her breasts and she also had on a short red skirt. Heiro had a very hard time not staring at her.

"So how is Ashe your daughter? You're not a mystic." Zander asked.

"I was walking through the forest on the outside of the Capital and found an abandoned house; she had been there all alone." Thesia said thinking back to that day.

"She had no family so I decided to take her in as my daughter, she was only two years old at the time." she added looking over at Ashe smiling.

"I'm so sorry Ashe." Kerra said looking over at her.

"I'm not sorry; I have a mother." Ashe said pointing to Thesia.

"You'll have to forgive her; she can be a bit blunt and rude." She said glaring at her daughter.

"So what's our plan of action, what do we do next?" Zander asked.

Thesia pulled out a map and laid it on the table. "I believe Ashe and I will take some soldiers and go up to the city of Rygoth and speak to the Duke there. We will try to get more help." She explained.

"So what do you want us to do in the mean time?" Heiro asked.

She pointed to an empty area on the map, "You will take the cave under the northern waterfall, until you get to the Order's underground hideout and wait for us there. We should meet there around the same time." The Baroness explained.

There was a knock at the door, Ashe opened it and Ryder walked inside. He had been gone the entire time even during the attack from the Militia.

"Where have you been?" Heiro asked.

Ryder bowed courteously to them and took the Baroness's hand and kissed it gently. "Forgive me; I had gotten bored so I took a walk outside of the city." Ryder said.

Heiro jumped across the table and pushed Ryder up against the wall with his hand on his neck. "We were fighting for our lives and defending the city, while you were picking flowers and seeing the sights!" He shouted.

Ryder's expression never changed, "I do believe fighting in a room full of woman is quite rude." Ryder said smiling.

"Heiro calm down." Kerra said.

Heiro released him and walked back over to his seat. "I didn't realize there was another in your group." Thesia said.

"There isn't, Ryder had just guided us to the city." Zander said.

Ryder gathered himself from the floor, "I don't mind sticking around and helping out a little longer, I didn't mean to eavesdrop but I can help you get to that cave at least." He said.

"I don't think that's a good idea." Heiro said.

Zander sat and thought about it a moment, and as much as he didn't like Ryder or trust him; they could use his battle experience. "No its fine, Ryder can help us but only until we get to the waterfall." Zander said.

"I am in agreement with those conditions." Ryder said as he walked out the door to wait outside.

Thesia grabbed Zander's hand, "Zander I want to thank you again for helping us." She said.

"We would do anything to protect V'nairia, you can count on us." He said.

"Pretty confident aren't you?" Ashe asked.

Zander gave her a dirty look; he didn't like her or her attitude. "We shall see you at the hideout." The Baroness said as the three of them left the room and walked out of the inn.

"Are we ready to depart?" Ryder asked.

"Yes and the sooner we get there the better." Heiro said angrily walking past him.

They began to walk down the street out of the city entrance, and after walking a few miles they had finally made their way to the waterfall to the north. They luckily hadn't seen any sign of Militia soldiers.

"How much farther is the waterfall Ryder?" Zander asked.

"It is just up ahead." Ryder said.

"Zander do you honestly think we can trust this organization?" Heiro asked quietly.

"I don't believe she would deceive us." Zander said.

***

They had finally come to the waterfall. Zander could see the cave underneath the water. Zander suddenly felt uneasy, there was something off about their trip. He felt a chill down his spine, and there was an overwhelming weight on his chest.

A figure appeared before them, Zander saw who it was and wasn't surprised he had felt his presence; it was Vallus.

"Hello brother." He said.

"Vallus." Zander said under his breath.

Their meeting had finally come.

CHAPTER X

Vallus had finally shown his face. Zander hadn't seen him since he fled the city after the fight with his father. He had suddenly felt nauseous and weak in the knees. Vallus had a sadistic looking smile on his face that had made Zander cringe. He knew just how powerful his friend was and he knew that now he was probably even more powerful than he had been before.

"Well isn't this a joyous reunion." Vallus said.

"Why are you here Vallus?" Zander asked.

"Can I not check up on you? After all we are friends aren't we?" He asked.

"That depends, are you going to come back home with us?" Zander asked him.

"Now why would it be in my best interest to do that? So I can go back and be executed by my father and you can all go about your precious little lives while our leaders still control everything?" Vallus asked.

Zander could hear the hate in his voice, he was very bitter towards his father and what he was doing to all of the mystics. Zander was glad that at least that part of him was still intact. "We can stop the genocide together and bring peace back to V'nairia but it can be done a different way." Zander explained.

Vallus began to laugh hysterically, "I don't just want to abolish the government, I want to obliterate every living thing in this world and watch as it is reborn under my rule." He said. He had sounded like a madman, to destroy the entire world? Zander had never heard him speak of this before.

"Vallus please come back to the Capital with us." Kerra spoke up; she was still in a state of shock.

Vallus turned to her and smiled, "Kerra, poor and innocent Kerra. I'm afraid I can't do that but you can always come with me if you wish." He said.

It was like a knife had pierced Zander's heart. "Come with you?" She asked. She seemed different, almost as if she had been under mind control or something. Vallus must have been using the dark powers of his sword Ebony to control her mind.

"Come with me and together we can make this world pure again. Humans and mystics will once again live in harmony and I will become a god." Vallus said smiling devilishly.

"There are no gods, only foolish men!" Heiro shouted.

"Not yet perhaps." Vallus said.

Kerra began to walk towards him; she had looked lifeless almost as if she was a puppet. "I'll come with you Vallus." She said.

"Zander do something!" Heiro shouted.

Zander grabbed her by the shoulders and began to shake her, "Kerra wake up, its Zander don't go with him." He said.

She continued to push forward under Ebony's evil spell, "I'll come with you." She repeated.

Zander didn't know what to do, he was going to lose her; he couldn't bear to think about not having her with him. He wrapped his arms around her and held her tightly, "Stay with me, I need you Kerra." He whispered in her ear as tears began to run down his cheeks. At that very moment he could feel her put her arms around him as well.

"Zander I'll always be here with you." Kerra said to him softly.

She had turned to look at Vallus with an angered look on her face, "You're not Vallus at all, and we will stop you." She said to him clenching her fists.

"Fine, have it your way. You can just die with everyone else." Vallus said.

It was if Zander's love for her that had awakened her once from her trance. He was relieved, the warmth rushed back into him and he could feel again. He had her and he was never going to let her go.

"I guess it's time to finish you." Vallus said.

"Well it's four against one I believe we can take you." Heiro said.

Ryder stepped forward, "I believe you need to rethink your odds boy." He said in a deeper voice than usual. His appearance had quickly changed, "I am Raphael personal servant to Lord Diaboro and accomplice to Vallus." The man said.

This had changed everything, he had been reporting back to Vallus the entire time. Vallus had known everything that was going on before they had even reached Talias. That is how he knew they would be arriving at the waterfall.

"Raphael deal with them, I'm going on ahead." Vallus said.

Zander was furious, "You bastard!" He shouted as he ran at Vallus with his weapon drawn.

Vallus blocked the strike, grabbed him by the arm and threw him across the water. Vallus knew Zander wasn't strong enough to defeat him. Something held him back from killing Zander in that moment. Zander had realized that maybe Vallus wasn't completely taken over by the darkness. However,

Vallus had wanted him to become stronger, hating him even more. He wanted Zander to be able to put up a fight before he killed him. Vallus turned his back on them, the very friends that were always there for him. He began to walk toward the waterfall and disappeared into the cave without even looking back.

Zander slowly got to his feet, it was far from over but for now their man focus was getting through the cave. "Which one of you wants to go first? I can make it quick and painless if you wish." Raphael said.

Zander drew his sword, "Both of you stay back, I'll handle him." He said. Kerra and Heiro had never seen him like this. He was enraged and unpredictable. Zander could feel the energy inside of him rising.

"Zander, be careful." Kerra said.

"I won't be long Kerra." He said.

He raised his sword to Raphael, "I swear on everything I care for, I will end you!" Zander shouted running at Raphael. As their blades collided the energy had caused the water to raise and then fall back down in an instant. It was almost as if it had been raining, but only for a brief moment.

"I'm going to eliminate you three and bring the sword to Vallus myself." Raphael said.

"Not if I kill you first." Zander said.

Zander tripped him and grabbed his leg, with a burst of incredible strength he threw Raphael over his head into the side of the mountain. His anger had increased his magick tenfold, thus increasing his strength and speed.

Heiro looked at Kerra in amazement, "No normal person should be able to do that." He said.

"Zander has never been normal." She said.

Raphael gathered himself from the rubble. "Such strength, it has to be his magick essence." Raphael thought. Zander suddenly appeared behind him to strike him from his blind spot; Raphael barely had enough time to block the attack. Zander hauled off and punched him so hard in the face it sent him flying backward. Raphael stood up unwavering, "Water Art: Tidal Surge!" He said as the water began to rise and a wave swept Zander up and pushed him up against the mountain. "Earth Art: Body Coffin." Raphael said grabbing Zander's chest with his hand. The mountain began to cover Zander's body all except his head. Raphael walked over and stabbed Zander in his shoulder with his sword, he cried out in pain. "How does that feel, not so confident now are you?" Raphael asked.

"Zander!" Kerra shouted.

Raphael turned his head quickly looking over at them, "Quiet! You two are next." He screamed.

Kerra and Heiro couldn't help Zander they were frozen with fear; it must have been some kind of ability that Raphael had used on them. Raphael kept stabbing Zander over and over in the same wound, to Kerra it had been a nightmare. The spell she was under didn't allow her to even cry out; she could only feel the stream of tears running down her face. She had known Zander since they were children, she loved him and now she was going to watch him die in front of her very eyes. She was experiencing the ultimate torture.

"I've never had so much fun, I'm going to bleed you dry boy." Raphael said as he continued to impale Zander.

He cried out in pain, Raphael had also spelled his body as well so he could not faint from the excruciating agony. He was clever enough not to hit any vital spots to keep from killing him too quickly. This was Raphael's favorite game to play with his prey, he reveled in it. He was bleeding profusely; His friends couldn't bear it anymore. After gathering energy, Heiro managed to use part of his magick energy to break himself out of the spell.

"Flame Art: Fire Stream!" he shouted.

The flames had reached Raphael but he had dodged them just in time. This had broken his concentration and his spell along with it. Kerra had also been released as well as Zander but he was still unable to move due to the earth spell.

"Lightning Art: Thunder Crash!" Kerra said as her lightning spell headed for Raphael.

Raphael blocked her attack with his sword. He was quicker and stronger than any enemy they had faced thus far. "Kerra don't let his blade touch you." Heiro said.

She remembered when he fought the bounty hunters before and used the technique to steal their souls. They couldn't take any chances; he was certainly a formidable foe.

"Resistance is futile, your lives are mine." Raphael said laughing.

Kerra engaged him in close combat, being very careful not to get struck by his blade. She delivered a punch to his face and a kick to his abdomen. Heiro followed up with a fire spell, burning him. Raphael got to his feet, he was damaged but not by much.

"Something isn't right; our attacks should be affecting him." Heiro said.

"I'll hold him off, you cut Zander out of the rock." Kerra said charging at Raphael with her fist drawn.

He grabbed her arm holding her fist down and delivered a blow with his elbow. Kerra flew across the water and landed below the waterfall. The force of his strike was so powerful it had knocked her unconscious. Heiro used his sword to cut Zander out of the rock covering his body; he was weak and had lost a lot of blood. He wouldn't be of any use to him the remainder of the fight.

"We will handle this, lay here and rest buddy." Heiro whispered to him. He looked over and saw Kerra lying on the ground.

"Well, then there was one." Raphael said.

"I guess I have no choice, Demonic Art: Blood Sword." Heiro said as the blade of blood formed in his hand. He threw the sword into the air and it had become the crimson orb once again. The sphere of blood had begun to float overhead.

"What the hell is that?" Raphael asked. The tendrils from the sphere began to come after him, but Raphael was nimble enough to dodge them. "That's quite an impressive skill you have, and it's a demonic art no less." Raphael said.

The strikes from the tendrils came even quicker this time around, but with each move Raphael became quicker as well. It was almost as if he could read its movements entirely.

"I have quite a few tricks up my sleeve; don't count me out just yet." Heiro said.

Heiro began using his fire spell as his blood sword technique raged on.

"He's clever trying to distract me with the flames while his other attack tries to connect." Raphael thought.

He could also see the fact that his special technique took quite a toll on Heiro as long as it was being used; he was trying to use this to his advantage. Raphael allowed the flames to hit him as he held off the blood sword's tendrils.

"I'm wearing down; I'm going to have to finish this now." Heiro thought. "Earth Art: Stone Binding." He said as Raphael became immobilized.

The blood swords tendrils stuck through his flesh, he had tried to struggle but couldn't move. Heiro leapt in to the air grabbing the sphere as it transformed into a giant axe. He had struck Raphael from overhead with the axe, he had thought the attacked had worked; but he was wrong.

Raphael had used most of his energy to offset the attack merely three inches from his body. Heiro was exhausted; his technique had disappeared as he fell to his knees.

Raphael was also out of breath; he had used up quite a bit of magick himself during the fight. "You three are lucky, but you will meet your end soon." He said as he disappeared into a thick fog.

"I held him off, at least it's over." Heiro thought to himself before falling over and blacking out. The three of them had made it out of the battle alive, but only just barely.

***

A knock came to Judge Vallerus' door, "Come in." he said. The door opened and Lieutenant Omak entered.

"I'm here to report my recent findings sir." He said saluting the judge.

"At ease, please explain." Vallerus said.

Omak took a seat in front of the judge's desk. "It seems as though Zander and the others had recently passed through the town of Durea and had a run in with the Iron Claw Bandits." The Lieutenant explained.

"It seems as though they have been busy, and what of them now? What of the bandits?" the judge asked.

"They had defeated the entire clan even their mystic leader, it seems as though the boy has grown in strength." Omak said.

"What of the Slaughter twins?" Vallerus asked.

"Zander and the others had defeated them as well, they are getting a lot stronger sir." Omak said.

"Well I guess that means it's time to put the first segment of my plan into motion, Make sure she meets me at the abandoned warehouse tomorrow evening." Vallerus instructed.

Omak had gotten up out of the chair and made his way out the door, "Yes sir, it will be done." He said as he closed the door behind him.

"Now everything is finally coming together." Vallerus said.

CHAPTER XI

Kiarra had walked home from the office late the next evening; she had been caught up in her paperwork for the numerous riots that had begun to happen in the city. People were beginning to understand mystics, and really didn't care if they could use magick or not; they just saw them as any other person. The Supreme Judge didn't like this at all; he ordered the Militia to arrest the "Mystic Lovers". Kiarra had noticed footsteps aside from her own, halfway home she quickly stopped to look around but saw no one.

"I know your there, come on out." She said.

Lieutenant Omak appeared from the shadows, he had been following her. "Sneaking up on someone this late at night could get you killed Lieutenant, especially a judge of the High Court." She said.

"My apologies your honor, I didn't mean to startle you." He said.

"Why are you out here in the middle of the night?" she asked.

He handed her a folded sheet of paper, "It is a report from the small hospital in Durea, your daughter is being treated there for serious injuries." Omak said.

This news was devastating to her; Kerra was all she had left after her husband died. "What else do you have to report? What happened?" she asked frantically.

"It's not best to talk here, someone might overhear us." He whispered.

He was right Vallerus wanted to know their location, and to capture them and bring them back so they had to discuss the matter in private. "Where shall we go to discuss the matter?" she asked.

"Follow me to the abandoned warehouse down by the docks, we can speak freely there." He said as he led her down the street. She didn't understand why the Lieutenant was helping her; she never really did particularly like him but she was grateful none the less.

They had finally made it to the warehouse, it was old and worn down; abandoned really wasn't the word for it. They came to the door and he opened it for her and motioned her to walk in first. She never recalled him being the gentlemen type. She walked inside the warehouse, it was dark and quiet. Suddenly the door behind her slammed shut.

She began to bang on the door, "Omak let me out of here at once!" she shouted. She could hear him laughing on the other side of the door; she already couldn't wait to strangle the old fool.

"Come now Kiarra stay awhile." A voice said.

A chill ran down her spine, she knew that voice and suddenly it had occurred to her why she was brought here. The figure walked out from the shadows, it was Vallerus.

"Why have you locked me up in here?" she asked.

"This is your trial my dear, and from what I know I don't need a confession." He said.

"I can just blow the door off." She said.

He waved a finger in front of her, "I've spelled the door closed, and the only one who can get out is me." Vallerus explained.

"So you mean to kill me, is that it?" Kiarra asked.

He smiled widely, "You always were a clever girl. Even as the outcast of our little group of friends." He said.

She pulled out her sword to defend herself, "Even if you kill me, you won't stop them." She said.

"I was lenient enough to allow your daughter to live after finding out she was one of them, and this is how you repay me?" he asked.

She knew the extent of his power as well as her own, the odds were against her. "So I'm the last and you've come to finish it after all this time?" she asked. "Don't speak to me about betrayal!"

"I had to it was for the good of this world, first was Lillian and Zephyr then there was Heiro's parents Hyo and Aeria, it's a shame I never had the pleasure of ending Mik's life as well. Now it will all end with you." He explained.

"You bastard!" she shouted.

Vallerus smiled devilishly.

She began to inch her way backward to keep her distance from him, "So how did you find out about the order?" she asked him.

"Thesia never was one to keep a good secret; I had informants working at her estate. I sent a hundred soldiers to Talias to burn the mansion down and kill the children and everyone else inside it." The Supreme Judge said.

"Enough talk lets end this!" she said enraged.

Vallerus pulled out his sword, "As you wish, may the sentencing begin." He said.

A battle between two judges under these circumstances had never been seen in the history of V'nairia. Their power was on a whole other level, and you could see it with each blow. Kiarra was fast, and she was good but not as good as Vallerus. The rate at which they exchanged blows was incredible; if you blinked you could miss it.

"Lightning Art: Thunder Crash!" she shouted as the spell headed for the judge, who had dodged it just in time.

"Flame Art: Fire Stream." Vallerus said as he spat the flames at her, she was also able to dodge the spell successfully.

Neither of their attacks was connecting, Kiarra became frustrated. She had lowered her guard for a split second and the Supreme Judge made his move. He had punched her in the gut, and threw her into the back wall. She could feel some of her bones cracking from the impact; she tried to fight through the pain. He had been using his magickal essence to increase his strength. She regained her composure and jumped back in the fight.

"You're more resilient than I thought." Vallerus said acknowledging her abilities.

"Lightning Art: Thunders Dance of Madness!" she shouted.

Several bolts of electricity had struck Vallerus and threw him into the wall behind him. He seemed to be unharmed, "So you do pack quite the punch after all." He said.

He was only toying with her; this hadn't been his true power at all. They ran at each other and exchanged blows again. She began to throw lightning spells trying to hit him but none were successful.

"Surely by now you've used at least half of your magick, feeling tired yet?" Vallerus asked.

"No I'm fine; I won't stop until your dead." She said confidently hiding the fact she had been drained

He came at her ready to strike; she quickly appeared behind him and delivered a kick so powerful it sent him flying through the wall and outside the warehouse. They clashed swords from the docks all the way up to the street.

"With one kick she was able to break through my spelled wall? She is impressive." Vallerus thought to himself.

"Flame Art: Flash Fire!" Vallerus shouted as three fireballs struck Kiarra, damaging her greatly.

She cried out in pain, he was so powerful she couldn't overpower him. She could barely stand; he began to kick her repeatedly. All she could think of was Kerra and how much she loved her and prayed that Zander had kept her safe. She was bruised, burned, and bloodied; Vallerus picked her up by her neck and lifted her off the ground.

"Well how did we know it would come to this?" He asked her.

She spat Blood on his face, this had infuriated him. He shoved his blade into her, "Now you won't have to worry, you'll be seeing your daughter sometime soon." He said smiling.

Tears began to run down her face. She managed to let out one word before the light left her eyes, "Kerra."

He pulled his sword out of her and wiped the blood off with a cloth and threw the bloodied cloth on her body. "Such a shame." Vallerus said shaking his head as he looked upon her dead body. He picked her up and dumped her into the sea off the side of the docks. The very same sea that was said to hold the thousands of bodies of Vallerus' enemies from the Great War. Vallerus had finally what he had started over fifteen years ago. All of their parents were finally dead.

***

Zander and the others had recovered from their fight with Raphael, but stayed by the waterfall to camp for the night. Heiro was fast asleep, nothing in the world could wake him; not even the fiercest of battles.

Zander couldn't sleep; he saw Kerra sitting under a tree near the waterfall and walked over to sit by her.

"Hey, you couldn't sleep either?" she asked him.

"Nope, not a wink what are you doing way over here?" he asked her.

He sat down next to her and gazed off into the distance. "I just came up here to look at the moon, its beautiful tonight." She said.

It was the first time they had ever seen the moon this close before, in the Capital it was hard to see such beauty at night for all the tall buildings. "Yeah it is." He agreed.

Suddenly it began to rain and thunder boomed throughout the area. "The weather sure did change quickly." He said.

"Something's not right." Kerra said feeling an odd chill.

A large lightning bolt struck a tree nearby setting it on fire. Kerra felt a strange feeling in her heart, and it moved throughout her whole body and then it hit her. She began to cry,

"Kerra what's wrong?" Zander asked.

Kerra was silent for a moment and then spoke up, "My mother is dead."

CHAPTER XII

"What do you mean your mother is dead? How could you possibly know that?" Zander asked her. She was still crying, she was so upset she couldn't speak. Zander couldn't imagine the pain she felt, he had never known his parents in the first place. "Kerra talk to me." He said calmly as he hugged her tightly.

"Our family has always had the ability to sense the deaths of our own bloodline; we are connected through the natural energy that comes from lightning. It is what helps us channel our magick; the moment that lightning struck that tree I felt my mother's heart stop beating." She explained.

Zander had never known that her family had such a unique yet disturbing ability, knowing that she wasn't there with her mother while she died must have been a horrible feeling. "That's not all Zander; we can also sense how they die." She said. She had a frightened look on her face; Zander assumed that the worst of the news was coming. "It was Vallus' father's sword that killed her." Kerra said and began to cry again.

This made perfect sense to him, Kiarra had helped them break Heiro out of the underground holding cell; of course he would want her dead but this wasn't the time to bring that up. The storm had finally woken Heiro up, "What's going on?" He asked them as he walked over to where they were sitting.

"Vallerus killed Kerra's mother." Zander explained.

Heiro's expression completely changed, "Kerra I'm so sorry." He said sympathetically. She didn't respond she was still in shock, "So what should we do? Should we go back to the city and confront him?" Heiro asked.

Kerra wiped her eyes and looked up at him, "No we aren't going to stop, we will go get Vallus and go face him together, the four of us." She said.

Zander could understand what she was saying, if we faced him now the three of them would surely be killed. He was ruthless; he wouldn't spare any of their lives. "There has to be a connection here, Thesia said that all of our parents were mystics." Heiro said.

"Vallerus told me when I was young that he and my parents were friends, up until he became Supreme Judge then they had drifted apart." Zander said.

"My mother told me that my father had fought in the Militia with Vallus' father." Kerra said.

Zander thought for a moment, and then it hit him. He fell to his knees slamming his fist into the dirt, "Dammit!" he shouted.

"Zander what's wrong?" Heiro asked.

Zander stood up and faced them; he had tears running down his face. "Don't you see what's going on? Vallerus was the one who killed our parents." Zander said.

"Are you serious!?" Heiro asked.

"Look at what we know, all the pieces fit." Zander was right. He wasn't a fool; Zander knew exactly what was going on, now the others knew as well. "We will find Vallus and end this." Zander said clenching his fist.

"When do we leave?" Heiro asked.

"We leave now." Zander said walking over and grabbing Ivory and strapping it to his side. The three of them packed up the camp and began their trip through the cave under the waterfall.

The cave was dark; they couldn't even see their hands in front of their faces. Heiro picked up a stick and used a fire spell to light it. "So where do you suppose Vallus went?" Kerra asked.

"There may be more than one path in this cave." Heiro said.

Zander began to feel pain in his left shoulder, he was still sore from when Raphael had stabbed him. His shoulder wasn't the only part of him that was wounded, so was his pride. He wasn't able to protect Kerra he could have gotten them all killed. He still wasn't strong enough and it ate at him. They walked on through the cave trying to find the way out.

***

To the north in the snowy city of Rygoth the Baroness and Ashe rode to the Duke's palace. Rygoth had been the third most populated city in all of V'nairia but that didn't mean that it exactly had a lot of money. The Duke that ruled over Rygoth was a very vain and greedy man; he could care less about the sick or homeless. The Duke's personal assistant greeted them outside, "Madam Thesia such a pleasure to see you." The man said as he helped the Baroness off her horse.

"Thank you for your kind words, I need to speak with Duke Agarath at once." Thesia said.

"Yes my lady right this way." The man said as he shown her to the palace doors. It was hardly a palace in comparison to Thesia's mansion but the Duke loved to call his home a palace.

Inside, the palace was brightly lit, paintings from very famous artist hung from the walls; the Duke was quite fond of

The Fated Swords

the arts. The assistant walked them into the main hall where the Duke sat at the long dining table eating his evening meal.

"My lord, the Baroness Thesia, and her daughter Ashlyn." The man said making their presence known. The assistant left the room and closed the double doors behind him.

"Ladies Thesia and Ashe, please have a seat." The Duke said motioning them to a chair.

They both sat down and the servants poured each of them a glass of wine. "We thank you for your hospitality your grace." Thesia said.

"You are always welcome in my hall milady." Duke Agarath said before biting into a lamb's leg.

The Baron never had been visually appealing, he was a short, portly disgusting man with a long black braided beard; Ashe couldn't stand to be in the same room with him. They had always tried to avoid him at social functions; he was very loud and vulgar. He had always treated women like they were his property. The only thing he loved more than eating and drinking wine, was bedding the many whores at his disposal. He knew of the order but never played any part in anything worth honoring someone for; for the Duke even though wealthy, was not an honorable man.

"What brings you to the city of Rygoth?" He asked them.

Thesia took a sip of wine from her glass and gently laid it back on the table, "We have come to warn you of the dangers that ride from the south." Thesia said.

"What sort of dangers do you speak of milady?" he asked.

"The Supreme Judge's son Vallus is going to the shrine north of this city to resurrect Diaboro." The Baroness explained.

The Duke laughed, "That's impossible he would need the key and the cursed blades." He said.

She shown him the key she had fashioned into a necklace that hung just above her breasts. "When he finds out I have the key he will come for me, he also has possession of Ebony." Thesia said.

Ashe seemed to not be a part of the conversation; she kept eating and drinking. She always did act like one of the boys, Thesia had despised this. "Well without Ivory he has nothing, have you located the other sword?" Agarath asked while still stuffing his fat face.

"The wielder of Ivory is on our side actually, it is Lillian and Zephyr's son; Zander." Thesia said.

"Well fuck me; he's finally grown up has he? Where's he been all this time?" The Duke asked.

"He was in the care of the Supreme Judge; he had just graduated from the Militia's academy a few months back. He's a fine soldier and swords master now." The Baroness stated.

"So I take it the boy is after Vallus and Vallus is after the sword the boy has?" Agarath asked.

She nodded politely. "That does pose a problem doesn't it? What can I do to help?" he asked.

"We simply meant to come and warn you, I have everything else under control; just please have your men ready for anything." Thesia said as she and Ashe rose from their seats.

"Thank you for your information and concern milady but Rygoth has nothing to be worried about, please have a safe trip back." Agarath said.

"Duke Agarath I implore you to reconsider the seriousness of this situation." Thesia said.

The Duke could tell how serious she was by her tone. "Alright Thesia ill put out more guards and have them survey the area." The Duke said trying to put her mind at ease.

"Thank you." She said.

The assistant came in as they had made their way over to the door, "Milady these soldiers will accompany you back to your horses." He said showing them out the door. The soldiers walked them outside; they had gotten on their steeds and rode off for the hideout.

"Well that was easier than expected." The Duke said.

The assistant began to change shape, it was Raphael. Raphael threw a large bag of Yol on the table in front of the Duke. Agarath began to go through the money counting it.

"So she does have the key to the shrine?" Raphael asked.

"Yes she carries it around her neck." The Duke said as he began sniffing the money. "If there's one thing better than wine or women, its money."Agarath said.

"Clearly." Raphael said disgusted by the man's indulgences.

"So you won't kill her right? That's what we agreed upon." The Duke asked.

Raphael gave a courteous bow, "Cross my heart." Raphael said as he turned to leave.

The Duke whistled and a woman walked in the room, she had long blonde hair and was topless. She walked over to him and kissed him on the cheek. "How can I serve you my lord?" she asked.

"Be a dear and wait for me in my chambers, will you?" He asked. She gave a small nod and he slapped her on the behind as she turned to walk out. "So Raphael, should I do anything to slow the boy and the others down?" he asked.

Raphael turned his head slightly, "I already have that covered." He said walking out of the great hall.

CHAPTER XIII

"How much further Zander? My feet are getting sore." Kerra asked.

"Just a little further it shouldn't be long." He said. He was just guessing he had never been here before; he was just trying to get her to relax.

"Quit complaining Kerra, save your breath before you run out of it." Heiro said. She became angry and ran up behind him and knocked him in the back of the head.

"That will do you some good asshole!" she shouted.

Zander wasn't in the mood for bickering; he was sweating profusely and had no idea why his breathing had suddenly became heavy.

"Now apologize." Kerra demanded.

Heiro let out a hard sigh, "Fine I'm sorry." He said.

Kerra smiled, "Thank you." She said. They had finally seen a light in the back of the cave, it was the outside. They ran for the exit and finally made it out, Heiro drew in the fresh air appreciating the fact he was no longer smothering. "It took us long enough." Kerra said. "It seemed to go on forever."

Zander and Heiro agreed, it felt as though it was forever before they would have escaped the pitch black cave. Zander began to see two of everything; Heiro waved his hand in front of his face. "Hey Zander, you feeling okay?" He asked.

Zander didn't respond, he just walked forward not even knowing where he was going; stumbling along the way.

Finally he had passed out, the others rushed over to him; Kerra immediately dampened a cloth from her pack and put it on his head.

"This is strange, he hasn't been sick the whole trip and suddenly he collapses." Heiro said.

Kerra was patting him down with the cloth, when she noticed something on his skin. She pulled down his shirt a little, revealing a strange black mark below his right shoulder; almost like a bruise.

"What is that?" Heiro asked.

"I don't know I've never seen anything like it." Kerra said.

Heiro examined the spot more closely and saw that it had appeared over the scar where Raphael had stabbed him. "Kerra this is no ordinary mark, he's been poisoned." Heiro explained.

"What do you mean he's been poisoned?" Kerra asked. "How?"

Heiro pointed to the center of the black mark, "There in the center do you see the cut that's healed?" he asked her.

She examined the mark more closely, "This is where he was stabbed by Raphael." Kerra said.

"He's been poisoned by Raphael's sword, we have to find a hospital soon." Heiro explained.

Kerra pulled out the map that Thesia gave them and examined it. "There is a small village east of here, it's just south of the hideout." She said.

Heiro lifted Zander onto his back. "Okay lets go we don't have any time to waste." He said.

They crossed the plain until nightfall, unsure of what wild beasts could be out waiting for them; they still kept moving. Finally they had made it to the small village of Eo. It was a very small village in the middle of the plain. It was a poor village, not very many residents of V'nairia had even heard of it. A short older lady came to meet them at the entrance of the village, "Hello there dears." She said.

"Madam our friend is very ill, he has been poisoned." Hciro said. "Do you have somewhere we can take him?"

"Yes dear right this way, and hurry." The little old woman said leading them to her hut.

They carried him into her small hut and placed him on the straw bed in the corner. The woman had dampened a cloth and placed it on his head to help quell the fever.

"What was it that poisoned the boy?" she asked.

"He was struck by a blade in the shoulder; were not sure." Kerra explained. "We don't know anything about poisons."

The woman grabbed a small iron dagger from a box sitting on the floor across the room. She had taken the dagger and made a small cut into Zander's arm. She tasted the drop of blood from the blade, "It is Xernarin root, one of the deadliest plants in V'nairia." The old woman said. "He has at least three hours to live at best."

"What can you do for him?" Kerra asked, begging for her help.

The old woman shook her head, "I am afraid there is nothing I can do dear, but there is an old mystic that lives to the far side of the village." She said. "He is skilled in healing magick, if anyone could help the boy it would be him."

"Healing magick?" Heiro asked. "I thought that there weren't any mystics left who practiced healing magicks."

"He is the last of his bloodline, but he has become somewhat of a hermit." She said. "He never leaves his home."

"Come on Heiro we at least have to try and get his help, it's the only way to save Zander." Kerra said. She had been a mess right now the person she had loved most in the world could die at any moment.

The Fated Swords

The old woman led them out of her hut and across the village to the home of V'nairia's last healer. Kerra wasn't about to let him die, no matter what. She was determined to see this through. They walked over to the hut; there were animal bones hanging from the trees surrounding the hut. It gave Kerra the creeps; she had almost turned back if it weren't for her thinking about Zander.

"Hello is anyone there?" Heiro asked.

A tall, thin figure came out from the hut. "What the hell do you want at this hour?" the figure asked.

"Our friend has been poisoned and we need your help, we were told that you can perform healing magick." Kerra said.

The man shook his head, "I'm sorry I don't know what you're talking about. Go away!" he shouted and walked back into the hut.

"It was Xernarin root poison, he will die please." Kerra begged.

The man poked his head out, "Only voidshades carry that kind of poison, what were you doing messing around with one of them?" He asked.

"What's a Voideshade?" Heiro asked.

"It is a shape shifter that takes the form of a human; they feed off the souls of the living." The man explained.

"That definitely describes the guy I fought." Heiro said.

Kerra got down on her knees and begged the man for his help and he finally gave in. "Take me to him." He said.

They took the healer to the hut of the older woman and he examined Zander, "You're lucky you brought him in time, another hour and he'd be dead." He said.

"Thank you so much for helping us, I'm Kerra and this is Heiro." She said smiling.

"I am called Ferian, pleased to meet you both." He said. Ferian placed his wrinkled hands over Zander's body and a green light began to glow. In moments the black bruise had faded and his fever was gone, Ferian had pulled the poison right out of his mouth using magick. He placed the poison in a glass vile and threw it into the fire.

Zander shot up gasping for air, he coughed ferociously and after a minute or two he was fine. "What happened?" he asked. "Where are we?"

"You had been poisoned during the battle with Raphael and collapsed. We brought you here and Ferian healed you." Kerra explained.

Zander looked over at Ferian, "Thank you for saving my life." He said

"Do not thank me young man, thank your friend's quick thinking and determination." Ferian said smiling at him.

The older lady walked into the hut, "Why don't you stay the night dears, we have plenty of food." She said.

"I'm definitely not arguing with that." Heiro said as he followed her and Ferian outside.

"Are you alright?" Kerra asked him placing her hand on his. He had noticed a tear run down her check.

He had taken his hand and wiped the tear from her face, "Of course, it'll take a lot more than that to finish me." He said smiling at her.

"You made a promise to protect me remember?" Kerra asked. "You can't die now"

"I'm not going anywhere I promise." He said.

"Good." She said smiling, practically blushing. "Would you like me to bring you something to eat?"

Zander shook his head, "No you go on ahead I think I'm going to rest up a bit longer." He said lying back down.

She rose from the side of the bed and walked towards the door of the hut, she turned back to glance at him and smiled. She had never been happier to have him by her side than that very moment.

***

Later that night, Kerra saw Zander sitting on a hill looking up at the moon. She had walked over to join him, "Ah ha, I caught you." she said sneaking up on him.

"What exactly did you catch me doing Ms. Lyale?" He asked.

"You're out of bed." She said.

"Yeah I couldn't sleep, thinking about everything that Thesia said has me confused." Zander said.

"What do you mean?" Kerra asked curiously.

"Do you really think Vallus is doing this to take over the kingdom?" Zander asked. "It doesn't sound like him at all."

"Zander that is not Vallus." Kerra said. "I know you felt it to back at the waterfall. I didn't feel Vallus at all."

"Your right, we will just have to drive the evil out of him." Zander said smiling at her.

She sat across from him just staring; he was so handsome, she could just drift away into his eyes. "Kerra there's something I've been meaning to tell you." He said as he grabbed her hand.

"Yes Zander?" she asked.

"After all this time, after everything we have been through your still here with me; and I'm glad I didn't leave you back in the Capital." He said.

She smiled, "I'm glad you didn't either, I believe we have both matured on this journey; you most of all." She explained.

He looked into her eyes and held her close to him, "I love you." He said. These three words went straight through her ears and pierced her heart like an arrow, she could hear it in his voice; he meant it.

"I love you too." She said.

The two of them began to kiss passionately in the moonlight. She held him close to her and didn't let go, they just sat staring at the moon; never wanting the moment to end.

CHAPTER XIV

The next morning they had gotten up early, said goodbye to the villagers and were on their way. They actually hadn't been too far from the hideout now. After a couple of hours they had finally reached the hideout of the order. As they arrived they had saw Ashe and Thesia's horse's drinking water from a stream beside a tall rock monument.

"Is this the place?" Heiro asked. "There's nothing here."

"I'm not sure, but this is the location on the map." Zander said.

Kerra had begun to examine the rock, but there was no door. Suddenly a figure jumped off the top of the monument, sword drawn. Their target had been Heiro first; he dodged the strike by quickly jumping backwards.

"What the hell!?" Heiro shouted.

Ashe stood there with her famous pissed off look, watching him freak out. "Oh excuse me sexy I didn't see you standing there." He said winking at her.

She delivered a roundhouse kick to his face knocking him to the ground He slowly got to his feet, "Always playing hard to get." He said.

"Heiro, you idiot she's the one that attacked you." Kerra said.

"Men are so stupid." Ashe said walking over to Zander. "My mother is waiting inside." Ashe said as she pulled up an iron gate on the floor of the plain that was covered in grass.

"Camouflage, very nice." Zander said. The three of them followed her down the torch lit hallway of the passage.

They came to a large room with even more books than the last. There were weapons and armor lining the walls and various paintings of heroes and battles. They had saw Thesia sitting at a small square table drinking tea.

"Hello everyone, I see you made it in one piece." She said greeting them.

They knelt before her and she motioned them to rise. "Well I hope you had no trouble getting here." She said.

"Actually we did, Ryder turned out to be a voidshade named Raphael that has been working with Vallus the entire time." Zander said. "He attacked us at the waterfall; we just barely made it out alive."

"Not to mention Zander was poisoned." Kerra said.

"My apologies, I hadn't known the path would be so dangerous." Thesia said.

"Everything is fine now milady how was the trip to Rygoth?" Zander asked.

"Cold." Ashe spoke up.

Thesia turned and glared at her, she had to always manage to get a negative comment in. "It was fine, I had warned the Duke and he is well aware of the situation." She said. She paused for a moment and looked nervous, "Before we proceed there is something I must explain to Ashe and Zander if no one minds." The Baroness said.

They each shook their head, "It is very difficult for me to deliver this news to you." She said biting her lower lip. "I never could quite figure out how to say it."

"It is okay Thesia you can tell us." Zander said.

"Zander, Ashe is your sister." Thesia said as calmly as she could. "Zephyr and Lillian Kyre were your birth parents."

Ashe jumped up in a rage, "What the fuck!?" she shouted.

"Ashlyn, that is not the language of a lady!" the Baroness shouted.

Zander sat there frozen, he had no idea what to say. Ashe stormed out of the hideout slamming the door behind her. "Zander are you alright?" Kerra asked.

"Yeah I am, actually I'm happy." He said rising cheerfully.

"That didn't just shock you? Cause it shocked us." Heiro said.

"Well of course I'm shocked but at the same time, I have family." He said.

"Yes well by the time I had gotten to Ashe and taken her in Vallerus had already taken you." The Baroness explained. "It was your mother's dying wish that I take care of you both."

"Thank you for finally telling me." Zander said.

Thesia smiled and was pleased with at least one of their reactions. "Now, the next thing I'm going to tell you is very important, I believe I've found a way to bring Vallus back unharmed." She said.

Zander leapt over the chair and sat down, "How?!" he asked excitedly.

"We can use a purifying seal technique." Thesia said.

"What kind of spell is that?" Heiro asked.

Kerra rummaged through a few old books on the shelf and opened one. "The purifying seal is much like the ability of Ivory, the holy sword; it destroys the evil essence inside not just the person's heart but their very soul." She read.

Thesia pulled out a scroll from her pocket, "You will need this and ivory to complete the seal, but I must warn you that this spell can only be used once every five-hundred years." Thesia explained.

"There was one other thing we forgot to mention, Vallerus killed my mother." Kerra said trying to hold back her emotions.

"What did you say?! How can this be?" Thesia asked she seemed severely upset about Kiarra's death.

"It's true; he killed all of our parents because they were mystics." Zander said.

"So you had finally figured out Vallerus secret?" Thesia asked.

"Yes I had put all of the pieces together back at the waterfall." Zander said.

Thesia didn't know what to say she was stunned. "I am so sorry, Kerra your mother made me swear that if we had ever met that I wouldn't tell you three what had happened." The Baroness explained.

Zander shook his head, "It is fine milady, we understand." Zander said.

"So it really was fate that we all had met." Heiro said.

"Yes the five of you and your parents were a part of the destined bond." Thesia said.

"What is that?" Kerra asked.

"It is a spell that is passed from husband to wife and then to child." The Baroness explained. "Your families are a part of a centuries old prophecy."

"Can you tell us anything about the prophecy?" Zander asked.

Thesia had sipped her tea, "No sadly I cannot. I had only heard of the prophecy from my father the Baron." She said. "We don't know exactly what the prophecy had held for your families."

Growing up Zander had always wanted to be a war hero just like his father. He had no idea that his destiny was

The Fated Swords

going to be far greater than that of a war hero. He was always destined for greatness, all of them were. Zander was determined to find out more about the prophecy and learn of his destiny. "I'm going to go find Ashe." He said as he rose from the chair and headed down the passage after her.

***

Back in Rygoth, Vallus was enjoying his visit to the city. He stopped at the inn and walked inside. "Welcome sir, how can I help you?" the clerk asked.

"I'll need a room, and do you have a young woman named Lyra working here?" Vallus asked.

"We certainly do sir." The clerk said pointing to a girl with straight brown hair that came to her shoulders; she was sweeping in the corner.

"I've heard she's one of the most talented maids in the kingdom, would you mind sending her to my room?" Vallus asked handing the man a sack full of Yol.

"Right away sir." He said excitedly as he showed Vallus to his room personally.

He hated the room; he had much better rooms back in the Capital. He had taken off his long coat and placed Ebony up against the bedside table. There was a knock at the door,

"Come in." he said.

It was Lyra; she was shaking as if she was frightened. "You wanted to see me sir?" she asked in a soft voice.

A fragile little thing she was, Vallus could change that. "How old are you Lyra?" He asked her.

"I'm seventeen." She replied.

"I've heard you can do extraordinary things, can you show me?" he asked her.

Suddenly she disappeared, he could not see her body at all; and then she reappeared again. "Wonderful, what other skills do you have my dear?" Vallus asked.

"I can also use water magicks." She said. "Please don't tell anyone, mystics are forbidden to live in the kingdom."

"Oh you shouldn't worry about that, things are about to change my dear." Vallus said smiling at her.

This was delightful; it was exactly what he had heard about her. He walked over to her and gazed deep into her eyes. Lyra had noticed that his eyes had glowed a bright purple for a moment and then faded. In that moment she was no longer nervous or afraid, she was no longer herself.

He was using Ebony's ability once again to control her mind and put her at ease. It was the same ability that he had used on Kerra at the waterfall to control her mind. Zander was able to break Ebony's spell because he wields Ivory. Vallus had raised his hand to Lyra's chest and pressed his palm against it. His hand began to glow with a purple aura and he watched as his hand had passed through her skin and inside her body. He had taken hold of her heart, seeping his dark energy into it, turning it black.

He had looked into Lyra's eyes as they began to glow purple. He had removed his hand from her chest and watched as her expression changed. He had used Ebony's power to take over the goodness in her heart.

"You're going to do exactly as I say." He said to her as he looked into her eyes. "You're my slave now and you will fight for me."

"Yes Lord Vallus." She said smiling up at him menacingly.

"Good girl, now get your things. We are leaving." He said. "There's someone you need to meet."

Lyra had gathered up her belongings and followed Vallus down the stairs of the inn and out the door into the streets of Rygoth.

***

Zander walked outside the hideout and saw Ashe across the field gazing off into the distance. He walked over and stood beside her for a few moments thinking of what to say, "Hey Ashe, are you alright?" he finally asked.

She slowly turned to look at him, "Oh so now you want to play the brother card?" she asked sharply.

"No I was just checking on you, you stormed out pretty quickly." Zander said.

"I'm fine alright; you can just go back inside." Ashe said. "You don't have to check on me."

"Ashe you're the only family I have, and five minutes ago I didn't have any. Do you understand what that means for me?" He asked her.

"Well I don't need anyone." Ashe said.

Zander could tell the feelings between them were not mutual, he was excited to have a sibling and she certainly was not. "I know you don't like me or the fact that were family, but I never knew our parents either it's just as hard for me as it is for you." Zander said.

Ashe then realized that he was just like her; he didn't have any family either. "I'm sorry Zander, I just don't know how to deal with this news, I thought she was my mother all this time until now." She explained.

"I understand Ashe but we can work through it together we are family after all." Zander said.

They both looked at each other and began to laugh.

"She had looked down at his hand and noticed his four elemental markings. "So you can use fire magick?" Ashe asked.

"Apparently I can but I haven't learned any fire spells yet." Zander said.

"You know if you wanted me to, I could teach you a couple of spells." Ashe offered.

"That would be great Ashe." Zander said grateful for her help. "Thank you."

"Don't mention it." She said smiling at him.

They had spent the rest of the day getting to know each other and training. Zander was glad he had finally figured out what it meant to have family.

The next morning they had left the hideout with Ashe and Thesia; their next destination was Rygoth. They had hoped to find Vallus there so they could finally settle things. Zander prayed that the purification spell worked, it was their only hope.

CHAPTER XV

  Vallus walked up to the palace gates in the cold city of Rygoth. The guards walked down the stairs to bar his path, "No one is allowed in, the Duke is not accepting visitors today." One guard said.
  "I wasn't asking for an invitation." Vallus said as he thrust his sword into the stomach of one guard and quickly decapitated the other.
  He kicked in the double doors of the palace and began to set everything on fire with his fire spells as he gallantly walked through the hall. The Barons precious paintings began to melt from the heat of the flames. He opened the doors to the main hall and saw Duke Agarath, he was sitting at his large dining table eating and drinking surrounded by his whores.
  "What is the meaning of this!?" He asked startled. "Who the hell are you?"
  "Food and woman, do you know nothing else pig?" Vallus asked.
  Agarath quickly recognized Vallus from his conversations with Raphael. "You're the Supreme Judge's son, Vallus." The Duke said.
  "Well you are well informed sir." Vallus said with a devilish grin. He pulled the tablecloth off of the large table along with it came the food and silverware.

"I did everything you asked, why are you doing this?" Agarath asked whimpering. His whores had already run to the back of the palace in a panic.

"I've already murdered the other diplomats, why not you?" Vallus asked.

"I'll do anything, I'll give you anything you want please spar me." The Duke begged as he got on his knees.

Vallus sheathed Ebony and smiled, "What do you think Raphael, should we spare him?" He asked.

Raphael came up behind the Duke and grabbed him, slicing his throat open with a dagger. The blood sprayed on the marble floor of the hall like a crimson mist. "I don't believe in sparing cowards, or anyone for that matter." Raphael said.

"Well said." Vallus agreed.

Suddenly a fire spell had erupted through the double doors of the main hall. Walking into the room through the flames was his father, Vallerus. This was definitely an unexpected surprise to Vallus, but a welcomed one none the less.

"So good of you to join us old man." Vallus said.

He had figured his father would come for him sooner or later. "I'm here to end this foolishness." Vallerus said.

"Well I'm glad you're here, it saves me the trouble of traveling to the Capital to find you." Vallus said releasing Ebony from its black prison. "Raphael you may go." He added.

Raphael gave a courteous bow to Vallus and the judge and evaporated into thin air. "First you can conjure demons and now you're working with voidshades." Vallerus said. "What's next Vallus?"

"That is none of your concern father; you won't be here long enough for it to matter." Vallus reassured him.

Vallerus pulled out his sword; it had a crimson colored hilt and a red and black scabbard. "Ah yes, the famous sword of Supreme Judge Vallerus Arvello, Death Bringer." Vallus said.

"Do not mock me boy." Vallerus said angrily.

"I never understood why you named your ridiculous excuse of a weapon in the first place, it's not like it's a cursed sword like mine." Vallus scoffed.

"I will show you the true meaning of its name, just as I have with others before you." His father said.

Vallus was cocky, he knew he had more power than his father could imagine. With incredible speed they came at each other, swords clashing against one another. Sparks flew as their steel had collided. Maybe this was fate for one of them to die at the others hand, after all their family never was perfect. Both men retreated a few steps backward,

"Flame Art: Fire Stream!" Vallerus shouted as the flames engulfed Vallus. "I'm going to burn you to a crisp." He said.

The flames quickly subsided and Vallus appeared unharmed. "Demonic Art: Black Prison." Vallus said as his dark energy created a black cage around Vallerus. "Just try to get out of that cage, that spell is stronger than any sealing magick." Vallus explained.

With all his strength Vallerus managed to slice through the black bars of energy. Vallus wasn't shocked at all, he knew even though his father was a middle aged man; he was the Supreme Judge for a reason. Vallerus came up and punched him then grabbed him by his coat, he threw him through the doors and out through the walls of the palace. Vallus rose from the ground wiping the river of blood flowing from his nose and lower lip.

"I've always preferred an open arena." Vallus said.

By this time Zander and the rest of the group had showed up in the city and quickly rushed over when they had seen the smoke from the burning palace.

"Vallus!" Zander shouted.

Vallus glanced over at them and turned his attention back to his father. "Look father, brother came to watch the show." He said.

Vallerus did not respond, he only stared at what was left of his son, now only seeing a monster. "Get out of here Zander, or you and the others shall be next." Vallus warned him.

"Vallus he has lied to us our whole lives. From his hatred of mystics he had slaughtered our parents in cold blood." Zander said. "He killed Kerra's mother."

This news struck a chord in Vallus and a shred of humanity had shone through the darkness inside him. "Is this true?" Vallus asked his father.

Vallerus did not answer yet again, merely stood there staring at him silently. "Dammit you bastard!" Vallus shouted "Is it true?"

"Mystics should not be allowed to live; it is for the good of V'nairia." Vallerus said.

"Zander if its revenge you want; I will be the one to take it for you." Vallus said as he used his magick to place a barrier around the group, not allowing them to escape.

"Vallus no!" Kerra shouted.

"Vallus don't do this!" Zander shouted.

"Before you die, I will allow you to witness the death of the man that destroyed your lives." Vallus explained. Vallerus and his son drew their swords.

"Flame Art: Fire Stream." Both warriors said as their flames collided, pushing against each other.

"Great Fire Stream!" Vallerus shouted as his spell grew larger.

Vallus jumped out of the way just in time. "Demonic Art: Dark Aura." Vallus said firing a blast of dark magick at Vallerus.

As the spell hit his father it knocked him into a nearby building in front of the Duke's palace which by this time had been a pile of smoldering debris. Vallerus appeared from the wreckage, "Flame Art: Flaming Pillars." He said.

The ground beneath Vallus began to shift and from it sprang multiple pillars of fire. Vallus dodged each one perfectly.

"Demonic Art: Dark Aura." Vallus said firing another round of dark magick.

His father deflected the blast with his blade while running towards him. He used his blade to strike Vallus' left arm and delivered a kick to his abdomen, throwing him off balance. "Flame Art: Great Fire Stream." Vallerus said as he spat the flames upon Vallus, this time the flames had finally damaged him.

"Man they mean business, it's incredible." Heiro said watching the fight.

So this is the power of the Flame Hammer?" Ashe asked.

Excuse me Ashe, what is the Flame Hammer?" Kerra asked.

"That is what they call the Supreme Judge in Talias. Vallerus the Flame Hammer." She explained.

"The Supreme Judge is mighty; he will not go down easily." Thesia said.

Zander couldn't help but think of what would happen to them if Vallus were to die, Zander couldn't stand to lose a friend it would kill him. "Vallus will win; I have to believe that he will." Zander said.

"You're certainly relentless old man." Vallus said exchanging blows with Vallerus.

"I never would have thought you would have lasted this long." Vallerus said. Their strength and speed was unmatched, the others could barely see what was going on. Vallus ran and jumped over Vallerus,

"Sword Art: Blade Extend." He said as Ebony's blade grew closing in on his father's heart. Vallerus quickly turned and the sword went through his shoulder instead. Vallus retracted the blade as he landed.

"Enough of this." Vallerus said as he held two fingers to his face.

Zander knew what was coming next, it was surely over. "It's his secret technique, it will end this fight." Zander said.

"No Vallus! Run away!" Kerra shouted but Vallus ignored her cries.

"Sacred Art: Dance of a Thousand Blades!" Vallerus shouted as the blade from his sword disappeared.

He snapped his fingers and Vallus had vanished, he had thought it strange there was no blood or traces of his body. Suddenly Vallus appeared before him and stuck his blade into his father's chest.

"That was my Mirror Shadow spell, pretty convincing wasn't it?" he asked.

"It's not possible." Vallerus said.

He began to cough up blood, and spat at Vallus' face. Vallus pushed the blade in further as his father cried out in agony. "Such a shame, your famed technique failed." Vallus said smiling.

He drove the blade in all the way to the hilt; Vallerus couldn't feel anything anymore he was fading quickly. "I'll see you in hell." His father whispered.

"I'll rule hell." Vallus said as he removed his blade and sliced his head clean off. He had killed his father, Zander's revenge was complete. The man that had killed each of their parents, his very friends that he swore to protect was finally dead.

CHAPTER XVI

The barrier had finally vanished, Zander watched as Vallus stood over his father's body laughing. He was enjoying this, he was free and so was the rest of the world. The tyrant judge was no more. They had seen and heard of too much death already, it was starting to get to all of them. Zander couldn't have imagined how Kerra felt, she had never seen someone die in front of her eyes before let alone someone being butchered like Vallerus had been. Suddenly there was a scream from behind them, Zander was no longer spacing out.

Vallus was gone and no longer next to the body. Zander turned around to see a blade protruding through the Baroness' abdomen. Vallus was behind her holding the other end of it. He ripped the key off of her neck and tucked it into his coat pocket.

"Vallus, what are you doing!?" Zander shouted.

"Mother!" Ashe screamed as tears ran down her rose colored cheeks.

He had removed Ebony from Thesia's body and placed it back in its scabbard. Thesia fell to the ground, she was dying quickly. "Now I have what I came here for." Vallus said.

"You fucking bastard!" Ashe shouted as she ran up to him and tried to strike him with her sword.

He quickly grabbed her by the neck and lifted her up off the ground, "Foolish girl." Vallus said as he tightened his grip.

She couldn't breathe; she kept flailing her arms and legs trying to break free. "Please Vallus don't kill her." Zander said.

"Why shouldn't I put her out of her misery, she can be reborn in my new world; they all can." He said.

Zander began to break down, "Vallus please she's my sister, the only family I have." He begged. Ashe began to lose color in her face, she was fading. "Brother please I'm begging you don't kill her." Zander said a final time.

Zander's words seemed to get through to him; he began to have flashbacks of the two of them growing up together and training in the courtyard. They use to have so much fun together; they were each other's family.

"Brother." Vallus whispered.

He loosened his grip around Ashe's neck and she fell to the ground, she started to cough trying to catch her breath. Heiro ran over and picked her up,

"It's okay your safe now." He said as he stroked the side of her face with his fingers. Vallus began to feel many emotions at once and was frightened. He turned and looked at Zander one last time. A black portal of darkness appeared behind him.

"You know what you have to do Zander." Vallus said.

"Yes, I know." Zander said.

Vallus hadn't turned to look at his friend he simply walked through the black portal and vanished. The portal had disappeared and Zander turned his attention to his friends.

He had failed, and he didn't just fail himself but he had also failed everyone else that he had cared about. He had finally had Vallus there in front of him and could have ended everything and brought him back home to the Capital but he choked. He could tell that his words had somehow gotten past the darkness in Vallus and his humanity had shone through even if only for a moment. That was his only chance and he had failed. Kerra's mother was dead; now Thesia was dying. How many others have to die before this conflict was resolved? He had often asked himself this question and many others. He had to find Vallus again, being no easy task; but Vallus now had the key so it didn't take a genius to figure out his next destination. He was going to have to confront him and fight him long enough to wear him down and use the sealing spell. Saying it was once thing, doing it was another.

Ashe finally came to, she saw Thesia lying across from them on the ground; she was still alive. She immediately ran over to her,

"Mother hold on, stay with me." She said frantically shaking Thesia to keep her awake. "We can find some way to heal you."

Thesia looked up at her and moved the hair from in front of her face, "No sweet child, this is as far as I go." She said weakly. "You and your brother have so far to go."

Ashe began to cry, Thesia was the only family she had ever had; she had raised her. This was the hardest thing she has ever had to deal with. "There is a stone on the peak of the mountain north of here, it can increase the power of each of your magicks; you must go there." She said. "Without the stone you will not be strong enough for the fight ahead of you."

"We will get the stone mother I promise." Ashe said wiping her eyes.

"I love you Ashlyn; the two of you will succeed, I just know you will." The Baroness said with her last breath.

"And I love you mother, be at peace now." Ashe said kissing her forehead. She sat on the cold snow covered ground weeping over her mother's body.

"Ashe we should give her a proper burial." Zander said.

Ashe nodded slowly looking at Thesia and smiling, "She would have wanted that."

Zander helped her to her feet and together they carried Thesia's body outside of the city; to a little snowy hill just west of the city's entrance and buried her. "We will camp here for the night and allow Ashe some time to mourn." Zander said. "We all need to rest after today."

"No, I want to leave now." Ashe said.

Kerra knelt down beside her and tried to embrace her but Ashe had shrugged her off. "Ashe we understand you're upset, but there is no reason to leave yet." Heiro said.

"Dammit!" Ashe shouted as she forced her fist into the snow covering the ground.

They had said nothing, they knew how determined she was to end the fighting. Her mother had already been killed, who next?

Zander?

She couldn't bear the thought of losing anyone else close to her.

"We will leave now, we have to." She said as she rose from the cold blanket of snow that covered the hillside.

"Ashe I swear to you I will protect you with my life." Zander said.

"No Zander I'm going to protect you, you're the only one who can end this." His sister said.

He was glad he finally had someone by blood to call his family. "So what is the deal with this stone Thesia was talking about?" Heiro asked.

"You're referring to the Stone of Hylkroft?" Ashe asked.

"You mean Hylkroft the Godsage?" Kerra asked.

Ashe turned to her and nodded, "The most powerful mystic to ever walk this very kingdom." She said.

"I've never heard of him." Zander said.

"Mother use to read me stories about him when I was very young, he was the only mystic to ever control all five elements of magick." Kerra explained.

"So what does the stone actually do?" Heiro asked.

"The stone is said to grant a mystic immeasurable power." Ashe said.

Zander knew they had to get their hands on this stone; there was no way they were the only ones who knew about it.

"Where is the stone hidden?" Kerra asked.

Ashe pointed to a mountain range just north of their position, "We need to travel to the peak of that mountain, and there is a temple there where the stone is hidden." She said.

"Then we will leave now, we need to get our hands on that stone before someone else does." Zander said.

The others agreed and began to follow him down the path away from the city. It would be a day's journey at least before they reached the mountain, and possibly another day to reach the peak. Zander was determined to see this through to the end; he wasn't going to allow anyone else to die. He was going to end the fighting.

They had almost made it to the mountain when they saw a Militia squad up ahead, leading it was Omak. The soldiers readied their weapons.

"Well if it isn't the little piss ants." Omak said.

"What do you want Omak?" Zander asked.

"Well we were on our way to Rygoth to meet up with the Judge but here you all are." He said.

"Vallerus is dead, Vallus son killed him." Heiro said.

The lieutenant was shocked by the news, "That's impossible, Vallerus is the strongest man in V'nairia." The Lieutenant said. "You're bluffing."

"It's true his body and his sword are lying in front of Duke Agarath's palace." Ashe spoke up.

Omak began to laugh, "So I guess that leaves me in charge of the kingdom, now doesn't it." He said.

"What are you getting at? The other judges are back at the Capital right?" Zander asked.

"After he skewered that bitch he had all the other judges executed, death by firing squad." The Lieutenant said.

"That bastard." Heiro said.

It may have surprised everyone else but it hadn't surprised Zander at all. Of course Vallerus had wanted everyone else out of the way. The current judges had known too much, he had thought to kill them and just appoint five new judges.

Kerra became angry and clenched her fist; even now he would talk ill of the dead in front of her. He was just like Vallerus, he had no heart. "So you mean to kill us too is that it?" Ashe asked.

"Well I don't see any reason to let any of you live." He said.

Zander looked back at the others, "You three take care of the soldier." He said. "I'll deal with Omak myself." The three of them nodded in agreement and prepared to fight.

"Be careful Zander." Kerra said. Zander looked back at her and smiled. She had believed in him and she knew that he wouldn't let her down; not now and not ever.

"Let's finish this Omak!" Zander shouted.

"Try not to piss yourself, you snot-nosed brat." The Lieutenant said pulling his rocket launcher off his back.

Zander unsheathed Ivory as he ran toward the Lieutenant, but his strike was blocked by the large barrel of the launcher. Omak took out his small pistol and began to fire at Zander, but he was quick enough to dodge the bullets. He spun around and struck Omak's hand with Ivory's scabbard knocking the gun up into the air. Zander was quicker than the last time they had fought, but that wasn't going to stop the Lieutenant.

While Zander was distracted with his fight with the Lieutenant, the others were having a tough time with the Militia's numbers. Omak had brought some of the Capital's strongest soldiers to fight alongside him and in great number as well. They had to make it to the stone; the only thing standing in their way was the Militia and Omak.

"Lightning Art: Thunder Crash!" Kerra shouted firing a bolt of lightning at a group of soldiers.

"Earth Art: Stone Spike." Heiro said as he stomped the ground causing spikes made of rock to come up from the earth impaling some of the soldiers.

"Flame Art: Fire Dragon." Ashe said as the flames engulfed another group of soldiers. They were making a dent in the enemy forces but for now it wasn't enough.

Zander had his hands full; Omak began firing rockets at him. The explosions had a wide radius and were hard to escape. Zander was caught in the middle of one and was thrown back against the rocks hitting his head. Blood streamed down his forehead as he turned over and looked at Omak who was preparing his last shot. "It's over boy, you're finished." He said.

This could have been it, Zander knew he could die. He at least had hoped that the others would press on and try to stop Vallus. All he could think about was Ashe and how she was about to lose someone else important to her. He couldn't bear the thought of her being alone. He had hoped to survive.

CHAPTER XVII

The Lieutenant fired the rocket, he laughed as he pictured Zander exploding into a million bloody pieces. They had escaped him before but this time he would finally have their heads. The rocket exploded as it hit its mark, shaking the side of the mountain range. Boulders began to tumble down the mountain. Luckily no one was in the way of the falling rubble. As the smoke cleared Omak saw Zander standing behind a rock wall covered in water.

"He used two defensive spells of two different elements together?" The Lieutenant asked himself. *"His magick had grown stronger."*

"Wind Style: Slicing Gale!" Zander shouted as the blades of wind came from Ivory.

He followed up with a fire spell to combine the two. "Combination Art: Flame Vortex!" Zander shouted. The flames came for Omak who tried to dodge the spell but failed, leaving his left arm and leg severely burned. He winced at the pain and tried to ignore it.

"So you can control four different types of magick, your full of surprises aren't you?" Omak asked.

Zander pointed Ivory's blade at the Lieutenant, "I'm just getting started."

He ran towards the lieutenant while gripping Ivory tightly. Omak fired a rocket in his direction, trying to distract him. Zander ran up to the rocket and in one quick motion slashed right through it, he barely had time to escape the blast. He used the force of the blast to increase his momentum, "It's over Omak!" he shouted as he reached Omak and pierced him through the chest with his blade nailing him against the mountain. The Lieutenant had died almost instantly by the sheer force of the blow.

Zander stopped to catch his breath, he had never taken a life before at least not a life of someone that he had known better than foot soldiers, but it felt different than he had imagined it. Somehow he thought he would feel more remorse, but he didn't feel anything. The Lieutenant had it coming to him; he had helped Vallerus organize the hunt so he believed that he actually had done V'nairia a public service. He knew that now maybe V'nairia had a chance at redemption, all he had to do now was stop Vallus. He removed Ivory from Omak's body and placed it back in its scabbard.

By this time the others had defeated the other soldiers and walked over to find him sitting on the ground staring at the body. "Zander are you okay?" Kerra asked him.

He didn't respond, he seemed as though he was in some kind of trance. Heiro placed his hand on Zander's shoulder, "He deserved to die Zander, you didn't do anything wrong." He said.

"I understand that he deserved it, it's just this strange feeling." He said.

"What strange feeling?" Kerra asked him.

"It was satisfying to watch him die, it gave me closure." Zander explained. "I guess it hadn't really hit me that Vallerus was finally dead, at least not until now."

They had never seen this side of him before, it was almost terrifying. It was like Vallus' words were coming from Zander's body, it had disturbed them. He was somehow darker than he was before; they feared that his heart would turn evil like his friends. Kerra knew something like that could never happen, she loved him and would never let him drift into the darkness.

"We are alright now, because of you Zander." Kerra said bending down to kiss him gently on the lips. This had awoken him from whatever dark place he was drifting off to. He was alright, the feeling had suddenly subsided.

"I guess everyone reacts differently to killing a man." Heiro said.

"I guess your right Heiro." Zander said standing up and dusting himself off. He strapped Ivory to his side and walked out ahead of them. "We should get going."

The three of them looked at each other and proceeded to follow Zander up the mountain path. After only walking just a few moments they had noticed a change in the weather on the mountain.

"Zander I think we should camp." Ashe said trying to see the path ahead of her that had been obstructed by falling snow.

"Ashe we don't have time, we need to get that stone." Zander said disagreeing with his sister.

"Zander she's right, the higher up we go the colder it gets." Heiro explained. "We need to build a fire and camp for the night."

Zander let out a deep sigh and rolled his eyes in frustration, "Fine we will make camp and leave early tomorrow morning."

Kerra and Ashe began to set up the tents while Heiro started a fire. Zander had stood over the side of the mountain staring out into the snowy wasteland below him. The cave where Vallus had waited for him hadn't been far from their position. The end was almost near, what the end had in store for him he didn't know, and that terrified him.

***

Zander, Heiro and Kerra awoke the next morning feeling better than they had been the day before. The snow storm on the mountain had subsided for now and they were ready to press on up the mountain. Kerra was still worried about Zander; she had wondered what had happened to his mind after killing the Lieutenant. They had seen no sign of Ashe, she had probably gotten up earlier to scout ahead; she was still mourning Thesia's death and was not taking it easily. Zander knew to give her the space she needed and she would come around eventually.

"How are you feeling Zander?" Kerra asked.

Zander looked over at her and smiled, "I feel pretty great actually." He said stretching his legs.

His smile was definitely comforting; it eased some of the worry. She hadn't seen him smile like that in some time. "I bet he's ready for another fight, aren't you?" Heiro asked him jokingly.

"I wouldn't go that far." Zander said. "I'm still felling that fight from yesterday."

It was the happiest they had been in a while, they weren't worried about Vallus, or the reawakening of the Demon King. As much as they wanted to take a longer break from their journey they couldn't, they had to retrieve that stone from the mountain peak at any cost. The stone was the only way Zander would have enough power to defeat Vallus and save V'nairia. They began to pack up their belongings and walked up the mountain path.

"Do you think Ashe is okay?" Kerra asked.

"I'm not sure; Thesia was the only family she had known for most of her life. It's been pretty tough on her." Zander explained.

"Not to mention the hatred she feels for Vallus, what if she tries to take revenge?" Heiro asked.

Zander hadn't thought about that, what if she tried to kill him? Zander couldn't stop his sister; she was his blood. On the other hand, Vallus was his friend; it was certainly something to think about. "Maybe I can talk to Ashe and see where her thoughts and feelings are now." Zander said.

The other two nodded, it was futile to try to convince him otherwise; but they both knew it was a wasted effort.

Up the path they saw Ashe sitting on the side of the mountain staring off into the distance. Zander could see the pain in her face; he could tell she had been crying from the puffiness around her eyes. Ashe wasn't the type to voice her feelings when she was sad; but anger had been a different story.

"Have you been out here long Ashe?" Zander asked.

She looked up at him and looked as though she was about to break down. "About half the night and all morning I'd say." she said softly and tilted her head back to look at the clouds.

"It's alright Ashe; you can talk about it if you want." Kerra said feeling sorry for her.

Ashe stood up and dusted herself off, "We had better get going if we want to reach the peak before nightfall." she said avoiding Kerra's kindness.

She began to walk ahead in silence, they others knew to drop the subject and they followed. "Have you eaten anything Ashe? You seem a bit pale." Heiro said.

"I ate some fish I had cooked from a nearby river." she said as if annoyed.

Zander knew she would blow up any minute; she was a hot head; so it was in his best interest not to say anything. "If you'd like I can carry your bag for you." Heiro said.

Ashe stopped and spun around, "Dammit! Can everyone just shut the hell up already?" Ashe asked her face the color of blood. "If I needed help I would ask for it."

"There it was; it was bound to happen sooner or later." Zander thought to himself.

The others just stood in amazement; they could see the veins in the side of her neck. They had never seen her so angry before. "I have eaten, and I can carry my own damn bag; let's just get to the peak and be done with it okay." Ashe continued.

"Alright, were sorry Ashe." Zander said as they began to follow her up the mountain.

When they had finally made it to the mountain peak they saw a large stone temple with four large columns that had stood on each side of the square perimeter. Beside of the temple sat a large tree with many branches. The tree was dead and had no leaves on it. The temple on the other hand had been extremely well kept for being at the very peak of the mountain.

"Sis did Thesia mention anyone living up here?" Zander asked.

"No all she said was that we could find the stone here." Ashe said.

"Maybe we should go see if anyone is here." Heiro said.

They walked over to the large double doors of the temple and Zander knocked on the door hard. There was no response, "Hello!" Kerra called out.

Zander knocked again, on the third knock the doors began to open slowly.

The door opened and they saw a short older man with graying hair and a long white beard standing in the doorway. He had walked with a cane and glared at them suspiciously. "Who are you?" he asked.

"I'm Zander and these are my friends; we're looking for the stone of Hylkroft the Godsage." He said.

The man stared at him for a moment, and then busted out into a hearty laugh. "You want the stone of the Godsage, ha that's rich." The man said.

"This is serious sir; we need it to save V'nairia." Heiro explained.

"So you believe you can stop your friend from awakening the Demon King?" the old man asked.

Zander had never mentioned that information, how could this man have known why they were here. "How did you know who we were?" Kerra asked.

"Ha, after two hundred years living in this world you know a great many things my dear." He said motioning them to come in. "Please come inside."

He showed them into his dining area and seated them at the table. "Tea?" he asked.

"Yes please." Zander said.

He poured each of them a cup of tea and he sat down with them. "I know each of you, I've seen you fight, and I know everything there is to know about you." The man said.

This man was well informed, but how could he know everything about them. To Zander it just wasn't possible; he must have been using magick. "So how do you know everything about us?" Heiro asked.

The man sipped his tea and placed the cup back on the saucer. "With my left eye I can see things that happen in the present, I'm a mystic just like each of you." He explained. They studied his eye; it was made of pure crystal. "I am Einkroft, the Godsage's younger brother." The man said.

This was shocking to each of them, they had never heard of the Godsage having any siblings. "So if your Hylkroft's brother than you must be pretty powerful." Ashe said.

Einkroft laughed, "Who knows really, I have never used my magick for combat." The old man said. "I'm what you'd call a pacifist."

"Have you ever been in a battle?" Heiro asked.

"Once or twice, but the Militia mainly used me for training the mystic forces."

"So why are you all the way up here on the mountain?" Kerra asked.

Einkroft had taken another sip of tea, "After the war was over and Vallerus had killed my brother I fled the capital and build this temple." He said. "I have been here ever since."

"What about the stone?" Zander asked. "Is it here?"

"Yes, the stone is here but you aren't ready to wield such power." Einkroft said. "Not yet at least."

"Will you train us then?" Ashe asked.

"You two are just like your parents, quick to the point. Although, your father had more wits about him." The man said.

This must have meant he knew about the organization, this is what Thesia had meant when she said to come after the stone; she knew that Einkroft would train them.

"So you will train us?" Zander asked.

"Yes we shall start tomorrow at sunrise; you all had better rest up." Einkroft said.

"Thank you sir." Kerra said. He smiled and nodded, "You can take the two back bedrooms." He added.

Each of them went to their rooms and unpacked their things and had gotten into bed early. The next day they would start to grow stronger and Zander knew it was just a matter of time before he brought finally brought Vallus back home.

CHAPTER XVIII

The next morning they had gotten up at sunrise and met Einkroft outside the temple to train. They could feel the breeze brush against their faces as it passed by. It hadn't been too cold the sun was shining brightly warming the peak of the mountain. They could barely keep their eyes open they were all so tired from walking the day before, not to mention none of them have ever been woken up at the crack of dawn. Zander yawned, "It's so early, can't we wait awhile to train?" he asked.

Einkroft hit him over the head with his long wooden cane. "Hey what was that for?" Zander asked rubbing the sore spot in his head.

"You want to train to use the stone, we do it my way." the old man said."Understand?"

"Yes we understand." Zander said rolling his eyes as if annoyed.

Einkroft walked around them studying each of their features, "Well at least the four of you look like you eat after coming such a long way, you will need your strength for this training." he said laughing.

"Would you like us to explain our skills sir?" Heiro asked.

"I already know all there is to know about each of you Heiro, such as your deadly Blood Sword technique." Einkroft said. Heiro was surprised not many knew about the spell he had created. "It is indeed powerful, but it takes so much energy to control; so it would be difficult to sustain in your current condition." Einkroft said.

Heiro nodded, "Yes, I can only sustain it for about five minutes or so." he said.

"Then we will definitely have to fix that." Einkroft said. "It's a good trump card but can easily be a double-edged sword."

He stopped at Kerra, "You child, you can use lightning magick correct?" he asked.

Kerra looked down at her feet; he held a finger to her chin to lift her head. "Eyes up here child, your enemy could take you out swiftly if you're not looking." Einkroft said.

"Yes sir, lightning magick is my family's specialty." Kerra said.

"You look just like your mother, I bet you have her spark also." he said making a joke which made her smile.

He walked over to Ashe who had a stern look on her face. He examined her closely, "A woman as beautiful as you should smile more, firecracker." Einkroft said.

Ashe became angry, "Who the hell are you calling firecracker, old man!" Ashe shouted.

He whacked Ashe in the head with the cane, "I'm calling you firecracker, you're a hotheaded fire magick user." he said. Zander realized then that he and Ashe were not so different.

He finally walked over to Zander, "So it seems you are the only one here without an original technique." Einkroft said.

"Original technique?" Zander asked.

"Yes. Something that you have made your own that no other warrior has in their arsenal." the old man said.

"I can use four types of magicks." Zander said.

Einkroft chuckled and smacked him on the head again, "You fool, elemental magick is all fine and dandy; but it won't give you the upper hand in a fight." Einkroft said.

Zander thought back to Vallerus' most powerful technique and thought about how devastating it was. It must have taken him years to perfect and a lot of enemies to test it on. He would definitely have to train hard to achieve something that powerful. He doubted he could produce something of that magnitude. There must be a way to speed up the process, and then it hit him; there was the stone. The stone could help him achieve the technique he needed, but he would have to train with Einkroft to meet his standards before receiving it.

"So how do you propose we train?" Ashe said.

"The men and women will fight each other separately; I want to see your skills in action." The old man said walking to the side out of the way of the fighters. "First will be the men."

Heiro and Zander faced each other, Heiro began to stretch. "It's been awhile since we fought." Heiro said.

"So it has, I wonder if you can keep up with me now?" Zander asked grinning at him.

They both drew their swords, "Now this is a friendly fight boy, no killing blows." Einkroft said as he called for them to begin.

Zander quickly sheathed his blade and ran at Heiro with his bare fists. "Changing tactics huh? The blade was to throw me off." Heiro said while dodging his punches.

"You catch on quick." Zander said as he gave a roundhouse to the side of Heiro's face.

Zander threw a punch but Heiro blocked it, and then swept Zander's legs out from under him. Heiro came down with his sword but Zander blocked it with his own. Zander stuck his foot into Heiro's abdomen lifting him over his head and throwing him backward.

Heiro quickly rose from the ground, "Flame Art: Fire Stream!" he shouted.

"Water Art: Water Wall!" Zander screamed as the wall came up from the ground drowning out the fire.

The steam filled the space around them. "So he's using the steam to obstruct my vision, clever boy." Heiro said.

Zander appeared behind him with his blade drawn, "I've got you now." He said.

"Earth Art: Stone Spikes." Heiro said as the spikes came up from the ground behind him, Zander quickly maneuvered out of harm's way.

"I saw that coming, but I've got to hand it to you; you've certainly grown." Heiro said.

"I'm not finished yet, Flame Art: Triple Fireball!" Zander shouted.

Heiro then had figured out that Ashe had been teaching him a few new tricks. The three balls of flame came towards him. They were coming from three different directions so that Heiro was surrounded. Suddenly Einkroft jumped in and used a water spell to quell the roaring flames.

"Enough. That was an excellent display of elemental control for both of you." The old man said.

Heiro and Zander knelt before him to show their respect and appreciation. "Zander your use of defensive and offensive spells is astounding for your age, but you still need that ace in the hole; remember that." Einkroft said.

The two guys moved out of the way as the two ladies took their places on the field. "Kerra since you're not using a weapon I won't either." Ashe said.

Kerra smiled, "Okay that sounds fair I guess." She said.

"Okay now let the second fight begin!" Einkroft shouted.

Neither of the girls moved a muscle, the stared at each other to see who would strike first. "Flame Art: Fire Stream!" Ashe shouted as she spat flames at Kerra.

"Lightning Art: Thunder Blade." Kerra said as energy shot out from her open hand that formed a blade of electricity.

She used the energy to cut through the flames, while extending another blade from her other hand. "That's an impressive technique." Ashe said.

Kerra was fast; she kept on thrusting the blades at Ashe hoping to connect. She was lucky she could dodge them easily; they could paralyze her ending the match. Kerra's skill in magicks was fair, but her hand to hand combat skills were unmatched. Her mother had trained her in the art herself, there was no better when it came to a closed fist.

"Lightning Art: Thunder Crash!" Kerra shouted firing a bolt of electricity.

"Flame Art: Fireball!" Ashe said as she blew the ball of flame from her lips. The two spells collided causing a small explosion.

After the smoke had cleared they saw the two woman still standing in the same spots as before. The guys were certainly impressed; especially with Kerra, she could hold her own against the Fire Drake herself.

"Flame Art: Flare Surge." Ashe said as she threw a tiny ball of flame to the ground in front of Kerra.

"It's over." Ashe said as she snapped her fingers. The small flame burst causing another small explosion that knocked Kerra backward.

Before falling to the ground, Einkroft jumped and grabbed her laying her safely on the ground. "Enough Ashe." He said.

"I believe that is enough training for today, I will make us some tea." The old man said as he wobbled inside the small house.

The guys walked over to meet up with the girls. "Wow you guys were great." Zander said.

"You really think so?" Kerra asked.

"He's right Kerra you certainly held your own against me, I was impressed." Ashe said grinning a little.

The four of them walked inside and sat with Einkroft at the table. He had hot tea and cookies waiting on them, the entire house was filled with the scent of vanilla and cinnamon. "So what is your plan once you get the stone and obtain its power?" Einkroft asked.

"We will make our way to the shrine below the northern mountains, and stop Vallus from awakening the demon." Zander said.

"You understand that he wants you to meet him there, he means to kill you and take Ivory from you." The old man said.

"He won't die; the three of us will be there to back the kid up." Heiro said. "Well what about Vallus' bodyguards?" Einkroft asked.

"What bodyguards?" Ashe asked him.

"He has the voidshade, Raphael and Lyra from Rygoth." Einkroft explained.

"So who is this Lyra?" Heiro asked. "What are her abilities?"

Einkroft sipped his tea and bit off the end of a cookie, "All I know is that she possesses water magick."

"Ashe and I can handle Lyra." Kerra said.

"Then I guess I'll finish off Raphael, I have a score to settle with that one." Heiro explained.

"So that leaves me with Vallus." Zander said.

The others nodded in agreement. So the battle plan was set, each of them knew their enemy. It was just a matter of time before Vallus figured out where they were and why they were there. They needed to hurry and grow stronger so they could use the stone. There wasn't much time left. "For now you all can relax, I have a story to tell you." Einkroft said.

"What kind of story?" Zander asked.

Einkroft leaned forward in his chair, "The tale of the cursed blades, Ebony and Ivory." He said smiling.

CHAPTER XIX

Centuries ago the land of V'nairia had once been called Astaria. There were no judges or Supreme Judge, only a king who ruled over the kingdom. The king dwelled in the city of Syterian along with the queen and their two sons. That king was Ardour the Third and his sons, the princes were named Archon and Geinedor. The brothers had never gotten along and the king had often had to break up the quarreling boys. Archon followed the path of righteousness and was a healer. He believed in doing well by others and good deeds would bless him, giving him a long and prosperous life.

Geinedor was mischievous; he was always getting himself into trouble. He had dreamed of ruling the kingdom and enslaving all those who did not possess magick. He saw the human race as weak and useless.

The king's family were the first mystics, they were said to have been blessed from birth by the gods of old. As they had gotten older the kings made the boys read books and study the world. Archon loved learning about the world and building on his own knowledge, he learned to control his magick quickly.

Geinedor on the other hand never liked to study and was often caught practicing his sword skills or hanging around the city's whore house. Geinedor was often scolded and whipped but he didn't care, his only goals were to grow stronger than his brother so that he could succeed his father and steal the throne. At sixteen Geinedor was even worse, he began to kill livestock and blame one of the villagers. The king beheaded each villager that was accused. The dark child loved to kill and loved the sight of blood even more so.

One day the boys sat in the study and were being taught about Astaria's history by one of the king's disciples. Geinedor began to kick the side of Archon's leg. "Looks like father will die any day; I wonder which one of us he will choose to succeed him." His brother hissed.

"I have no doubt that I will be chosen, you're a terrible diplomat." Archon said.

"One doesn't need a diplomat's tongue to rule, you need an iron fist." Geinedor said.

Archon then had an idea, "Why don't we have a quick duel after our lessons to see who is best fit to rule Astaria." Archon said.

He knew his idiot brother wouldn't refuse a challenge; it would be a mistake on his part. Geinedor had brawn there was no doubt about that but Archon was quicker and by far cleverer, giving him the upper hand.

After their lessons they met in the courtyard in front of the castle. Archon carried a knight's sword with a white handle, while Geinedor held a large broad sword. They drew their swords, circling each other waiting for an opening. To no surprise Geinedor struck first, Archon had anticipated this and blocked the strike with his blade. He did however underestimate his brother's strength; he realized this as the broad sword began to inch closer to his body.

He quickly broke the clash between them and jumped out of the way. He ran at Geinedor with his blade in his hand, he thrust it outwards towards his brother's sternum. Geinedor grabbed the blade with his bare hand to stop the attack. His blood ran down the side of the blade, he didn't seem to flinch at all. He retracted his sword and came after him a second time. They exchanged blow after blow, sparks flew as the steel scraped against one another.

Suddenly the king appeared. "What is the meaning of this?" He asked.

They stopped the fighting and immediately knelt before him. "It was merely a game father." Archon said.

"A game? When a battle consists of cold steel, it is no game my boy." His father said.

Geinedor looked up at his father who was now glaring back at him. "I'm assuming this was your idea stupid boy?" The king asked.

Geinedor did not respond but only looked the king in the eyes with a fiery hatred. Archon was always the favorite son, their father hated Geinedor. "Stand and draw your blade boy." Ardour said still looking at Geinedor.

"Father it was nothing I swear!" Archon shouted. The king motioned for his silence as Geinedor rose in front of him. He picked up his broad sword off of the ground and held it.

The king drew his blade as well, "I'll show you what games cost you." He said.

Geinedor ran at his father swinging his blade. His father dodged the strike and sliced the boy's arm. The king came with his blade again and struck his leg with his blade. The blood dripped from his wounds, hitting the cold autumn ground. The king swept his feet out from under him, and watched him fall to the ground.

"The enemy will not be so merciless; you might just lose your head." The king said as he started back toward the castle.

The rain began to fall hard, the drops pounding on Geinedor face. Archon sat and watched his brother, defeated and broken. He loved his brother despite his wickedness, but love could not fix him.

"Archon lets go, leave him be." Ardour said. Archon said nothing as he followed his father back to the castle.

Geinedor's hatred for his family began to grow at an unhealthy rate. One evening in the midst of his plotting, Geinedor crept into his parent's bedroom. He walked over to his mother's side of the bed and pulled out a small dagger from his belt. He covered her mouth, and her eyes sprung open in terror. He held a finger to his lips motioning for her to remain quiet, and then with one quick stroke he slit her throat wide open. He reveled in the sight as the blood flowed from her corpse. To him it was almost poetic, killing off the ones who gave him life; what a wretched life he had. He moved on to his father's side next, he despised the sight of the old fool lying there sleeping peacefully, unaware of what was about to happen. He covered his mouth like he did his mother only to find the same reaction. This time he pulled out a sword, his father gazed up at him in terror.

"You might just lose your head eh father." Geinedor whispered to his father and with one blow, sliced off his head. He quickly and quietly snuck out of the room carrying his father's decapitated head.

The next morning there was a knock at Archon's door, "Prince Archon come quickly!" one of the guards shouted.

Archon rose out of bed and dressed himself and ran down the stairs. He opened the double doors to the throne room, he glanced over at the throne and saw something; but couldn't quite tell what it was. He looked closer and it was his father's head dripping blood from the seat of the throne.

"What the hell happened? Who has done this?" Archon asked frantically.

"There was no sign of a break in sir." The guards reported.

Then it hit him, and he knew then what had happened. "Guards search every inch of the castle for Prince Geinedor and bring him to me at once." Archon said.

They nodded and hastened out of the throne room to search the castle. Archon walked over and knelt before his father's remains, "I swear on my honor father, I will avenge you." He said.

A soldier walked in with a grim look across his face. "Sire, it's your mother we found her in her chambers with her throat cut." The man said sorrowfully.

Archon sat at the throne and thought for a moment, and the more he thought the more tears ran down his face. He began to weep over his dead parents, the only love he had in the world was gone. They guards had come back shortly and reported nothing, Geinedor had fled the castle.

Geinedor had gotten word of an old tree on a mountain top that could grant a person any power they desired. It was a large oak tree that bared no leaves, and had three faces imprinted in the trunk. It was said to have been grown by a powerful shaman that was linked with underworld. Geinedor wanted the power for himself to overthrow his brother as king and enslave all of humanity.

Archon and Geinedor had met at the mountain top where the tree stood to finish their childhood rivalry once and for all. Archon had an idea, and again knew his brother would accept.

"I have a proposition my brother, I propose that the shaman craft us two weapons of incredible might and power and we shall fight to the death on this very peak." Archon said.

Geinedor hated to wait but certainly agreed to the terms. "If I defeat you I will become king and enslave the entire human race." Geinedor said.

"If I defeat you, you will transfer your magick to me and will be exiled from this land until the day you die." Archon said. Both sides agreed and the brothers parted ways.

After a month had passed the shaman had finally created the powerful weapons they required. Archon's blade had a white scabbard and was known as Ivory, the holy blade. Geinedor's sword was known as Ebony, the blade of hellspawn. However the blades were cursed, the chosen wielders of the swords were said to be eternal rivals until death itself claimed one of their lives.

Ebony used Geinedor's anger and hatred to consume him; transforming him into the Demon King known as Diaboro. Ebony consumes the heart of its wielder until finally no humanity is left. Ivory's power comes from the purest of hearts, it is said to lead its wielder down the path of righteousness and justice. The purer the heart, the stronger the wielder. Their battle raged on for days, until Archon used Ivory's power to seal away Diaboro in a shrine below the northern mountain. He also used Ebony's power to make the seal even stronger, thus the seal can only be broken by having both cursed swords. After defeating his brother, the two blades disappeared across the kingdom never to be found again, except for those wielders the swords choose. Archon was so stricken by grief he had fled the kingdom and was never heard of again.

CHAPTER XX

"That is a tragic story." Kerra said.

"Yes, very tragic and true." Einkroft said agreeing with her.

"So after all this time no one has ever heard of what happened to Archon?" Zander asked.

Einkroft began to pour himself some more tea, "No my boy not a soul, I would imagine his bones are dust by now." He said.

"So what ever happened to the tree?" Heiro asked.

"Come with me." The old man said rising from his chair.

As they walked outside the temple they were surprised to see that the sky had turned color, It was now a dark purple in color. The clouds were pitch black and the winds had started to pick up.

"What's going on?" Kerra asked.

"It seems as though your friend has opened Diaboro's shrine." Einkroft said.

They followed him around the side of the temple to the old dead tree. "This was the very tree that the shaman had grown, but it has long since lost its power." Einkroft said.

"There! I can see the imprint of the faces." Kerra shouted pointing to the trunk of the tree.

"So then Geinedor did absorb the power from the tree?" Zander asked.

"No, Archon confronted him before he could absorb its strength, after sealing his brother away Archon had killed the shaman and the tree lost its power." Einkroft explained.

"After hearing the story I think I know what I have to do." Zander said turning to them.

"So you have figured out the meaning, have you?" the old man asked.

"If I have to kill Vallus to save the kingdom from the reawakening, then that is what I must do." Zander said.

He had thought Kerra would have been shocked and became angry, but instead she lowered her head and stared at her feet. She knew the truth and she knew that it would eventually come to this.

"The longer Vallus possesses the demon sword, the faster his heart fades to darkness." Einkroft said.

"Zander we are right behind you, we won't let the kingdom fall." Heiro said punching him in the shoulder.

"Thanks Heiro." He replied.

"Hey I may be a thief but that doesn't mean I don't have a heart." Heiro said.

"Kerra?" Zander said. "Are you okay with that decision?"

She looked up at him and smiled and he instantly felt relief from the pain in his gut. "Yes we have to save V'nairia no matter what the cost." She said.

"I don't care what we have to do, let's just go kick some ass." Ashe said. That was Zander's sister that's for sure, hotheaded as always.

"The training I normally provide can take months, but given the kingdom's current state; we don't have time to dawdle." Einkroft said.

"You're giving us the stone?" Ashe asked.

"Yes I have faith in the four of you; I know you will save the kingdom." The old man said as he walked up to the tree. "Sacred Art: Binding Seal, Release!" he shouted.

The others watched as he placed his hand through the tree, Zander began to rub his eyes. Einkroft actually put his hand through the tree without any force. As he began to pull his hand out of the tree they could see something in his palm, was the stone. It was beautiful, different parts of the stone were different colors to represent a different elemental magick. He had brought it over and gave it to Zander.

"Now my boy there is one more thing you must know, there is another way to defeat Vallus other than the purifying seal." Einkroft said.

This was surprising, they thought the seal was the only way to stop Vallus and restore his heart. "What is it?" Zander asked.

"You must pierce the evil heart and Ivory will purify it." The old man said.

"Well that sounds easy enough." Heiro said.

"There is however a condition that must be met; you must sacrifice a pure heart to complete the process." The old man explained.

"Meaning what exactly?" Heiro asked.

"Someone with a pure heart has to be the one to pierce Vallus' heart." Zander said stunned.

"Yes that is the condition." Einkroft said.

Zander shook his head, "No the purifying seal will work, no one else is dying." He said.

The others fell silent, they thought to each of themselves if they were worthy enough to help Zander with the purification. None of them were entirely certain if they had a pure heart.

"Now I can finally go in peace." Einkroft said.

"What? What do you mean go in peace?" Zander asked.

The old man began to laugh, "My life force is connected with that stone, it's a spell me and my brother cast ages ago that's why I've been around for so long." He said.

"So the Godsage had you protect the stone all this time." Ashe said.

"Yes he did." Einkroft said.

Kerra began to weep for him, they had only just met him and now he was going to die. Zander was depressed also, it seemed like everyone that had known anything about his past was dying around him; it was frustrating.

"One more thing, no matter how bleak the situation seems; there is always a solution to be found never forget that." The old man said smiling.

"Thank you Master Einkroft, for everything." Zander said.

The four of them gathered around the stone and placed their hands on it. There was a flash of light; they could feel the energy surging through them. They were completely refreshed, as if there was new life breathed into them. After the transfer of power was complete they looked over at Einkroft, he had begun to fade into particles of light.

"Einkroft don't go please!" Kerra shouted.

"Protect each other always." He said as the last of his spirit faded.

Zander had saw a tear fall from his eye just before he faded, he truly believed in them and now they would have to believe in their selves. They immediately left the mountain peak in search of the shrine.

As they walked north to find the shrine, Zander's mind began to wonder. He began thinking about everyone who has lost their lives to the Vallerus and Vallus. So many have died and he would finally have the chance to avenge them. Kiarra,

Thesia, and Einkroft; their deaths would not be for nothing. Soon they would all be back in the Capital in warm beds and be called heroes by the people of V'nairia.

"Zander are you okay?" Kerra asked him.

"Yeah I'm fine." he responded.

She was always good at picking up on strange vibes he had put off. "We will be home soon Kerra I promise." Zander said smiling at her.

"I love you." she said smiling back.

"I love you too." he replied.

Their love for each other had definitely grown, Kerra often thought about marriage or having children with him. This journey had taught them many things, but for Zander it had definitely matured him. "Is everyone prepared? Do you know the plan?" Zander asked.

"I will take Raphael." Heiro said.

"Kerra and I will take Lyra." Ashe said.

"Zander are you sure you want to fight Vallus alone?" Kerra asked.

"I have to it's the only way, I will wait on you three to finish off the bodyguards and then we will prepare the seal." Zander explained.

Their plan would soon be set into motion. They were nearing the shrine; Zander could feel a sharp pain in his stomach. The very sight of Vallus at this point would pain him, not just the fact that he missed his friend but he was angry and wanted to end the fighting. He was going to save V'nairia even at the cost of his own life. He had already decided that he was going to sacrifice himself to save Vallus but he wasn't going to tell anyone that.

They had finally come up on the entrance to the cave where the shrine was. It was dark; Ashe and Heiro used fire magick to light the torches on the sides of the cave.

After they had lit up the path to the shrine, Kerra froze and didn't move.

"Kerra what's wrong?" Zander asked.

"What if we don't make it out of here, what if one of us dies?" she asked as she began to sob.

"The purifying seal will work Kerra you just need to have faith." Ashe said.

Zander grabbed her chin and kissed her, it was if she was instantly brought back to life. "You okay now?" he asked her.

"Yes I'm fine, just a momentary freak out." she said as they continued on.

They came up on the shrine, on top of it was a stone statue of a large demon with long horns and it was holding a broad sword. "It's just like the story, that's Geinedor after his transformation." Heiro said.

"He was a pretty big demon." Ashe said.

"Pretty goddamn ugly if you ask me." Heiro said looking at the statue.

"So glad of you to join us." a voice said.

They looked behind them and saw Raphael walking over to greet them. He glanced over at Heiro and smirked,

"Still kicking I see." he said.

"The only kicking around here will be of your shady ass." Heiro said.

"Quite a temper you have, it matters not you will all perish soon." Raphael said.

"Where is Vallus?" Zander asked as he drew his sword."

Master Vallus isn't ready for you yet." Another voice said.

They turned back at the shrine and saw a young girl in a blue dress; it was Lyra. "Just who the hell are you?" Ashe asked.

Lyra began to giggle, "I'm Lyra, one of Master Vallus' guardians." She said.

"I'll ask again, where is Vallus?" Zander asked her.

"The master did say you had a bit of a temper, if you must know he believes this party is a little too crowded." Lyra explained.

"What do you mean?" Heiro asked her.

"I'll show you what she means." Raphael said as he snapped his fingers.

Portals of darkness began to appear below each of them except for Zander. The darkness had begun to pull them in,

"Guys are you okay?" Zander asked.

"Don't worry about us; they are just trying to separate us." Heiro said struggling to get out of the portal that was swallowing him up.

"Zander stall Vallus until we get back." Ashe said.

Kerra looked over at him and didn't speak; he could tell she was frightened. Before he knew it, he was the only one left in the cave.

***

Ashe had awoken from what seemed like a long sleep, but she was in a strange place. She was in a forest near a waterfall surrounded by trees. Across from her she saw Kerra lying on the ground asleep, she ran over to wake her.

"Kerra wake up!" Ashe shouted shaking her.

Kerra rose up and turned to see Ashe sitting beside her, "Where are we?" she asked.

"It's some kind of forest, but not one that I've ever been too." Ashe said.

They got to their feet and began to look around; their location was unfamiliar, they had never seen a more beautiful place before. "I wonder how long we have been here." Ashe said.

"Only a few minutes." A voice said, it was Lyra's but they couldn't see her.

"Where are you, you little bitch?" Ashe asked.

"A lady mustn't use such terrible language you know." Lyra said.

"Show yourself!" Ashe shouted as flames began to surround her body.

"Temper temper." Lyra said.

They looked around but still saw no one; she had to be playing games with them. "Oh and there is the shy little virgin." Lyra said referring to Kerra.

Her voice swirled around them; they were getting quite annoyed by it. "So you're supposed to be Zander's lover. That's interesting you don't look like you would know the first thing about being one." Lyra said provoking her.

Kerra became angry; her words were like needle pricking her in the back of the neck. "Why don't you come out and fight you cunt?" Ashe asked.

"If that's what you wish." Lyra said. They looked over toward the waterfall and there she stood ready for a fight, "Shall we begin?" she asked.

CHAPTER XXI

"Where did she appear from?" Ashe asked looking over in Kerra's direction.

"I'm not really sure; I hadn't seen her before now." She said.

"Water Art: Water Spear." Lyra said as the water rose to form a long bladed weapon.

She grabbed the spear and ran after them, "If I were you I would concentrate on your enemy." She said.

Lyra had come after Kerra but Ashe deflected her attack with her sword. Ashe was surprised at how powerful Lyra's magick was, her spear was as hard as steel.

"You're incredibly strong for a little bitch." Ashe said as she used the force of her weight to push Lyra back and disconnect from her.

"That's not exactly a term of endearment." Lyra said.

"What's your fucking point?" Ashe asked.

"Lightning Art: Thunder Crash!" Kerra shouted as she fired a bolt of lightning in Lyra's Direction.

Lyra threw her spear at the attack absorbing the blow. The spear dissolved into the earth, and in its place another had appeared. "As long as there is water around I have unlimited weaponry at my disposal." Lyra said.

"It was really smart to put a flame magick user against a water user." Ashe said smarting off.

"You can't worry about that now, focus on the battle." Kerra said.

Lyra began to summon multiple spears and threw them at the two of them. Ashe dodged most of them and watched as they went right through the trunk of a tree. One flew past Kerra and gashed her side; she started to bleed, but only a little.

"Kerra you okay?" Ashe asked.

"Yes, it's only a flesh wound." She replied.

They looked around and didn't see Lyra anywhere. "Where did she go?" Ashe asked.

Kerra had begun to flail around like a ragdoll, but Ashe noticed that Kerra was incurring injuries on her face and other parts of her body. "Kerra get down!" Ashe shouted as she used a fire spell and blew it towards Kerra.

Kerra quickly ducked out of the flames path and suddenly the air caught fire. It was Lyra she had turned herself invisible to throw them off. Lyra commanded the water to rise from the ground and cover her to put out the flames.

"That's great, she's a water magick master and she can turn invisible." Ashe said. Things had begun to get worse for them, who knew what other tricks Lyra had up her sleeve.

***

Zander walked through various parts of the cave trying to find the others and had no luck. It was as if they were transported to another dimension beyond his reach. He had come to an exit that he hadn't been through before, it lead to a cliff that protruded outside of the mountain with a river flowing below him He heard footsteps behind him; he quickly turned to see who was there. Out of the darkness of the cave came Vallus.

"Welcome brother." He said greeting him.

"I'm not your damn brother!" Zander shouted.

Vallus wasn't offended; he had actually produced a smile. The very same smile that Zander had always hated growing up. "Come on Zander, don't be angry with me; I'm doing this for the good of the world." Vallus explained.

"Your way is not the right one; you can't play with people's lives." Zander said.

"On the contrary, I can do what I want when I rule this world." Vallus said.

Zander drew Ivory from its long white scabbard, "Not if I have anything to say about it." He said.

"Put your sword away, I'm not here to kill you." Vallus said.

Zander was puzzled; he thought that had been the entire reason behind luring him to the shrine. "What do you mean?" Zander asked.

"I want you to become my guardian and together we will pull this world out of its dark cloud and into the light." Vallus proposed.

"I don't want any part of the kingdom's bloodshed." Zander said.

Vallus shook his head, "Your nobility is incredibly annoying." He stated.

"I know what I have to do, and I won't back down now." Zander said.

"Fine if you're offering me your life, then I guess I will have to take it." Vallus said raising his hand.

Another black portal appeared beneath Zander. "What are you doing?" Zander asked struggling to free himself.

"It's simply a change of scenery." Vallus said as the black swallowed him.

***

"Flame Art: Great Fire Stream!" Ashe shouted as she blew fire through the forest, Lyra had turned invisible yet again.

The spell caught some of the trees on fire; Lyra had used her water magick to put them out. "You shouldn't harm nature you know." She said.

"I'll do whatever I have to do to kill you." Ashe said.

"You can try hothead." Lyra said throwing more of her water spears.

Ashe and Kerra were wiser this time around and saw the attack coming, they dodged each spear perfectly. "So you have figured out my attack, I guess I'll have to resort to something else." Lyra said.

She began to gather energy and released a stream of high pressurized water. It was very narrow and could barely be seen, the girls ducked just before it hit them. It had sliced through the some of the trees behind them. Ashe and Kerra turned their heads slightly and watched the trees fall. They had made a loud thud as they hit the forest floor.

"What spell was that?" Kerra asked.

"That was my Matter Slicer spell, I can use my magick to pressurize the stream and it will cut just as good as any blade." Lyra explained.

"Kerra we need to be careful of that attack, one wrong move and were dead." Ashe said.

"Okay." Kerra said nodding in agreement.

"I have tricks of my own." Ashe said.

A small ball of flame appeared on her finger tip, she threw it toward Lyra and it fell to the ground before her. "What do you call that? Are you out of energy already?" Lyra asked laughing.

"Flame Art: Flare Surge!" Ashe said snapping her fingers.

The Fated Swords

The tiny flame burst with incredible force, throwing Lyra backwards into the waterfall behind her. Her body hit the stone behind the water and made a loud crushing sound. Kerra followed up with her lightning spell blasting her even further into the rock.

"That was a pretty nice follow up Kerra." Ashe said praising her.

Kerra smiled, "Thanks Ashe."

Lyra pushed herself out of the stone and landed in the river. "You actually struck me, congratulations. I'm afraid it's going to take a lot more than that to finish me." She sneered.

Kerra rushed in to strike her with her fist and Lyra blocked it with a water wall defensive spell. Lyra kicked her across the face knocking her back a few feet. Kerra wiped the blood from her nose and jumped back in. The two girls exchanged blows until Kerra finally landed a hit. She had struck Lyra in the stomach with her knee; while she was bent over she came down with an axe kick to her head. Ashe could see Kerra growing stronger before her eyes; she knew she wanted to hurry back to Zander.

"Water Art: Matter Slicer." Lyra said weakly as the water shot out from the river and through Kerra's right shoulder. Kerra cried out in pain,

"Kerra!" Ashe shouted running over to her.

"I'm fine, it's just my shoulder. Kerra said as she slowly rose to her feet.

She pulled out a scroll from her bag, "It's time to end this." Kerra said angrily.

Kerra rolled out the scroll along the ground, and placed her hand over it. A light came from the sky and shone on Lyra creating a box shaped barrier sealing her in.

"What the hell? What is this?" Lyra asked.

"This is the technique that has been passed down in my family for many generations; this will be the last thing you ever see." Kerra said.

Her tone had completely changed, it was darker. Ashe had never seen this side of her before nor did she realize she had this much power. "Lightning Art: Thunder God's Devastation!" Kerra shouted.

The thunder boomed through the forest, it was louder than any thunder they had ever heard before. Suddenly lightning appeared from the sky in the shape of a giant sword, it came crashing down until it struck the barrier. Kerra clenched her fist that she had been holding over the scroll to finish the attack. The barrier exploded causing some of the trees around them to catch on fire, but strangely enough Ashe and Kerra were unharmed by the explosion.

"Why were we not harmed?" Ashe asked.

"The thunder god will not harm me or my comrades." Kerra explained. Something began to move around in the smoke, it was Lyra she was still alive. She was badly injured and bleeding,

"I'm not dead yet you stupid bitch!" she shouted. She stumbled towards them unarmed, she could barely walk. Ashe and Kerra joined hands,

"Combination Art: Electrical Firestorm." They said. A blast of lightning and flame magick was released and struck Lyra obliterating her. They could hear her screaming in agony only for a moment and then she was gone, there was nothing left of her. Suddenly the illusion faded and they were back in the cave.

"We need to find Zander and Heiro." Ashe said. "Right lets go." Kerra said as they began to search for their friends.

CHAPTER XXII

Heiro awoke in a desert; he had no recollection of how he had gotten there. The last thing he remembered was that he and the others were at the shrine before the darkness swallowed them. So it must have been that portal that brought him here, but why was he alone?

"Hello?" Heiro called out, but there was no response.

He tried calling out again, there was still no response. All he could see was sand for miles, no water to quench his thirst, no sign of any town or even another person.

"There's no one here, besides me that is." A voice said. He knew the voice, and wasn't disappointed. He turned to see Raphael standing behind him, ready for a fight.

"It's time I settle the score with you." Heiro said.

"Not before I bleed you dry." Raphael replied. Heiro knew he had more of a chance this time around with the power of the stone. He had an ace up his sleeve, but wouldn't reveal it unless absolutely necessary. Heiro knew that the last time they fought he hadn't seen the full extent of a voidshades power but he knew that today would be a different story.

"Are you afraid of death boy?" Raphael asked him.

"Ya know, I've learned a lot traveling with Zander and the others, and the most important thing I have learned from them is friendship." Heiro said.

"What does a useless thing like friendship have to do with death?" the voidshade asked.

"Because I would gladly give my life for any of my friends and if I die, then I can go in peace knowing that one of them will destroy you in my place." Heiro explained.

Raphael began to laugh, "You won't have any friends once Vallus is done with them." He said.

Heiro pulled out his sword, "I'm tired of talking." He said.

Raphael removed his weapon from his side as well, "So am I."

"Earth Art: Stone Binding." Heiro said.

The ground covered Raphael's legs and hardened. With the power of his magick he removed himself from his bindings.

"I am a voidshade boy, only sealing spells can restrain me." He said.

"Of course I missed that lesson." Heiro said running up to him with his blade drawn. The two warriors crossed blades repeatedly. Heiro grabbed Raphael by the shoulders and kneed him in the gut,

"Flame Art: Fire Stream!" Heiro shouted dousing the voidshade in flame.

Raphael had noticed the flames were more intense than before and quickly used a water spell to put himself out.

"So your magick has grown?" he asked.

"Oh you noticed." Heiro said smiling.

"Soul Cutter!" Raphael screamed as he ran past Heiro trying to strike him.

He had dodged the blade only an inch away from his body. Heiro had quickly remembered what happened to the bounty hunters when he had used that technique on them before. If Raphael were to absorb his magick and the stones

The Fated Swords

power, Zander would never defeat them. He can't screw up now, this fight is crucial to their victory.

"Wind Art: Slicing Gale." Heiro said as he released the blades of wind from his sword. The spell had hit Raphael, damaging him only a little.

"You call that wind magick? This is wind magick." Raphael said as he began to gather energy.

"Wind Art: Sandstorm Gust." The voidshade said as the wind began to pick up. It had swept Heiro up into the air, the sand was so thick in the air he couldn't see anything. Raphael jumped into the air above him and grabbed his arm; with all his strength he threw Heiro into the sand below. As he landed he had made a large crater in the sand below.

Heiro rose to his feet, "Lucky for me the sand broke my fall." He said stumbling.

The impact had done more damage than he had let on. He could tell just by moving around that four of his ribs were cracked.

"Flame Art: Great Fire Stream." Heiro said as he blew the flames from his lips toward the enemy.

"Water Art: Tidal Surge." Raphael said as the water from deep beneath the sand shot out at the flames.

The two spells collided causing the desert to fill with steam. This had turned the temperature up even higher, and the heat was already wearing on Heiro.

The sweat began to pour from his body; it was weakening him he needed to end this quickly. "Is it too hot for you boy?" Raphael asked.

Heiro didn't reply he was trying to conserve breath and energy. "I figured a thief rat like you would be right at home considering they found you in that desert village." The voidshade continued.

"As long as I am still breathing I will not give up, my friends are counting on me." Heiro said.

He had thought about Zander and Kerra and how strong they had gotten since the beginning of their journey. Each of them, including Heiro himself had matured and learned more about themselves than they had ever known before. Then he thought of Ashe, from the moment he met her had known there was something special about her. He hadn't cared that she was definitely far more powerful or skilled than he had been; he had begun to fall for her. He had told himself that as soon as this fight was over he was going to ask her to out on a date.

"This conversation is over, I'm ending this now!" Raphael shouted as he charged at Heiro with his sword extended.

Heiro stood his ground and braced himself for the incoming attack. "Soul Cutter." Raphael said as he tried to slice Heiro across his chest.

Heiro quickly grabbed the blade with his bare hand. The blade sunk into his flesh as his palm kept bleeding more and more. He gripped the blade hard and increased his energy output. He pulled the blade with his hand and watched the steel break in half.

"How is that possible? How could you shatter my blade with only your hand?" Raphael asked as though he was surprised.

"My friends are the only family I have; you will not take them away from me!" Heiro screamed as he grabbed Raphael's hand and picked him up off the ground and over his head.

Heiro threw Raphael into the air and watched as he landed at least one-hundred feet away. The blood from Heiro's wounded hand had run up his arm and had begun to cover his body as if it was some form of armor. Wings of blood sprouted from his back like those of a great dragon.

The Fated Swords

"Demonic Art: Blood Knight Armor." Heiro said. A large lance also formed from the blood within his hand.

Raphael rose to his feet, *"His energy is spiking, and I have never felt so much power before."* He thought to himself.

He had begun to cast multiple elemental spells and launched them at Heiro. Each spell hit him and bounced off, it had been his new armor. He had hardened it like he had his own body in the battle with Zander and Vallus before.

Heiro's wings began to flap and lifted him off of the ground. He had gathered momentum and flew towards Raphael.

"Flame Art: Great Fire Stream!" Raphael shouted blowing the flames at Heiro as he swooped in. The armor was unaffected by the spell, Heiro readied his lance to strike.

"How the hell is he able to fly?" Raphael asked himself.

"Blood Lance." Heiro said as he struck Raphael in the chest with his new bloody spear. The attack had shattered Raphael's magick damage reducing barrier.

Overwhelmed by Heiro's newfound power, Raphael began to run away for him and search for the exit of the dimension. "No way, you're not getting away this time." Heiro said as he threw his blood lance into the air with great force.

The sky quickly turned a dark crimson color, and Raphael looked up in terror. "Demonic Art: Bloody Carnival!" Heiro shouted.

The lance burst into thousands of tiny needles that rained down upon the sand. The needles impaled Raphael's body and stained the sand with the color of blood. Raphael hadn't moved, Heiro watched as his body quickly faded away into black particles of dust. The dimension started to warp and burst open; before he knew it Heiro was back in the cave.

Kerra and Ashe ran over to him and helped him up. "Are you alright?" Kerra asked.

He grabbed Ashe by the waist and pulled her in close and kissed her. At first she tried to fight it and then gave in, "Now I'm okay." He said. She had been speechless; the only thing that she had known was that he had certainly been growing on her.

"We need to hurry and find Zander before he goes and gets himself killed." Heiro said.

The two girls nodded slightly and the three of them ran off into the cave to find Zander and Vallus. They had prayed they weren't too late.

CHAPTER XXIII

Zander had woken up from what seemed like a deep sleep and found himself leaning on the edge of a tall cliff overlooking a body of water. He quickly rolled back from the edge and caught his breath, one more roll and he could have fallen to his death. Of course, Vallus would toy with him like that; but he also wouldn't want to kill him so quickly. He rose to his feet and looked around; the cliff he was standing on was connected to a mountain path that formed a square around the large reservoir. There wasn't very much room to move around let alone fight, perhaps this was Vallus' plan.

"Vallus!?" he shouted.

There was no response; the only sound he heard was of the birds chirping that flew overhead. "How do you like my battleground?" A voice said.

It was Vallus again; he enjoyed sneaking up on people a little too much. "Is this your idea of a joke?" Zander asked turning to look at him.

Zander noticed he had taken down his ponytail, he was serious this time. "I will give you one last chance to join me." Vallus said.

"Vallus you know that I can't, I came here to finish this and I know what I have to do." Zander said.

"Ah so you mean to sacrifice yourself for the others, how foolish of you." Vallus said.

Zander released his sword and pointed it at Vallus, "It isn't foolish, I'm ensuring my friends safety and the safety of the rest of the kingdom." Zander explained.

Vallus ran his fingers through his hair to keep it from getting in his face. "So you believe that they will immortalize you just like they did your father? Have you ever heard anyone utter a word about that bastard?" Vallus asked, "You're no war hero, you're just a child".

Zander was furious, he clenched Ivory's handle hard and his breathing became heavy. "Say that again with my sword through your chest." Zander said. Vallus could certainly feel a change in him from when they were together back at the Capital; he was more mature and more powerful than ever. Zander was never seen as a threat to his plan before, but now he had to be more cautious than ever.

Vallus drew his sword and held it at his side; Zander watched the blade carefully because he knew that with Vallus' recent battles he had many tricks to work with. "I can see you watching my blade. Do you think I'm going to pull some sort of trick on you?" Vallus asked.

"Maybe it had crossed my mind." Zander replied. "I can feel that your magick is different from the last time I saw you, so you found the stone?" Vallus asked.

Zander wasn't surprised; Vallus was always five steps ahead of his enemies. "I'm just as powerful as you are, maybe even more powerful." Zander said.

Vallus chuckled a little, "Confidence is easily broken Zander." Vallus said glaring at him.

Vallus disappeared as quickly as Zander blinked, appearing behind him and holding a knife to his throat.

"Don't struggle, the blade might slip." Vallus warned him.

The silver blade kissed his pale white skin, with a slight movement the blade nicked the side of his neck. A small drop of blood ran from the cut down his shirt. Vallus released him and pushed him away, "I would never kill you in such a manor, we have known each other since we were babies I have more respect for you than that." Vallus said.

"It's good to know you have some humanity left in you." Zander said.

Vallus licked the blood from the knife and placed in back in the holster on his leg. "Not for long I'm afraid; I may just become the next demon king." He said.

"Then I guess I couldn't feel too bad about killing you." Zander said.

"So I guess it's that time, isn't it?" Vallus asked.

Zander got into stance, "I guess it is." he said.

Zander had made the first move, running up to his old friend and trying to strike him with a basic blow from Ivory's blade. Vallus anticipated this and blocked the blade with his boot. He had taken his leg and swung it to the side knocking the blade away, and struck Zander in the face with his fist. Zander quickly regained composure and came back with his blade once more, which was again blocked by Ebony. Sparks flew from the blades as Vallus and Zander stared into each other's eyes.

"Brother do you remember the day I gave you that blade?" Vallus asked.

"Of course I do." Zander said.

"Then I guess we will soon find out how the rivalry will end." Vallus said using the force of his weight and pushed Zander backward.

Zander quickly grabbed his arm and threw Vallus off the side of the cliff, "Flame Art: Fire Stream!" he shouted aiming the flames at Vallus.

"Demonic Art: Shadow Claw." Vallus said as he attached the spell to the side of the cliff.

He had used the claw to swing himself back up onto the cliff, thus dodging the flames. "Quick thinking." Zander said.

"As always." Vallus replied.

The earth below Vallus began to shift and cover his legs, hardening. "I knew you would try something." Zander said.

Vallus struggled to break free but the increase in Zander's magick further increased the spells hold. "Looks like I'm not the only quick one." Vallus said.

Vallus wouldn't be taken out so easily, "Demonic Art: Hellhounds!" Vallus shouted.

Three large, black hounds appeared from the ground in front of Vallus. They were the same type of hounds that appeared back in the Capital. Vallus whistled and they began to run after Zander. Zander threw Ivory and pierced one of the hounds and watched as it turned to dust. The remaining hounds continued the chase; they were almost on his heels. He quickly turned and kicked one aside and punched the other in its face, this was merely a diversion. He ran over and Grabbed Ivory from the ground,

"Wind Art: Slicing Gale." he said as the wind blade came from Ivory and sliced through another hound.

The third hound used this moment to run up and latch onto Zander's arm, biting down hard and piercing his skin. The blood dripped from his arm as he tried to shake the beast off, he had finally taken his sword and stabbed it through its skull. It had turned to dust and Zander had use of his arm once more.

"Well you have grown, haven't you?" Vallus asked.

"Enough! I'm going to end this." Zander shouted.

He raised Ivory's blade so that the tip of the steel had hovered just about his heart. "What are you waiting for?" Vallus asked calmly. "Go on, kill me Zander."

Zander hesitated; his hands began to shake along with the blade. "Kill me dammit!" Vallus screamed.

The blade pierced Vallus; Zander couldn't believe how easily it the blade had sunk into his skin. The blood began to flow from the wound as Zander pulled Ivory out of him. "So you couldn't do it?" Vallus said staring at Zander with disappointment.

Zander had only pierced his shoulder; he lowered his weapon and looked down at the ground. "Look at you, a helpless child. You're no soldier at all." Vallus said.

"What the hell happened to you!?" Zander shouted, so loud that it echoed throughout the area.

"What do you mean?" Vallus asked smiling.

"I loved you like a brother; you were the kindest person I had known." Zander said.

"Kind on the outside, filled with hatred on the inside." Vallus said.

Zander had known the pain that Vallus had to deal with growing up, he often tried to hide his feelings and for the most part he had. He had always disagreed with his father's views; Vallus had never seen the mystics as threats. Deep down Vallus was jealous of the power they had, and wanted the same power for himself. Zander knew looking into his friend's eyes that there was no kindness left in him, the hate had completely consumed him. The only way to rid the world of this evil would be to kill his best friend, and it was the hardest thing he had ever had to do.

"I knew you didn't have it in you." Vallus said looking down at Zander.

Ivory fell from Zander's hand and hit the ground. The blood from Vallus's wounds dripped on the ground in front of Zander. Zander's earth spell had ended, thus freeing Vallus from restraint. Vallus grabbed him by his hair and pulled him up off the ground. Zander struggled to break free of his grip; it felt as though he was ripping Zander's hair off his head. Vallus made a fist and punched him across the face. Blood flew from Zander's mouth and hit the ground nearby.

"I'm going to make your suffering unimaginable." Vallus said.

Vallus threw him to the ground and began to kick him repeatedly. Zander was helpless, his will was fading; he needed to think of something fast or else Vallus would kill him. He slowly rose to his feet; wounded and bleeding. "You still think you have a shot?" Vallus asked.

Zander wiped the blood from his face and picked up his sword. "I'm not going to give up, there are too many people betting on me." Zander said as he looked up at Vallus and smiled.

"I'll cut that smile right off of you!" Vallus shouted as he ran at Zander.

Suddenly a burst of magick came from Zander and had sent Vallus flying backward. *"So this must be the power of the stone."* Zander thought.

He gathered as much energy as he could and released it. The wave of magick had distorted the illusionary dimension they were in, destroying it. Zander lowered his hands from his face and looked around; he had noticed that they were back in the cave.

"Enough games Vallus, we're ending this now." Zander said.

CHAPTER XXIV

Vallus stood up and put his sword away, "So you managed to break out of my alternate dimension, impressive." Vallus said.

"I don't need your praise." Zander replied.

"Well I guess it would seem so." Vallus said.

Zander had also put away his blade; he was trying to stall him until the others had found them.

"I have to hand it to you; I never would have imagined we would be on the same level." Vallus remarked.

Zander kept his hand on Ivory's handle, preparing himself for a surprise attack. "The game is about to get even more interesting." Zander said.

"Zander!" a voice shouted from across the cave.

It was Kerra and the others coming to join him. "Good to see you're still alive." Heiro said.

"Yeah everything is just fine." Zander said not even taking his eyes off of Vallus.

"Those guardians were easier than we thought." Ashe said.

"Speak for yourselves." Heiro said looking over at her.

"It looks like your all here for the main event." Vallus said looking each of them in the eyes, he knew the odds and didn't care. He knew the extent of his power and theirs, the only one that had even a chance of defeating him was Zander.

"You guys stay out of this, I can handle him myself." Zander said.

"It looks like you have done a great job so far." Heiro said looking down at his wounds. Kerra walked up beside him and grabbed his hand,

"You forget that were all in this together, we will fight too." she said.

He could tell how strong she had gotten just by the tone of her voice, her pulse was racing but she was ready to risk it all for him. She loved him and it had been that very thought had kept him going.

"Kerra." Zander said uttering her name under his breath.

"We will buy you some time while you gather the energy needed for the seal." Ashe said as the three of them stood in front of Zander to guard him.

"Ashe once all of this is over I'm buying you dinner." Heiro said winking at her.

Even in the battle for the fate of V'nairia Heiro still had his devilish charm. "If you don't die, I'll think about it." Ashe said returning a smile. Vallus stood and watched them without even making a move.

Heiro moved in to attack first; he had always been the most impulsive of the four. "Flame Art: Great Fire Stream!" he shouted as he spat the flames in Vallus' direction.

Vallus however, in his quick thinking had rolled to the right thus dodging the attack. Heiro anticipated his next move and jumped above him. In mid-air he cast the spell again, the four of them watched as the flames had connected with their target this time around. The flames burned the flesh right off of Vallus' bones and disintegrated those as well. Of course they should have known it was an illusionary tactic to distract them.

Zander knew that a mere flame spell of that caliber could not even harm Vallus.

Suddenly Vallus had appeared behind Heiro, "Demonic Art: Shadow Claw." He said as the claw from his shadow had extended out and grabbed Heiro by the back of the neck.

Heiro struggled to break free but the more he struggled the tighter the claws grip had become. Vallus finally commanded the claw to throw Heiro into the cave wall.

"Heiro!" Ashe shouted, but he could not hear her he was unconscious from the force of the impact.

Zander slowly began to gather magickal energy in the back of the cave as he had watched the others battle Vallus. He couldn't believe how easily Heiro had been taken out, but he knew that Vallus wasn't playing around.

Kerra and Ashe were up next, they started off with a fire and lightning combination spell. This spell was more advanced and more powerful than Heiro's normal fire spells. The two spells had collided in the air and immediately the force and speed of the blast had increased dramatically. Vallus had not flinched; he simply waited for the right moment before the blast had hit him and unsheathed his sword. With one swing of Ebony's blade he had sliced right through the spell and cancelled it. That had been the very moment when they knew that he wasn't human any longer.

Kerra had quickly ran up to Vallus to deliver a roundhouse kick to the side of his head. The stone had also increased Kerra's agility and speed as well as her magick. Before the kick had hit him, he grabbed a hold of her leg and pushed it away. Ashe came down from above them with her sword to strike; Vallus had jumped out of the way and kicked her in the stomach. Ashe slowly got to her feet and pulled her bow from her back, she had loaded it with three arrows. She pulled the string back tightly,

"Flame Art: Triple Fire Shot!" she shouted as she released the string.

Vallus had swiftly dodged the first two arrows and caught the other in his hand. He crushed the arrow in his palm and threw the remains to the ground. Ashe's attack had been a diversion tactic; Kerra came flying through the air above Ashe.

"Lightning Art: Flying Thunder Kick." She said as the kick struck Vallus across the face and had slung him into the side of the cave.

"Combination Art: Thundering Firestorm!" the girls shouted as they cast their spell once more. The blast had hit the side of the cave where Vallus was, the shockwave had broken up the wall and rubble came tumbling down.

It had been too quiet, and there had been no sign of movement from Vallus. It was hard for Zander to believe that Ashe and Kerra had taken him out themselves although their teamwork was quite impressive. Suddenly, two shadow claw spells came from the wreckage. They had extended themselves up Ashe and Kerra's bodies and grabbed them by their necks. Vallus slowly pulled himself out of the rubble and walked toward them,

"You ladies are quick, I'll give you that. It's too bad you hadn't joined me." Vallus said lifting them up off of the ground. They could barely breathe the claws were strangling them so hard.

"Which one of you should I kill first?" Vallus asked looking to each of the girls.

Zander had felt useless; he still needed more energy for the seal. He couldn't save them, if he had broken concentration now all the collected magick would be lost.

"Blood Sword: Giant Axe!" Heiro shouted from behind Vallus. Heiro used the blood sword axe to cut right through Vallus. The shadows had disappeared and released the girls, as they fell to the ground they noticed that it was another one of Vallus' illusions.

"What the hell took you so long Heiro?" Ashe asked angrily.

"Hey give me a break, I was knocked unconscious." He said.

"Thank you Heiro." Kerra said smiling. Heiro walked over to them and caught his breath,

"How much longer you need back there buddy?" He asked yelling over at Zander.

"I just about have it; you'll need to restrain him." Zander said.

Vallus appeared out of nowhere and made his way towards Zander. The others quickly ran after him and grabbed a hold of his limbs. They had used their magick energy to add weight to their body to restrain him. They held their ground and gripped him tightly; Zander had been preparing the seal. The seal had to work; it was the only thing to bring him back without killing him. Zander unsheathed Ivory and pulled out the scroll that Einkroft had given them. Suddenly Vallus released a black burst of energy from his body that had sent out a shockwave, knocking back Heiro and the others. Their plan had seemed to fall through except that Zander had a plan B that no one else had been aware of.

He gathered all of his magick down his arm and into Ivory. The Blade had been encased in a blinding light; Vallus couldn't see anything around him. Ivory's blade had enlarged itself at least ten times its normal size. Despite the blades size it was light as a feather in Zander's hand, he held out the sword and ran towards Vallus.

"Sacred Art: Devil Slayer!" he shouted as he swung the blade of light through Vallus' body multiple times. While Vallus was stunned he quickly unrolled the scroll onto the ground. The incantation moved from the scroll and wrapped itself around Vallus. The binding part of the spell was complete, now all Zander had to do was seal the evil energy with his blade. He thrust Ivory into Vallus' chest as a powerful, warming light covered him. The sealing spell had captured him and began to purify him.

CHAPTER XXV

Heiro and the others picked themselves up off of the ground and walked over to join Zander. Zander stood in awe as he observed his best friend encased in a golden aura, slowly being purified back to his old self. "What kind of attack was that?" Heiro asked as he looked over at Zander.

"I believe that was his original technique." Ashe said.

"It was just as Master Einkroft said, everyone needs an original technique." Zander said.

Kerra came up behind him and hugged him, "You completed the seal, I was so worried about you." She said.

He turned and pulled her to him and she laid her head against his chest. "I'm alright, everything is alright now Kerra." He reassured her.

The golden aura faded from the body, they looked to find Vallus purified but it wasn't. It was Raphael; they had wasted the sealing spell on him. As he lay on the ground out of energy he looked up at them and began to laugh. "You idiots were so easy to fool, I took the form of Master Vallus and you believed it." He said.

"How the hell did this happen? It was him I was sure of it." Zander said as he fell to his knees.

Kerra leaned down and held him, he was in shock. "When you had broken the barrier and brought you and Master

Vallus back to this plane, I had quickly traded places with him and took on his appearance." Raphael explained.

"That doesn't explain how you could use Vallus' powers and spells." Ashe said.

"It is quite simple really, as a voidshade I can take on not just the appearance of another being but I can also mimic their powers and abilities just not to their owner's potency." He explained further.

Zander released Ivory from its sheath and held the blade to Raphael's throat, "I'll give you one chance to tell me, where is Vallus?" Zander asked angrily.

"Well I don't really know, in this cave somewhere I'm guessing." Raphael said smarting off.

Zander swiftly ran his sword across Raphael's throat and watched him fade into dust.

"What happens now? The seal is gone." Ashe asked her brother.

"I really don't know." Zander replied.

They had failed to save Vallus' life and now Zander had to come to the realization that they had to kill Vallus or the kingdom and the world was going to come to an end. The time had come; he had to kill his best friend. There was no turning back now. "It's done, now I have to kill him." Zander whispered.

Kerra had taken this hard but she knew eventually the day was going to come. The thing was that she was actually more upset because of the fact that Zander had to kill a part of his family. Her feelings for Vallus had long since faded away, Zander was the only one who had stayed true to her and she loved him more than he could ever fathom.

"We need to hurry and find Vallus and finish this." Heiro said.

"Is everyone still able to fight?" Zander asked them.

They looked at each other and nodded. "We had used up a lot of magick during the fight with the fake, but we should be alright for now." Ashe said.

Zander looked around, "Vallus! Where are you?" he shouted.

There was no response, he had shouted again and still nothing. "Maybe he fled the cave?" Kerra asked.

"No you're forgetting the sole purpose of leading us here." Zander said looking at the shrine.

They had almost forgotten about Diaboro's shrine and the awakening that Vallus was trying to make happen. Vallus had wanted Diaboro to give him the power to destroy the world and give life to it again under his rule. Zander and the others weren't about to let that happen. "Zander look!" Heiro shouted and pointed towards the shrine. It was Vallus with his trademark smile across his face.

"Looking for me?" he asked.

"You knew about the sealing spell, didn't you?" Zander asked.

"Of course I did, don't you remember when we used to play chess growing up brother? The pawns are always sent out to protect the king." Vallus said.

"I hated chess." Zander said.

Vallus laughed, "That's because you were terrible at the game, you were never a tactician." He said.

"You think your some kind of god." Heiro said.

"I'm no god, not yet at least." Vallus said grinning.

Zander kept his hand on the handle of his sword, "What makes you think Diaboro will even help you accomplish this?" Zander asked.

"I'm going to offer him your souls, each and every one of you." Vallus said.

"I'm not going to let you do this." Zander said.

Vallus jumped down from the shrine, "What do you plan to do? Kill me with your special technique? Vallus asked. "Oh how foolish you are."

"Enough of this lets kick his ass." Heiro said.

Zander motioned them to not move. "I've got an original technique of my own brother, wanna see?" Vallus asked.

Within the blink of an eye Vallus was gone. He quickly appeared in front of Zander and knocked him in the air with an uppercut. He jumped up above Zander and unsheathed his sword, a purple aura covered Ebony's blade and curved like a scythe. "Demonic Art: Angel Killer!" Vallus screamed as he came through the air and sliced right through Zander.

Zander fell to the ground on his back; Ivory had hit the ground a few feet from him. Vallus hovered over his body, "Sleep now brother, the rest will see you soon." He said smiling as he lunged Ebony's blade into Zander's heart.

Zander coughed up blood and fought to take the blade out of him but it was too late. His arms fell from the blade and onto his chest, he had stopped breathing. There was no longer any light within his eyes, there was only darkness. Zander was gone.

"Zander! No!" Kerra shrieked.

It was a scream that could have shattered glass. Her world was ending; her heart was being torn right from her chest. They could never spend the rest of their life together; there was no marriage now or any children to be had. Her life was over; she had watched the love of her life die before her very eyes. The tears overcame her, and you could not hear over the sound of her screams.

She immediately ran to his side and held him kissing his lips as if it would bring him back to life. Vallus reveled in her agony; all of their pain was his pleasure. He used a piece of cloth from his back pocket to clean Ebony's blade and sheathed it. He walked over from Kerra and Zander's body and picked Ivory up off of the ground. The sorrow now overcame his sister, whom he had only known for a short time. Now Thesia and Zander were gone, she had no one left. Her screams mixed with Kerra's wailing. The symphony of sorrowful moans filled the cave, and echoed. They were all overcome by their grief, even Heiro who did not weep but was in shock of what had happened within the last moment of Zander's life.

Vallus ignored the rest of the group and walked over to the shrine, and unsheathed the swords. He had stuck both of the blades into the man-made slots on the side of the silver statue. The swords began to glow with white and black auras.

"In a matter of minutes Lord Diaboro will rise from his resting place and I shall be the new king of V'nairia." Vallus said.

"We can't hope to beat him without Zander, its over." Heiro said.

"Your right he was the strongest out of the four of us, even with our power combined we can't defeat him." Ashe said wiping the tears from her eyes.

Kerra ran her hands through Zander's hair and kissed his forehead; tears came from her eyes and dripped down onto his face. "We need to get out of here." Heiro said lifting Ashe up off of the ground.

She nodded and took his hand, "Heiro's right lets go Kerra." She said.

They started to walk out when they noticed she hadn't been following them. They turned to see her still sitting beside Zander's body. "Kerra, we have to go." Heiro said.

Kerra shook her head, "There's only one thing we can do now, and we have to give in to him." She said.

They were shocked; she was ready to give up so easily. After working so hard the entire journey Kerra was ready to give up and sit by Vallus' side? She had clearly gone mad they thought. She stood slowly and looked over at Vallus, who had been watching her.

She walked over and knelt before him, "Master I beg your forgiveness and I pledge myself to you." Kerra said.

It was almost as if she was in a trance or under a spell of some kind. "Kerra, what are you doing?" Ashe asked.

"Kerra get away from him!" Heiro shouted.

She turned to look at them, "Vallus is all of our hopes for this world, and he is our king now." She said and turned back to him.

She walked up the stone stairs to the shrine and stood before him. "Your soul belongs to me now Kerra." Vallus whispered to her.

"I will do as you command your highness." Kerra said.

"I command you to embrace me as your king." Vallus said holding his arms out.

She wrapped her arms around his waist and held onto him. He placed his hands on her back and held her tightly. He looked down into her eyes, they were kind eyes. He was happy she had finally chosen him. He leaned in and kissed her to make Kerra his slave. Heiro and Ashe couldn't bear to watch, she had betrayed Zander's love so easily. It had made them sick.

"It's good to see you have chosen the side of the strong." Vallus said looking at her.

"It is true that Zander was not strong enough, but you are forgetting something my king." Kerra said.

Vallus was captivated by her beauty, "What is that my love?" he asked.

"I am pure of heart." She said as she pulled Ivory from the statue and thrust the blade into his back, the blade had also gone through her as well.

"Why did you?" Vallus asked but couldn't finish what he had been saying.

"You may have killed Zander, but that doesn't mean that you're a monster. You have a heart and I just found it, your free Vallus." Kerra said as the blade holding them together let off a tremendous light.

It was warm, she could feel no pain and there was no blood. This had been the Ivory's special ability Einkroft had spoken of. It was Kerra's love and her pure heart that allowed her to release it. Kerra looked to Heiro and Ashe, who were standing in front of the altar stunned. "Please watch over him, he will need you both." She said smiling.

Her body began to fade into particles of light just as Einkroft had done before. The fragments of light had surrounded Zander's body and covered him. The color had come back to his face and his wounds were healed. Zander opened his eyes, he was alive.

CHAPTER XXVI

    Zander lay on the floor of the cave, he hadn't moved or spoke. His best friend had actually killed him. He was dead, so why was he here now? What had happened since the time his heart had stopped and started beating again? Now that he thought about it he was afraid to know. There were a hundred questions floating through his mind all at once. He had died and went to the other side and the only thing he had seen was darkness.
    There is no other side, no better place to move on too; once you die it's over. It was a very lonely place, he was glad to be back. He had a mission to complete and he was ready to fulfill it no matter what it had taken. He sat up and looked around; the only thing he could see in front of him was Vallus standing at the altar. There was a light coming through his chest, Zander had looked a little closer and he could see that the light was emanating from Ivory. Someone had stabbed Vallus and taken him down that easily? It just wasn't possible he thought to himself. He watched as Vallus pulled the sword out of him and fell to the ground unconscious. Maybe it was finally over? They could go back to the Capital, he and Kerra could get married and have babies and everything would be right in the world.

It was as if everything was moving in slow motion and there was a ringing in his ear. For a moment he could have sworn he had heard Kerra's voice whisper "I love you." He hadn't understood anything that was going on, he felt like he was in a dream. He had saw Heiro and Ashe run over to him and grab hold of him.

"Zander your alive!" he heard Ashe shout as she smiled at him.

He then looked over at Heiro, "Good to have you back tough guy." He said punching him in his shoulder.

He was glad to see them, it let him know that it hadn't been a dream he was actually alive. Somehow he felt empty inside, he looked around for Kerra and didn't see her anywhere.

He looked at Ashe and grabbed her hand, "Where is Kerra?" he asked.

Her facial expression suddenly changed, she seemed very distraught. There had been no response to his question; both of them had fallen silent. "Dammit! Where is Kerra?" Zander asked shouting this time.

"Zander, I'm so sorry." Ashe spoke up.

He watched as a single tear left her eye and rolled down her cheek. "What are you saying?" Zander asked.

"Zander calm down." Heiro said as he placed his hand on his shoulder.

"Don't tell me to fucking calm down!" Zander shouted shrugging away from him.

He made a fist and slammed it into the cave floor; he had punched it so hard his hand went through the rock. "She saved you, she saved all of us." Ashe said.

Zander now had tears streaming down his face. "Please tell me Ashe, what happened?" he asked weakly.

"Because she was pure of heart she unlocked Ivory's secret power and purified Vallus and saved your life." She explained.

"She had loved you so much that her life force brought you back from the dead." Heiro said.

"You don't understand there's nothing on the other side. She will be lonely." He said.

"Zander she faded into you, her life force joined with you. She will never be lonely." Ashe said reassuring him.

She held him close to comfort him, "It will be okay, I promise." She added.

"I love her, I can't lose her." Zander said.

"She will always be there Zander, she loves you too." Heiro said. It was odd for Zander to hear empathetic words coming from him but he was glad Heiro had been there for him.

"What about Vallus, do you think it worked?" Zander asked.

"I believe it did." Vallus said from behind them.

Zander turned to see his best friend standing behind them carrying the two swords. "Your back." Zander said smiling faintly. "Is it really you?"

"I think so." Vallus said patting himself down.

Ashe took one look at Vallus and immediately became disgusted. She still had hatred towards him for killing the only mother she had ever known.

"I'm so sorry for everything I have done." Vallus said. "One moment I was in the hospital and then the next I am here."

"I'm just glad to have you back on our side." Zander said as he rose to his feet.

They both stared at each other for a moment allowing everything to finally sink in. "Kerra was very brave to save us like she did, she really loved you Zander." Vallus said.

"I will always miss her and I will always feel empty without her here." Zander said lowering his head.

"I will miss her as well but she will always be here with us in spirit." Vallus said smiling.

Zander was still sad about Kerra's death but at the same time he had gotten his friend back. Kerra had given him everything he wanted in life and in death.

Vallus walked up to Ashe and grabbed her by the hand, "Lady Ashe, I am so sorry for killing your mother but I was not in my right mind; I beg your forgiveness." Vallus asked kneeling in front of her.

Ashe looked down at him, "There is pain I still hold in my heart because of you, but for now I am just glad everyone is okay, including you." She said sternly.

"We have to go back to the Capital and rebuild the government and everything your father destroyed." Zander said.

Vallus nodded, "The revolution has ended and mystics will no longer be persecuted for who they are." He said.

"Yes, we had better get going the kingdom needs us." Ashe said.

Suddenly there was a purple aura emanating from the shrine. "What is going on?" Heiro asked.

The cave began to shake; there was a loud roar from deep in the ground. "The awakening ritual, Diaboro is coming." Vallus said.

The shrine had exploded pieces of stone and silver flew everywhere. A claw shot up from the ground and latched on to the side of the large whole. The beast pulled itself up out of the crevice. It was large and black with red piercing eyes and large horns. Its tail was razor sharp and it carried a large black broadsword. The beast had to have been at least eighteen feet tall, its horns had almost scraped the ceiling of the cave.

"After centuries I am finally free!" the beast roared. The group stared at the large beast in awe and terror.

"How are we supposed to beat that thing?" Zander asked.

"I am not sure but take this." Vallus said tossing Ivory to Zander.

"We have to be very careful in this fight." Vallus added. They nodded in agreement to his statement.

Diaboro looked down and saw them looking up at him, "You are not humans, I smell mystic blood in you four." The beast said.

Diaboro's attention was caught by the twin swords of legend. "How did a bastard like you end up with my Ebony?" Diaboro asked Vallus.

"That is none of your concern demon." Vallus said.

"How dare you speak to me with such insolence, I am Diaboro ruler of the fire planes and lord of demons." The beast said.

"We have come to put an end to you demon king." Ashe said.

Diaboro leaned his head in closer, "I would remain silent whore or I'll cut it off your shoulders." He roared.

Zander looked back at Heiro and Ashe, "Listen the two of you need to stay back, the legend says that only our blades can touch Diaboro and seal him away." He instructed.

"Zander is right; your spells won't work on him." Vallus said.

Heiro grabbed Ashe's hand and they ran to the back of the cave out of sight. "You think we can kill this demon brother?" Zander asked Vallus.

"I am not sure but were about to find out." Vallus said smiling.

Zander had always hated his smile until now; it was actually growing on him. They unsheathed Ebony and Ivory and prepared for battle. This was the most important battle of their lives, they had to win they had to save the kingdom from destruction. They were the only ones that could.

CHAPTER XXVII

They had to let go of their feelings long enough to finish this fight. If they were to make any mistake in this battle it would cost them their lives, and not just theirs but their friends and the kingdoms as well. They had to have a clear head and let go of all emotion. Zander had looked over at his friend, he had been so glad to have him back and on his side. They knew that they were ready no matter what happened, they were ready to die. Everything that had happened to them before this moment had prepared them for what was too come. They were stronger than they had been before, they were about to take on a god and not just that but they were going to win.

Vallus pulled a piece of white string from his pocket and pulled his hair back into a ponytail again. It had been just as Zander had remembered him; although his heart had been dark for a while Vallus had never really changed.

"Are you ready Zander?" Vallus asked.

"Yes, we will finish this." Zander replied.

Vallus shook his head, "No I meant are you prepared for the end?" he asked.

Zander looked down at the ground and then up at his friend. "Yes if it comes to that." He said.

They fist bumped each other and smiled, then looked up at Diaboro. The monstrous demon stood staring at them with rage, its eyes shone as bright as the sun in the dark cave. "Vallus, if we're going out lets go out with a bang." Zander said as he released Ivory.

Vallus also released Ebony, "Right brother." He said in agreement.

"If you think you can defeat the lord of demons then come and try." Diaboro bellowed.

Zander and Vallus had taken off toward the large demon. As they passed by his legs they struck him with their blades. The demon hadn't even flinched and proceeded to try and grab them with its large claws. Zander and Vallus had been much faster than Diaboro anticipated thanks to their magick boosting their speed and strength. Vallus thrust his sword into Diaboro's foot and twisted the blade, quickly pulling it back out. Diaboro had let out a loud roar as he felt the pain from Ebony's blade. The demon began to fire beams from its eyes that burned holes through anything they had touched.

"Zander watch out for that attack, it's fatal." Vallus shouted. Zander nodded quickly dodging an oncoming beam attack. Diaboro had swung his large broad sword; a gust of wind came and swept the two men into the back of the cave.

They rose to their feet unharmed, "We have to get to the heart, and it's the only way to kill him." Vallus said.

"How do you suppose we do that?" Zander asked.

"I'm not entirely sure at this point." Vallus said.

"Well that's not very comforting." Zander said.

"We could try a long range approach?" Vallus asked.

"Okay then let's go with that." Zander said rolling his eyes.

They ran up to Diaboro once more this time refraining from getting too close. "Flame Art: Great Fire Stream!" both of them shouted as they spat flames from their lips.

The flames ran up Diaboro's tall body and hit his face. The demon had begun to jump around trying to stomp them. The flames had made it hard for the demon to see them. Zander jumped up onto Diaboro's arm while Vallus kept him blind with his fire spell. Zander ran up his arm and finally reached his shoulder. Vallus released his spell and watched as Zander had taken his sword and sliced the side of Diaboro's neck.

Ignoring the pain from the gash in its neck the demon grabbed Zander and crushed him in his palm. Diaboro held him in front of his face, and glared at him, Zander was helpless.

"I have you now little man." The demon said squeezing Zander's tiny body.

The pain had become too much for Zander to bear, "Vallus!" he shouted in agony.

Vallus had to think of something quick or Zander would be crushed to death. "Demonic Art: Blood Axe!" Heiro shouted out of nowhere.

The blood axe came down and sliced right through the Demon's hand. Zander was released from its grasp and began to cough, gasping for air.

"Flame Art: Triple Fire Shot!" Ashe shouted firing the arrows into Diaboro's chest. The arrows exploded but the attack hadn't been very effective.

"I thought we told you two to stay back." Vallus said.

"So we can watch you both get killed? I don't think so." Heiro said.

"Besides we did save Zander and helped you out." Ashe said.

"Yes I guess that is true, I thank you." Vallus said.

Zander ran over and joined the four of them. "Are you alright?" Vallus asked him.

"Yes I'm fine." Zander replied.

Heiro had looked over and spotted something on Diaboro's chest, "Everyone look at that." He said.

They had looked over and noticed a crack that had appeared in the center of the large demon's chest. It must have been the explosions from Ashe's arrows that caused it.

"If we hit that exact spot, we may be able to break through to its heart." Heiro said.

"Alright Ashe you and Heiro use your spells once more to weaken the spot. Zander you will strike its body one finally time to break it open, after I can see the heart I will deliver the final blow." Vallus explained.

"Right." Zander said.

The four of them had prepared themselves; they didn't have much magick left. This was their last chance to finish the fight.

Ashe drew back her arrows, "Flame Art: Triple Fire Shot!" she shouted as she released the arrows. They watched as the arrows each pierced the spot on Diaboro's chest and exploded. The crack had gotten even larger.

Heiro was up next with his blood axe spell. He jumped up and swung the axe as hard as he could and almost shattered the demon's chest. Diaboro roared with anger.

"Go Zander." Vallus said.

Zander ran toward the demon and jumped at its chest; the demon tried to strike him with its claw in mid-air but was unsuccessful. Zander had been too quick for it to catch him. With one powerful swipe he struck the cracked spot with Ivory and broke open the demon's chest. Blood poured out of the large hole. As Zander came down he had grabbed a hold of the side of the massive wound. Inside he had saw Diaboro's large beating heart.

Suddenly out of nowhere he had saw a face inside the hole followed by a fist to his face. The punch was strong enough to remove him from the side of the hole and into the air just in front of the large demon. Diaboro had swung its great claw and struck Zander and threw him into the wall of the cave. He had fallen to the ground barely able to stand.

"Zander!" Vallus shouted as he ran up to the demon to avenge Zander. He had let his emotions get in the way of his careful thinking and the demon had struck him also, knocking him into the opposite wall. Both Zander and Vallus were lying on the ground on opposite sides of the room both barely able to move. The force of the blow was so powerful they hadn't expected to take that kind of a hit.

Ashe and Heiro had looked over at Diaboro, who by this time was acting strangely. Suddenly a broadsword had protruded through the top of the demon's chest and made a downward incision. The wound was ripped open by something from the inside. A figure had emerged out of the body of Diaboro and jumped to the ground below.

The figure had been a larger man with long black hair and massive muscles. He had donned a suit of armor and wore a black cape. He had carried a large broadsword on his back.

"Ashe, its Geinedor from the story." Heiro said.

"He came out of Diaboro." She said.

The large demon body behind Geinedor had become to deteriorate. Heiro and Ashe were defenseless against someone as powerful as Geinedor.

"Pathetic mystics." Geinedor said in a low bellowing voice. "Where is my sword?"

Ashe and Heiro looked over at Vallus who could barely stand. He was gripping Ebony in his hand. "What do we do Heiro?" Ashe asked.

"I don't know Ashe, Zander and Vallus are the only ones who stand a chance against him." He replied.

Geinedor had looked over at them impatiently; he could rush over and attack them at any moment. They had to think of something fast.

"Wait, what if we do a transfer spell?" Ashe asked.

"What's a transfer spell?" he asked.

"We transfer our magick to Zander and Vallus." Ashe said. It had been a great idea with what magick they had remaining plus the magick from the two of them they may have a chance. The only downside being that it would leave Heiro and Ashe vulnerable.

"The transfer spell is simple, you simple have to link yourself with the person your transferring your magick too." Ashe said.

"Aright, Ill transfer to Vallus and you with Zander." Heiro said.

Ashe nodded, "Alright."

The two of them had focused hard on their targets. "Transfer!" They shouted. Suddenly they could feel the magick slowly leaving their bodies. Zander and Vallus were siphoning it from them. Geinedor knew what they were doing and wasn't about to let it happen. He rushed over to them and with a powerful front kick, knocked Ashe inside the wall of the cave and knocked her unconscious. He had then used the flat end of his broadsword and struck Heiro knocking him into the wall also. With the two of them out of the way he was going for his sword.

Luckily for Ashe and Heiro the transfer spell had worked. Geinedor turned to find Zander and Vallus standing behind him with their weapons drawn.

"Ebony will be mine!" the dark prince shouted.

"Ebony has chosen me as its master." Vallus said. "I'm afraid it is no longer yours to take."

"We will see mystic." Geinedor said pointing his broadsword at Vallus.

"It all comes down to this brother." Zander said.

"Your right, the fate of our kingdom and the world rest in our hands." Vallus said.

"Are you ready?" Zander asked.

"As ready as ill ever be." Vallus said.

They smiled at one another and then with Ebony and Ivory in hand they prepared themselves for the final fight for V'nairia.

CHARACTER INDEX

AERIA EIRAN- Heiro's mother and wife of Hyo

AGARATH- The Duke of Rygoth who is obsessed with money and women.

ARCHON- One of the two princes of Astaria. Archon had defeated his brother Geinedor in battle after Geinedor had murdered their parents. He is known to many as the Prince of Light.

ASHLYN ROSENGRAD- Daughter of Lillian and Zephyr Kyre, and sister to Zander. She has earned the title of The Fire Drake by the people of Talias. She is also the adopted daughter of Thesia Rosengrad.

BALTHIER- The Supreme Judge of V'nairia that ruled before Vallerus Arvello assumed the title.

BLAZE- Ashe's best friend since they were infants. Blaze had joined Talia's Militia forces alongside his friend to better protect their city.

BLITZ & ACE- Twin brothers who had joined the Militia. They are two of the four members of the Extermination Squad.

BRONN & STELLIA ALENDAR- Heiro's grandparents that reside in Oaba Desert. The parents of Aeria Eiran.

BOSS ZUGO- A crime lord that owns Oaba Village.

CLYNE DAINES- A graduating soldier from the Academy that bullies Zander. He is also secretly a mystic.

DARRIEN- Also known as The Puppeteer, Darrien is a powerful mystic who can control other's bodies and minds to do his bidding.

DIABORO- Once Geinedor received his power from Ebony, he was transformed into Diaboro the King of Demons.

EINKROFT- Brother to Hylkroft the Godsage and once a famed mentor of the Militia.

FERIAN- The Last Healer known to exist in V'nairia

GEINEDOR- One of the two princes of Astaria. He had murdered his mother and father in cold blood trying to steal the throne from his brother Archon. He is known as the prince of Darkness.

HEADMASTER JERRISTON-Once a famed warrior and Lieutenant of the Militia, Jerriston has now retired and assumed the position of Headmaster of Militia Academy.

HEIRO ALENDAR- Known as the Rogue Mystic of Oaba, he befriends Zander and Kerra on their quest to save Vallus' soul.

HYO EIRAN- Father to Heiro and husband of Aeria. He is also one of the guardians of the prophecy.

HYLKROFT THE GODSAGE- The strongest mystic in history and the only mystic with the ability to control all five elements of magick.

KERRA LYALE- One of Zander and Vallus' best friends since they were infants. She is also the daughter of Judge Kiarra Lyale.

KIARRA LYALE- A Judge of V'nairia and mother of Kerra Lyale.

KNORR & CREGAN- Loyal bodyguards of Boss Zugo.

LILLIAN KYRE- Mother of Zander and Ashe, and wife of Zephyr Kyre.

LYRA- A quiet mystic whose heart was corrupted by Ebony's power and made into a bodyguard for Vallus.

OMAK- A Lieutenant of the V'nairian Militia.

RAPHAEL- A traitor to the Voidshade Colony and the guardians of the prophecy. He lurks in the shadows and tempts others with the power of darkness.

TERA ARVELLO- Mother of Vallus, and wife to Vallerus Arvello.

THESIA ROSENGRAD- The Baroness of Talias and the adoptive mother of Ashlyn Rosengrad.

TYRON ROSENGRAD- The Baron of Talias and father to Thesia.

VALLUS ARVELLO- Zander's best friend and the new Supreme Judge of V'nairia.

VALLERUS ARVELLO- Vallus' father, and husband of Tera. He is a previous Supreme Judge of V'nairia.

YAIGAMAT- A dark mystic who invades the kingdom of V'nairia with his army of evil warriors.

YEZAI- The shaman who had crafted Ebony and Ivory for the two princes of Astaria.

ZANDER KYRE-A young mystic with great power. He is best friends with Vallus and Kerra, and the brother of Ashe. He is the son of Zephyr and Lillian Kyre. He is also the newly appointed Lieutenant of the Militia.

ZEPHYR KYRE- Zander Ashe's father, and husband to Lillian Kyre.

If you enjoyed THE FATED SWORDS,
Look out for

THE CRUSADER KING
MYSTICS OF V'NAIRIA BOOK TWO
By: J.C. Ritchie

Coming Summer 2017!

Follow J.C. Ritchie

Facebook: www.facebook.com/jcritchienovels

Twitter: www.twitter.com/jcritchienovels

Amazon: www.amazon.com/jcritchie

Goodreads: www.goodreads.com/jcritchie

Email: jcritchienovels13@gmail.com

Printed in Great Britain
by Amazon